To Lori

From Annette's Mom

Phyllis Moore

Maxi's Choice

Phyllis H. Moore

authorHOUSE®

AuthorHouse™
1663 Liberty Drive, Suite 200
Bloomington, IN 47403
www.authorhouse.com
Phone: 1-800-839-8640

This book is a work of fiction. People, places, events, and situations are the product of the author's imagination. Any resemblance to actual persons, living or dead, or historical events, is purely coincidental.

First published by AuthorHouse 2/4/2008

ISBN: 978-1-4343-3232-5 (sc)
ISBN: 978-1-4343-6152-3 (hc)

Library of Congress Control Number: 2007910308

Printed in the United States of America
Bloomington, Indiana

This book is printed on acid-free paper.

Acknowledgements

Cover by Megan Robin Pfeffer

My Granddaughter

Thank you, Megan

Thanks to my husband Norval, who came up with solutions when my plot got me into trouble, helped with computer glitches, and came to my rescue numerous times. Thank you to my daughter, Annette, for her help with editing and her wonderful encouragement. Thanks to my son Dennis and his wife Bonita for giving me my computer, Dennis's special instruction in using it, and their support and encouragement. Without a computer, I would never have written a novel.

Prologue

SEPTEMBER 1985

THE FLOOD

The storm system began in the southern Caribbean where it swirled its way around in the warm waters, gathering moisture and building winds until it was declared Hurricane Edna. It built power in the Gulf of Mexico for three days before heading for Florida's Tampa Bay area.

High winds and water lashed at the coastal cities, leaving behind a wake of destruction as it traveled northeast. It cut through the Carolinas, veered off into the Atlantic where it renewed its force, then headed inland again towards the northwest.

Forest Hills, a small city nestled in the Appalachian Mountains along the Susquehanna River basin of central Pennsylvania, lay directly in its path. The residents were not alarmed as they watched the television news of the storm. These phenomena had happened before, and Pennsylvania's mountains soon calmed the storm's fury without major disasters.

On Tuesday Maxine Taylor woke to a heavy downpour of rain. It had started sometime in the night, she didn't know when, but the morning's light was dim. Her husband Jim had been up most of the night writing on his latest novel, so she didn't turn on the lights in the bedroom or bath before going downstairs to the kitchen. When Jim began a novel it was always like this. He became so pulled into the story he was creating that he couldn't sleep until he had written out whatever bent his mind had taken. He had explained early in their marriage that when getting started there were many ideas spinning around in his head, and he needed to get his thoughts on paper while they were still fresh in his mind. Later, when the core of the story and characters were established, his work schedule would become more in line with everyday life. But in the beginning, he had to go with the flow.

Tightening the belt to her white terry robe, Maxi moved barefoot around the kitchen, slowly waking up. Taking the coffee beans from the canister, she filled the coffee grinder, transferred the grounds to the coffee pot basket, added water and hit the on switch. Her movements were smooth and orderly. She headed for the front porch for the morning paper.

She glanced at the headline across the top of the front page, **HURRICANE EDNA HEADS INLAND**, with a sub-head, **Heavy Rain Expected Here.** *Thank goodness we don't live in an area with hurricanes,* Maxi thought as she poured her coffee, *we'll just get some rain from it, and maybe more wind than usual.*

Maxi and the other residents of Forest Hills had followed the progress of the storm on television and in the newspaper. It seemed certain they were in for some rain, but they were not much concerned about what was now termed an intense storm.

What they didn't know, and what the forecasters failed to realize, was that a low pressure system coming from the northwest would stall this tail end of the hurricane over the mountains of central Pennsylvania. It was fated to swirl around and around, dumping twenty inches of rain on the Susquehanna watershed in the next twenty-four hours.

So to Maxine and the other residents of Forest Hills this Tuesday was expected to be just another rainy day. They continued with their daily routine of going to work and getting the kids to school with their lunch boxes and the additional boots, raincoats and umbrellas.

Maxi headed toward the children's rooms and woke Michael first. He would be in and out of the bathroom in ten minutes, showered and dressed. Lorene, three years younger at fifteen, was taking longer these days to get ready for school or anything else for that matter. She could spend hours in the bathroom, but when pressed she could be out in a half-hour. Maxi quietly went into the walk-in closet off the master bedroom and came out a few minutes later dressed in jeans, pullover sweater and sneakers.

Back in the kitchen, she poured orange juice and took cereal from the pantry and set milk from the refrigerator onto the table. Maxi loved her kitchen; in fact, she loved the entire house. The two story Tudor style had been built to their specifications. They had moved in just a month ago. She had great plans for furnishing it and making it the home she pictured in her mind. Jim's first novel had been a moderate success and his second novel had made them financially secure. With the advance he had received on his third novel he was able to quit his bread and butter job as columnist on the Forest Hills Daily News. He was on his way to becoming a major novelist, and the money was making their lifestyle much more comfortable.

The 3500 square foot house was more than three times as large as their first home. The cracker box they had called home for nineteen years was in a development where all the houses looked alike. They had good times in it, but now it was great to be able to spread out and have 'elbow room,' as Michael put it. Maxi had quit her secretarial job so she would have the time to make it into a 'real home'.

By eight o'clock she was driving the kids to school. They were quieter than usual without the bickering they often did in the morning. The heavy rain and charcoal skies seemed to press down on them, making them mute. Driving across the river bridge, Maxi noted that the water was high; a second glance and she amended that thought to extremely high.

The rain was coming down too fast to run off. The curb gutters ran full, and in many places Maxi had to drive slowly through foot-deep water. She curbed her uneasy feelings as the kids got out of the car, giving her indulgent smiles. Maxine watched as they headed toward the school, splashing through puddles in places where puddles had never been. *They will sit all day with wet hair and wet feet. Their hair will dry in a little while, but their shoes won't. This kind of rain can't go on much longer; it will soon slack off.* As she drove away with these thoughts, she decided to stop at the local coffee shop for coffee and a donut before going to the grocery store. Maybe the atmosphere there would be more upbeat than her feelings this morning. The coffee shop was nearly empty so there was little conversation. Maxi skipped the donut, drank her coffee quickly, which she acknowledged to herself that she didn't need, then headed for the grocery store, overly caffeinated.

The rain continued. Little brooks among the mountains became raging streams, and creeks turned into overflowing rivers. It all ended in the Susquehanna River that began rising at an alarming rate. The overflowing streams flowed into the towns and over farmlands. The city fathers realized they were in trouble. Fire sirens sounded, church bells rang, and police and firemen were out in force. All emergency personnel were desperately busy in attempting to put into effect their heretofore unused plans.

By 11 o'clock Maxi was back at the school, waiting with the school buses and other parents in their cars to pick up children. When Michael and

Lorene spotted their mom's car they ran for it at a mad dash, getting completely soaked by the pounding rain as they splashed though the water at their feet. They looked half drowned by the time they got into the car. They huddled together in the back seat, looking scared.

"They said that we're having a flood, Mom." Lorene said in a trembling voice. "I thought we were not even going to get out of the school. There is water everywhere."

For once, Michael didn't say, "Don't be such a baby." His sister voiced feelings he felt he was too old to express. Instead, he hunched his shoulders and shivered.

Maxi wondered if Jim was still sleeping. She hadn't been home since she left with the kids for school. At the grocery store it had taken her a long time to get through the crowded checkout. While she was in line she heard the sirens and an announcement over the store's loud speakers that a flood alert had been declared and that schools were closing. She had been a nervous wreck by the time she loaded the bags of groceries in the trunk and headed for the school.

With her children in the car she felt a little calmer, but it still seemed to take forever to drive the three miles back home. They were eerily quiet during the drive. As she pulled into the garage she turned to the kids, "I want each of you to take as many bags of groceries as you can carry into the kitchen. Then go get hot showers and into dry clothes. Michael, use the shower in the laundry room so neither of you have to wait. I don't want you to be more chilled than you are already."

Maxi carried the rest of the grocery bags into the house and headed for the bedroom where she found Jim in a deep sleep, oblivious to the emergency.

"Jim, wake up." She shook him gently on the shoulder. He only grunted and rolled over. "Jim, wake up. We're having a flood." This time she shook him as hard as she could with both hands.

"Hmmmmm, yeah, I'm awake." He looked at her through slightly open eyes. "What's all the fuss? I didn't get to sleep until five o'clock."

"I know. But the school is closed and everything is in an uproar. We are having a flood. I need you to help me. I don't know what we have to do."

Soon the downstairs rooms flooded and they took refuge on the second floor where they were trapped for three days. The floodwaters had finally stopped rising halfway up the second floor stairs. They ate canned food cold and drank the cans of juice that she and Lorene had carried to the second floor. Jim and Michael had removed the furnace motor and what items they could from the basement. Everything had been piled on the kitchen floor and the gas and electricity shut off. There was no hot water for showers, but thankfully they were still able to use the toilet. Not knowing if the water system was contaminated, they didn't drink water and were thankful for the canned juice. They huddled in bed under blankets, trying to keep warm. The rain had brought unseasonably cool temperatures. They didn't have a battery-operated radio and were completely cut off from reports of what was happening.

Jim fell asleep Tuesday night, but Maxi could only lie awake, staring into total darkness. She hadn't realized how much light came into the house at night from the street lights. She listened to the rain and constant chop-chop sound of the helicopters as they traveled back and forth over the house, probably taking people to the emergency shelters and the hospital. The hospital was in the hill section as well as one of the elementary schools. She remembered that the school had been designated as an emergency headquarters and shelter. All night she lay listening to the helicopters -- the only sounds of civilization. *At least someone is out there doing something.*

By Friday they were able to venture downstairs. Mud covered everything. What they had brought from the basement lay on the kitchen floor, a total loss. Maxi broke down, crying. Jim looked at the mess and thought; *thank goodness my computer is on the second floor. My novel is saved.* Lorene was quiet. Michael remarked, "What a mess. Where do we start?" They toured the rooms with mud soaked furniture and curtains that hung wet and heavy with mud. Everything was cold, wet and dank.

At the sound of an engine they hurried to the door, slipping and sliding in the mud. A city bus was being driven slowly through the streets while volunteers looked for those who had been stranded.

"Are we glad to see you!" Jim shouted above the cries of the kids as they spotted friends on the bus. "Our cars were flooded as well as our house, so we had no transportation."

"We'll wait until you pack a bag with dry clothing and then we'll take you to Roosevelt Elementary. There you can get food and hot showers." The volunteer had a nametag fastened to his orange coveralls identifying him as "Buck".

As Maxi went back upstairs to pack she realized that things were always relative. They had dry clothing, while people whose homes had been completely under water or washed away had nothing. Along with the clothing she gathered up Jim's wallet and her purse, realizing that they needed credit cards to begin to get back to normal. They would need to replace their cars first and then go from there.

As she climbed aboard the bus the kids were talking excitedly with their friends, and Jim was catching up on all the news.

It was the beginning of the 'cleaning up and starting over' season.

Chapter 1

February 2001

(16 Years Later)

The silence of the cold, crisp air of an early February morning was shattered by the roar of the huge bulldozer as it sprang to life. The crowd of bystanders felt the frozen earth vibrate and tremble beneath their feet as they watched the huge machine rumble toward the vacant house. The operator aimed for the porch of the two-story, hundred-year-old building, tearing it away with a splintering crash. At the sound the crowd gave a collective murmur, not a cheer and not a groan, more like a sigh of acceptance, which left frozen vapor hanging in the air, unwilling to dissipate, like their hopes. The watchers saw the reality; the Project had begun.

Maxine Taylor and Helen McGuire stood amid the shivering crowd, seeing what had been a lovely Victorian house tumble into a pile of debris.

Maxi's thoughts went to the small, frail, elderly woman standing staunchly beside her. Helen was shaking from the cold despite her hooded and down-filled bright red coat that enveloped her from the top of her head to her ankles. Beige wool stockings under her signature red high-top sneakers covered her tiny feet.

Maxi's thoughts centered on her companion. *Was she thinking of the memories being tumbled into a pile* of debris? *Six months ago I had just met Helen, when she was the occupant of that house. I never expected my first contact to be a 96-year-old woman who had lived all her life in this house. What thoughts must be going through her mind?*

"Are you okay?" Maxi asked as she put her arm around Helen's shoulders and pulled the hood of her coat up closer around Helen's small, lined face.

"Yes, I'm fine. It's tough growing old, you know. But it happens and I would have had to move out of that house soon anyway. I couldn't keep up with the expense of it anymore. The memories are in my heart, dear, not in the house. I can take my memories with me anywhere." She turned away from the house and looked at Maxi. "Thank you for bringing me here this morning, Maxi. You're a sweet girl."

Maxi smiled at being called a girl. It was something she was not used to hearing, since she was a 54-year-old widow with two grown children.

"I needed to be here," Helen continued. "It's sort of like going to a funeral, you know. You have to say good-bye. Let's go now; it's cold this morning." Helen shivered and hugged her arms to her body.

As they turned away, a young, ill-kept man wearing a bulky black windbreaker and black watch cap, moved so that he bumped into Maxi, barring her way. Greasy dark hair fell over his forehead and his shadowy dark, mean eyes glared threateningly at Maxi as he said, "You happy now? Takin' away old folks' homes?"

"Now you be minding your own business, John. She's only doing the job she was hired to do and they couldn't have found a better person for it. Go on home now, be a good boy, and don't hassle the poor girl." Helen glared right back at John who gave way at Helen's rebuke.

He let them pass but it didn't stop him from continuing to stare at Maxi. She smelled his foul breath as he hissed at her as she moved past, "You'll get yours! Again!"

She stopped, giving him a hard look and felt a shot of fear course through her body at the malevolence in his dark, almost black, eyes.

Helen pulled at Maxi's arm, tugging her toward the car. "Come, dear, he's only blowing hot air, and I'm cold. I need my warm apartment now."

Reluctantly, Maxi turned her back on John and took Helen's arm as they walked the short distance to the car. She didn't like to admit it, but John had unnerved her. He wasn't completely responsible for his actions. He had been in a car accident several years ago and now lived with a metal plate in his forehead that sometimes caused pressure on his brain. Between the pressure and the pain medication, he acted a little crazy at times. The townspeople treated him as a harmless abnormality in their midst. Maxi also knew that Helen had taken him under her wing and he felt very protective of her. But despite knowing all this, Maxi couldn't shrug off the fear he left with her.

Could he be the one who blew up my home?

Before getting into her car with Helen, Maxi stood, slim and straight, dark auburn hair falling in a shining cascade to the collar of her chocolate brown, long wool coat, looking toward the center of Forest Hills. Shivering from the bone-chilling cold as well as the fear John had caused, she looked across the city being bathed in weak, early morning sunlight that glistened off the snow-covered buildings -- the buildings that wouldn't be there in a couple years. They housed businesses and apartment houses, as well as the many single-family homes that would meet the same fate as the one they had just watched being knocked down. All these buildings represented people she was responsible for getting moved into homes or helping them establish new business locations. *It's such a big job, especially the businesses. I'll be burning the midnight oil studying the relocation regulations on Eminent Domain.* Maxi shivered again as she got into the car beside Helen.

As she started the car, she smiled across at Helen and said, "I'll have the heater going in a minute. This car heats up fast.

"It's always the same isn't it, Helen," Maxi continued, "there's bound to be controversy over making changes in a town that was founded nearly 200 years ago. Most of the townspeople, including you and me, have lived here all their lives; their parents, grandparents, great-grandparents, and great-

great- grandparents have lived here before them. The Susquehanna River is part of their heritage.

"Forest Hills was built here because of the river", Maxi continued. "It provided central Pennsylvania with transportation, especially for the logging industry and coal mined in the mountains upstream.

"Some see the project as progress and others see it as taking away their history, even though the river flows as before, just not through the downtown area, which I see as progress," Maxi grinned at her own remarks. "I didn't mean to get so carried away."

Then she turned serious again, "You remember, Helen, how it was sixteen years ago, when Hurricane Edna nearly devastated our city?"

"You bet I do! That hurricane dumped 20 inches of rain here on the Susquehanna River Basin in a 24-hour period. I'll never forget. The water came into the second floor of my house. If it wasn't for all the help I got from the Red Cross, neighbors, and the federal grant money, I would have lost my house then. I was in good health then, too. I'd never be able to stand another flood. Getting through this treatment for breast cancer is just about takin' all I have left in me."

"I know, Helen, and I admire your courage tremendously. You are my role model. Did you know that?"

"Really!" A burst of surprised laughter rocked around the car. "I'm a dried-up, 96-year-old woman. There's not much piss and vinegar left in this old body."

Laughing with her, Maxi replied, "But there is! You're a real fighter. The difference is that you know when and what to fight and what to accept. We all have choices in life and you choose to live life, one day at a time, with an eye for tomorrow and what it will bring. I have great respect for the Serenity Prayer and you are the embodiment of that concept. I would probably never have gotten to know you but for this project and my part in it. It makes me wonder if it is true that some people come into your lives, like angels, to help you through difficult times."

"Well, you have certainly been my 'angel', Maxi. My biggest fear was not knowing what to do once I was certain that I was going to lose my home. You have made it all very easy. I love my little apartment at assisted living. I have my privacy and the comfort of knowing there are people there when I need them. And I have made new friends. The food is good, too. I don't cook much, even though I have a little kitchen, only when I get really hungry for homemade vegetable soup, chicken and waffles, or Pennsylvania Dutch potpie."

"You have no idea, Helen, of the problems I have with people in the prime of their life who not only drag their heels but dig them in at the prospect of moving. And the moves are to better housing in most cases and always at least comparable. I expected that people would welcome not living in a flood zone."

"It's not having any say about moving that makes them act that way." Helen responded.

"I know. And I sympathize with their feelings but there comes a time of facing reality and making the best of it. But I don't mean to put any of them down, most of them cooperate and we manage the move smoothly without too many glitches."

"I hear many good things about you, Maxi. Everyone is talking about the Project, and I have heard only good comments about how you are doing your job. People like you and know you are there to see that they get a fair shake, and have help in finding a new home and even getting moved. They trust you."

"Where do you hear all these 'good things'?" Maxi laughed, a bit embarrassed.

"Mostly at the hospital when I have the chemo treatments, but at the retirement center, too. And I have a few old friends who are still alive and have family here. You don't have a big ego, Maxi, but you are smart and have plenty of self-confidence about who you are. But most importantly, you have empathy with people. That is why people like and respect you and have confidence in your ability to help them. Those with the big egos turn people off."

"Thank you, Helen. You have just made my day!"

"Since I am telling you what others think about you, Maxi, I'll add that I admire the way you have been able to keep your life together through two tragedies and starting a difficult new job at the same time. Having a husband die is terrible, but one so unexpectedly in an auto accident and at a young age is worse. Then to have your home be completely destroyed, on top of that, would have been more than most people would have been able to endure."

"I almost didn't, Helen. I was in extended care for three weeks, in a depression that I almost didn't come out of. I wanted to die. Only the thought of what it would do to my family kept me from doing something about it. That was the only choice I had."

"But you did come out of it! That is what matters," Helen said as she opened the door to go into her apartment. "I would love to have you stay for a cup of coffee, but I know you have a lot to do today and I have to go to the hospital in an hour for a chemo treatment."

"Bye, Helen. Hope the chemo isn't too bad. I'll call you tomorrow." Maxi gave Helen a hug before turning to go back to her car. She passed Helen's bright yellow VW bug parked in the resident's parking lot. It looked like it just came off the assembly line. The mental picture of Helen driving around town in her yellow VW, wearing her high-top red sneakers, always brought Maxi a delighted smile.

Back at the office parking lot, Maxi found a space cleared of the snow that had been falling daily for the past two months. Running up the inside stairs to the second floor offices, she headed straight to Jake Reese's office. Fortunately, his door was open which meant staff was welcome to come in.

"I think I was just threatened!" Maxi was breathless from her dash up the stairs and her heart was pounding.

"What?" Jake had been working at his computer with his back to the door. It was a large, broad-shouldered back that went with his pro-football body. He turned his chair to stare at her. "What are you talking about? And slow down, catch your breath." Jake rolled his chair behind his desk and motioned Maxi to take a seat.

Maxi collapsed into one of the chairs facing Jake's desk, took a deep breath, and began. "I took Helen to watch the demolition of her house." At Jake's frown and negative shake of his head, Maxi hurried on. "She was fine. She called me yesterday and asked me to take her. She said it was like going to a funeral to say good-bye. And she was fine with it. Honestly!"

"Okay, she is fine. But what's your problem? You said you 'think' you were threatened. Were you or weren't you? And by whom?" Jake was always very direct, almost hard, when he thought someone was wasting his time, and especially when he was in the middle of writing reports.

Maxi wasn't intimidated by his gruffness. She knew from experience that he would always listen to her, even when they had differences of opinion. In fact, Maxi had won out a couple of times.

She proceeded to tell him what had happened when John confronted her. "And when he said, 'you'll get yours, **again**', I got goose bumps at the look he gave me. Could he be the one who caused the explosion that destroyed my home?"

Jake was already reaching for his phone and punching in the number for the police. It was answered on the first ring.

Jake wasted no time with preliminaries. "Marcy, get me the chief. This is Jake Reese."

The call was transferred immediately. "Chief Mark Fields here. Hello, Jake. What's up?"

"Get over here. It's an emergency!"

Ten minutes later, Maxi was retelling her encounter with John to Mark. "Do you think John is the one who destroyed my home?"

"I'll certainly check him out. He doesn't have a record of being violent, although his wild-eyed looks sometimes frighten people, especially people who don't know him. But you know him, Maxi. Have you ever been afraid of him?" Mark watched Maxi's reaction closely, her shaky hand movements, and her tense body, both indicating she was very upset.

"No. He never frightened me before. But today he scared the devil out of me."

"Maxi, you never had a devil in you!" Mark grinned. He couldn't help it. "I've known you since kindergarten and you never once did a devilish thing." He hoped he could joke her out of her nervousness but also felt her instincts about people were excellent. He wondered if anyone could have persuaded John to do something destructive.

"Mark, I don't think I could live through having my new home destroyed. I've just begun to feel at home again. I love my house." Maxi was near tears as she stood and began pacing back and forth.

"I know, Maxi." Mark stood, and being a long-time friend, felt it was all right to give her a hug. "I'll take care of it. I'll bring John in to the station today and grill him on his actions and his whereabouts when your house was blown up. We won't leave anything unanswered."

Maxi leaned into Mark's hug, comforted by the man who was built like a linebacker but had the heart of a teddy bear. He made her feel protected. Jake, too, made her feel safe. He was as tall as Mark but not as bulked up. Mark worked out regularly at the gym. Both men were well over six feet tall and had a confidence about them that inspired trust.

"Are you okay to work today or do you want a day off?" Jake asked, concerned about her general shakiness and pale complexion.

"I'll be okay. I have to do a bunch of comparable schedules so I'll be working in the office all day. No appointments are scheduled. Getting to work will help me settle down and I prefer being here with the staff around. I'm sorry to be such a baby. It was probably nothing, just John being John. He is very fond of Helen, and if he thought she was being mistreated, it could make him angry enough to confront me and say something stupid. I'm sure that's all it was and I just over-reacted. I'm sorry." Maxi stood and headed for the door.

"I hope that's all it was, Maxi, and you were right to come to me with your worries. I'll be in the office all day, too, so if you need to talk or think of anything that may or may not be connected to this, come in and talk to me. Okay?"

Jake and Mark waited until Maxi was in her office then turned toward each other. "I'll check him out, Jake. I can't believe that John is capable of thinking through all that would have been required to set off a gas explosion that destroyed an entire house. But he may have been influenced and directed by someone else. So I'll check all his activities back to the beginning of the summer."

"Thanks for coming right over, Mark. I'll do some checking on my own, and if I turn up anything at all, I'll get in touch with you. Do you think it's safe for her to be living out there all alone right now? That house she is remodeling is in the boonies, or almost anyway. If there is anyone after her…" Jake's voice trailed off, leaving unspoken the concern that lay between them like another presence in the room.

"I don't like the idea of her out there by herself either, but I don't have the manpower to put a guard on her. Jeff Knowles is watching her place as best he and his dog can. His house isn't far away, but not close enough for a constant watch."

"How well do you know Jeff? Is he trustworthy?" Jakes' concern was evident and sincere.

"I know Jeff very well and he's as trustworthy as one of my men, and probably better trained. That dog of his is well trained, too. There couldn't be anyone better to have nearby."

At Jake's questioning look, Mark continued. "He's an ex-FBI agent, Jake, and his dog was his partner. He quit when his wife had terminal cancer three years ago. He moved here after her death. He

15

used to visit his aunt and uncle here every summer when he was growing up. That's why he retired here. I have known him since he was a kid."

"Well, I'm relieved to hear that. Does Maxi know about him?"

"Yes, he's been a very friendly neighbor ever since she bought the place. And, yes, she knows his past and also that he was a friend of Jim's. There's something else I think I should fill you in on, Jake." Mark went to the door and closed it quietly.

Chapter 2

(Six Months Earlier)

Driving slowly along the River Road, Maxine Taylor experienced a comforting feeling of seclusion and protection under the arching branches of giant maples where the shadows of dusk were gathering. She pulled into a turn-around along the riverbank and turned off the engine. She was not sure why she had chosen to drive along this particular road, except that she had been driving aimlessly after finishing her day's work, not ready to go home to a house, empty except for her newly acquired kitten. Feeling lonely and terribly sad, she felt drawn to the place where as a child she had often walked to a swimming hole.

She sat still, looking at the river. She felt at peace here. Memories of long solitary walks along the river and up through the woods swept through her. Getting out of the car, she walked the few steps to a bench overlooking the water. It was dark now, but she remembered the path and the bench was still there. She wondered how many times it had been replaced in the last 40 years, surely a few. The house where she grew up an only child of parents in their 40's when she was born was not far away. It was on high ground and thus had been spared during the flood. Both her parents were gone now and the house sold. Her dad died first, only in his mid 60s. Her mother died a year later.

The water appeared black this late in the evening. Maxi sat and watched it slip silently by. The musky scent of damp earth and decayed leaves was heavy on the warm humid air that felt like velvet brushing Maxi's arm. Night sounds grew louder with the increasing darkness. Cicadas, crickets and katydids joined in a symphony, celebrating the warm humidity of the late August evening. She had always liked the night. Now it seemed to settle around her like a comforting blanket.

Unbidden, memories of the night that Jim had died in a one car crash came rushing over her. Tears slipped silently down her cheeks. Jim had told her that the novel he was just starting was based on new territory for him, a subject he hadn't explored before, and he would be spending a lot of time getting background information. So when he was late one evening she wasn't uneasy or fearful. But when the doorbell rang at 11:30, she had felt a zing of fear shiver down her spine, a foreboding. Jim would come in through the garage. Who could be ringing her doorbell at this time of night? When she opened the door to Mark Fields, Forest Hills Chief of Police, she knew something dreadful had happened. Mark, a lifelong friend stood on the porch, the porch light highlighting his blond, now showing some white, hair. His posture was ramrod straight; he held his hat in a grip that left his knuckles white. Maxi instinctively knew the news was terrible. It was, in truth, the ultimate nightmare.

Now, in the solitude and the comforting softness of a warm summer night, the silent tears gave way to great tearing sobs that shook her entire body. Later, cleansed and exhausted, she made her way slowly back to the car.

Maxi woke to brilliant sunlight streaming into the bedroom. A peek at the bedside digital clock showed 8:00. She didn't really remember driving home or going to bed. She stretched and recognized the feeling that comes only with a good night's sleep. It was the first sound sleep she had had since her husband's death four weeks ago.

Thinking of the night before, she knew her feelings this morning were because of the tears finally shed, letting out all the grief she had kept buried. It wouldn't last, she knew. People and places would engender unexpected moments of memories. The grief would build up again, but time would help.

She knew this from past experience, not from the trite words she heard from well-meaning people who now felt uncomfortable in her presence and were clueless in knowing what to say to her. In their unease, her friends were gradually drifting away, as though being widowed was contagious. She realized that the women didn't want to think about being in her situation. Also, some might regard her as a threat now, someone who could be interested in their husbands, and husbands who might follow up on their belief that widows needed a man.

Maxi didn't much care about losing friends that had been part of her life when she was the other half of a 'couple'. Everyone traveled in two's and she now felt out of place. She wasn't altogether without friends. Sue Marshall had been her friend ever since she could remember. She had lived next door and they had been a constant pair, in and out of each other's houses and treated by their parents as if they were all one family. Their quarrels never lasted more than a day. They were as close as twins. Sue and Rob and Maxi and Jim were married in a double wedding and were each other's bridesmaids. They had celebrated their 30th wedding anniversary together last June with a Caribbean cruise. It had been a wonderful week.

Maxi closed her eyes and savored the last heavy remnants of sleep and the dreams she had been having of the good times. As Maxi stretched, Beau, her newly acquired kitten of one week, woke at her movement to come and sit on her chest, poking his cold wet nose onto her closed eyelids while making kneading motions with his paws. She opened her eyes, smiled at him and ran her hand over the sleek head all the way to his tail.

"Okay, I'm awake. My eyes are open, see?" He was purring loudly, and switched to nuzzling her neck. It was something he did that made Maxi feel like he was kissing her.

"You are a handsome fella, dressed in a black satin tux," she told him as she stroked under his chin where a small patch of white fur marked his throat, the only white on his otherwise coal black coat. She had thought of naming him Georgie for his habit of nosing in her neck that made her think of the nursery rhyme, 'Georgie Porgie, pudding and pie, kissed the girls and made them cry,' but changed

21

her mind as she watched him dance, quick-stepping all around the house, so the name Beau Jangles came about. She was glad that her friend, Bonnie from her recent real estate days had talked her into taking him. At the time she thought a kitten was the last thing she wanted to be bothered with. But now he gave her a reason to come home. He needed to be fed and loved; he was lonely when she wasn't there.

Holding Beau in the crook of her arm, she threw back the sheet, swung her legs to the floor and stood, stretching before walking barefoot across the plush carpeting to the bathroom. She stared into the mirror, feeling like she was looking at a stranger. The dark auburn hair was past her shoulders and needed cut, and her dark brown eyes looked a bit puffy from the tears of the night before. She noted her creamy complexion was okay, no wrinkles yet, although instead of 54 at times she felt a million years older than she had a couple months ago. Shifting Beau from arm to arm, she put on a white silk robe and headed to the kitchen. She put Beau on the floor and started a pot of coffee before going to the front porch for the morning paper.

The ranch-style house seemed twice as big now that Jim was gone. She still had trouble accepting his sudden death. It had seemed larger, too, when

Michael left for college followed by Lorene three years later. Now they had careers and were married and in their own homes; they only visited on special occasions. *"It's too much house for me,"* Maxi mused as she turned back inside with the morning paper in her hand.

The suddenness of Jim's death had left her in a void of unreality; the only thing grounding her was her job. The Flood Protection Authority had employed her six weeks ago. Two weeks later, Jim had died in a car accident. She was off for a week to take care of his funeral and see their attorney. She still hadn't adjusted to thinking of herself as a widow, and often came home from work thinking of something that she wanted to share with Jim, and then realized that she would never share anything with him again. Each time it seemed like a fatal stab somewhere in the region of her heart.

She thought of her son and daughter and their spouses who had all been home for the week after their Dad's death and how they had helped each other through the initial shock. Now each called at least twice a week. She thought they had worked out a calling schedule as they always called on different days. She smiled, thinking what great adults they had become and how much she loved them, and their spouses. It would be nice if they didn't live so far away. Lorene and her husband, Kevin Lowe, lived in New York City, and Michael and his wife, Eve, in San Jose. But the important part was that they were happy with their lives.

With her thoughts turning to her own job, Maxi realized she still had so much to learn even though she had completed a week's training with the Federal Highway Department on Relocation just last week. Everything was so much more complicated than she had anticipated. The week's training only skimmed the surface. But it gave her a point of reference and people to contact when she ran into trouble.

In desperation during her first week of employment she had looked for help going through the volumes of material given to her by Jake Reese, her boss. Finding a brochure among those materials, she had called the number on it, making contact with Eleanor Fitzpatrick in the Federal Department of Transportation in Washington, D.C. It was through her that Maxi learned of the training offered and the schedule. The only training available in the immediate future was in Houston, Texas. So she had written a request for expenses and leave to fly to the training sessions. She submitted it to Jake, who in turn asked for approval at the next board meeting.

Two of the board members balked at the expense, but Jake explained that it was justified and necessary as she would be responsible for calculating relocation funds amounting to millions of dollars. Getting people moved would be the easiest part.

Jake also said, "I'm proud of her initiative in looking for ways to do her job well. I gave her information that I had from 10 years ago when I attended the same kind of training. But now I am too busy with my own work to give her much help and some of the laws had been amended. I apologize for not including an item in the budget to cover this expense."

On the personal side, Maxi mused, she was in fine shape financially, actually more than fine. She was rich! She still hadn't fully realized the extent of her wealth. It hadn't seemed important, given everything else that she had to think about. She had known that Jim's writing had made money; but she was now amazed at the amount and the investments he had made.

They had virtually started over after the flood 16 years ago. The newly built house they had just moved into was flooded nearly to the second floor. They had cleaned it up, made repairs and sold it.

Of course, they lost money on the sale, but Maxi could not feel safe after the flood, and Jim had been devastated that the house they had designed and built had been so violated.

The house where she lived now was free and clear, that she had known, and they had kept it well maintained. It was lavish by her old standards. It showed off their tastes and lifestyle. Her gardens were lush and expansive, displaying her hobby as a lover of flowers. The swimming pool and guesthouse beside it blended into the landscape.

Her new, fire engine red BMW convertible was paid for, as well as the Cadillac that she used for work. Jim's SUV still sat in the five-car garage and the three classic cars he had lovingly restored.

It was the investments that surprised her. She knew that Jim had made investments, but she hadn't paid much attention. She had worked as a realtor because she enjoyed it. If she had chosen to stay at home it would have been fine with Jim. They hadn't talked about money a great deal. Neither of them wanted an elaborate lifestyle and they were very comfortable. Maxi knew she didn't need to worry about Jim's income and he wrote because that was who he was, a writer.

To say that she was surprised when their attorney explained her financial status was a complete understatement. She still hadn't incorporated into her mindset the fact that she was rich! With the insurance, investments, savings and checking account, her assets were worth over twenty million dollars. And that didn't include the value of the house, which was close to another million.

She had known Jim's novels sold well, and she herself had enjoyed them immensely, but didn't realize that they brought in that much money. His writing evolved from his work as a reporter for the local newspaper. When he uncovered Mafia money laundering and trafficking in drugs, the Associated Press picked up his story. Investigations became his expertise. His novels later were based on subjects he had investigated. He had just started his eighth novel.

The advance on the started novel had already been returned to the publisher. She would continue to collect royalties from his previous works.

Even though she didn't need a job, she had to keep her mind occupied. She had to be too busy to think about Jim's death and her loneliness.

She was sure, most of the time, that she would enjoy the work of relocating families. And some of the time she was scared to death that she couldn't do it. She personally thought that to be told you had to give up your home, even for a fair price, would be traumatic. Jake called her his little social worker, teasingly of course, because that was one of the reasons he had recommended hiring her.

There had been many other applicants, but only two local people. She had the necessary skills in real estate, compassion for people and knew the area. She knew she would be walking a tightrope to be fair, seeing that everyone got their legally deserved moving expenses and the greedy ones did not get away with anything. Already she knew most people would prefer to stay where they were, flood area or not.

From the beginning of the planning for the project, Maxi had kept track of the process and had felt it was necessary for the area to survive. The last flood 16 years ago so devastated the city that if it hadn't been declared a national disaster area, it would be a ghost town today. Being declared a national disaster area made federal funds available for restoration. But along with the funds, notice was given that in the future no such money would be available, as flood insurance would be mandatory for anyone in the flood plain, which was now considerably expanded.

It was then the city fathers proposed that the Army Corps of Engineers study the area and devise a flood control plan. Eventually the Dike/Levee Project was born. It would protect the downtown business district, the beautiful historic homes and most of the residential district as well, keeping out flood waters from a large creek along one side and the Susquehanna River on the other. A total of 190 families and 20 businesses had to be relocated. As a city, it was small, but it was the largest in the county.

These thoughts ran through her mind as she showered and dressed. Ready to leave the house, she picked up her car keys from the kitchen counter where she had dropped them the night before. But her purse was not there.

"What did I do with it? I don't remember much about driving home and coming into the house," she mused. After a search of the car, it seemed the only possible answer was that it had dropped out of the car when she stopped at the river last evening. "I'd better have a look. I didn't have much money in it, but I would hate to have to go through everything needed to get a replacement driver's license and credit cards."

Again the River Road aroused childhood memories as she retraced her route of the night before. There were cottages along the road and a few year-round homes too. One she especially liked. Her mother had taken her to visit Mrs. Sterner when she was about 10 years old. She had decided then and there, that she would buy that house when she was grown up and made lots of money. The memory brought a smile. "I wonder who lives there now?" She murmured aloud.

Coming to the turnaround where she had stopped the evening before, she parked and got out. Almost immediately she spied her purse and went to pick it up.

"You're lucky!" At the sound of a male voice, she whirled around to see a man standing by her car smiling at her. Used to assessing situations and people quickly, her thought processes simultaneously registered his physical presence -- he was about her age, tall and good looking with sun-bleached light brown hair and a natural end-of-summer tan. Even though he seemed friendly and non-threatening, she felt vulnerable in this secluded place with this stranger who acted like he knew her. And the huge dog by his side was intimidating, too.

"Yes, I guess so," she replied. "I don't think I know you."

"Probably not. You're Maxine Taylor, Relocation Specialist, for the Flood Protection Authority. I've seen your picture in the newspaper and also I've seen you around town." He raised his eyebrows, seeking her acknowledgement. Adding, to himself, *and much prettier than the news photo.* He admired her compact, slim figure and guessed her to be about 5'3". Nearly perfect, he mused, watching the sun bring out rich auburn tones in her hair while her dark brown eyes grew wary.

"Yes". She was more nervous now. She had had a few run-ins with people who were vehemently against the Project. She hadn't been personally threatened, but had faced some very angry people and that in places where there were others around. Now this stranger, even though he seemed friendly, stood between her and her car in a relatively isolated area. "I do have an appointment that I have to get to if you don't mind. "

"I'm sorry. I have made you nervous and I didn't mean to do that. I was out walking last evening and saw you. I didn't want to intrude then, it being night and rather secluded. I didn't want to frighten you. I recognized your car just now and I apologize for the intrusion. My name is Jeff Knowles", he explained, as he gestured toward the road. "I live just down that way about a quarter mile." He backed away from her, holding his hands shoulder high with the palms toward her.

"Come Major," he ordered his dog that stayed close to his side.

Maxi lost no time in getting into her car. She was glad that the doors automatically locked when the engine was started. Quickly she backed out onto the dirt road and drove away. She immediately realized that she had turned the wrong direction and was heading toward the dead end. Pride kept her from backing up and turning around where she had been parked. She kept going down the dirt road knowing she would soon have to turn around, hoping that on her return he would not be where she had left him.

It was then she noticed the **For Sale** sign at the entrance to a long lane. She realized that it led to the Sterner house, the one she had visited with her mother. On impulse, she turned into the lane. It was at least a place to turn around, but then she couldn't resist going on to the house. The lane curved northward and upward away from the road and the river. She saw the sunroom with wide curving stairs leading up to it. She remembered sitting in that room and the spectacular view of the river with Bald Eagle Mountain on the other side.

Suddenly, her heart was thumping and excitement zipped through her. She wanted to see this house. She noted that the real estate sign was from her old office as she pulled into the parking area to turn around. Anxious to get back home and call for a viewing appointment, she never gave another thought to the man who had spoken to her just minutes before.

Jeff Knowles didn't forget her that easily as he took a trail through the woods that also led away from the river road; he often walked in the early morning and sometimes in the evenings, too. The walks helped him to think and plot. His thoughts now were of how he could meet Maxine Taylor again. He smiled as he noted that she had turned toward the dead end knowing that she would have to turn around to leave the river road. He was sure her appointment she had mentioned was not on that road. He had made her nervous. For that he was sorry.

"Hopefully, Major, we'll get to know her." He spoke to the dog at his side as if he were another human.

Chapter 3

Pulling into her driveway, Maxi jumped from the car and hurried into the house. She picked up the phone, dialing automatically the number she knew so well.

"Forest Hills Realty. This is Bonnie. How may I help you?" The voice was cheerful. Maxi smiled, recalling times when she worked with Bonnie.

"Hi Bonnie. This is Maxi. How are you?"

"Hello Maxi. I'm just fine. It's great to hear from you. How are you? I know there is nothing about Jim's death that I can say that you haven't already heard a dozen times. I feel devastated for you."

"I'm just going one day at a time. It's all I can do."

Wanting to skip more of the same awkwardness, Maxi jumped right in with her questions. "Bonnie, I'm calling about the house listed on River Road. I'd like to see it."

"Sure. You mean the Sterner Property, the big old Victorian?"

"Yes. That's the one. My mother took me there to visit when I was a kid. I remember I loved it then."

"Well, believe me; you will be in for a shock, because it's in terrible shape. When can you be available?"

"Since it's Saturday, I don't have to be in the office today. I'd like to go as soon as possible," Maxi replied, nearly shaking with excitement.

"That's fine. The house is vacant. We can go as soon as you get here. I'll get all the information on it and be waiting for you."

Ten minutes later, Maxi pulled into the parking lot. Bonnie was waiting with a file in one hand and her car keys in the other. "I'll drive. There is no use taking both cars." Bonnie said, sliding into the driver's seat of her town car. Maxi noted that she was her usual bouncy, happy self. Her naturally blonde hair skimmed the collar of her bright red

Ralph Lauren polo shirt tucked neatly into khaki slacks.

"So, how's your new job going?" Bonnie asked as she put the car into gear and drove from the parking lot.

"It's keeping me sane. I don't know what I would do since Jim's death if I didn't have it. There is so much to learn and the pressure is terrible. But when I am working I think of nothing else, so it is a life saver," Maxi confided.

"Well, it is going to be good for real estate business," Bonnie replied, sensing Maxi's need to get on to matters other than her recent widowhood. "As I understand it, even tenants get relocation money and moving expense; I am thinking there may be many renters becoming homeowners. If they are employed and have a good credit rating, they would have enough for a down payment for a HUD or Fanny Mae loan. I would appreciate any you can send my way." Bonnie grinned at her.

"I know you look after your clients, Bonnie, and won't sell them more than they can afford," Maxi replied. "I have to be careful of steering people to certain agencies or realtors, though, because we are using local, state and federal funds. But, personally, I hope you get most of them because you're one of the best in the business. I will suggest to my contacts the possibility that they may be eligible to purchase a home.

"I am sure you know that the Project is divided into areas for acquisition in conjunction with the construction schedule," Maxi continued. "Just keep on top of the areas being acquired and knock on doors. If you call me I can give you the schedule. That is the most help I can be." Maxi sighed and gave a slight shrug of her shoulders. "If anyone asks me about you, I will, of course, give you my highest recommendation. You can suggest they do that and I won't be breaking any laws."

"Are you thinking of this property we're going to look at might be good for someone you are relocating?" Bonnie asked as she turned into the lane leading to the house, "because it won't meet the standards required, at least as I understand them."

"Actually, no," Maxi grinned sheepishly. "I am probably taking up your time for my own curiosity. I remember coming here with my mother when I was 10. I loved the house and area so much even at that age that I promised myself I would own it some day when I was grown up and had lots of money."

"You are thinking of buying it for yourself?" Bonnie actually squealed in her surprise.

"I know. It's quite out of the question for me and I apologize for taking up your time on a wild goose chase. But I just felt this compulsion when I saw the sign this morning. I just had to see it." Maxi was leaning forward in her seat as they swung around the house to what Maxi had thought was the back door.

"I hadn't remembered that the back was really the front of the house. I remember sitting in the sunroom, which I now realize is the back, and being able to see the river and the mountain on the other side. I had forgotten what a lovely front porch there was and, of course, I didn't at that time think of it as Victorian architecture. All I knew was that I loved it"

Now Maxi was swept away by the view of the meadow sloping away from the front of the house, up a gentle rise and ending in the forest with a mountain beyond. Queen Anne's lace, golden rod and purple asters covered the meadow in a splash of color and the songs of meadowlarks rippled through the morning's silence. She breathed deeply of fresh, fragrant air as she started toward the house. Even though it was 10:30, dew was still heavy and their shoes and legs were soon wet as they walked through the knee-high grass to the porch.

Maxi's heart was pounding. She chided herself not to be silly. She was only looking out of curiosity. This would not be suitable for her at all. It was a huge place. She needed to stay where she was, or if she did sell and move, it should be something small.

Maxi's heart sank as she got her first good look at what she remembered as a beautiful, elegant home. Not only was it huge; it was in terrible condition. When they stepped onto the porch, Maxi's foot almost went through the rotted floorboards. She noted the siding hadn't been painted, probably since she had visited with her mother by the looks of it.

"What was the owner thinking?" Maxi murmured, taking in the rundown condition. "It was such a beautiful house."

"A nephew inherited it and he was a hermit. Never left the place and never did any maintenance, either. He died a month ago and it's being sold for back taxes, or to the highest bidder. Personally, I think someone will buy it for the location and the view and tear it down to build new."

Maxi was picking her way through rubble inside the house. The entrance hall had plaster missing and toadstools were growing from the crevices. But the beautiful mahogany paneling lining the central, curving stairway wall was intact. A massive chandelier hung from the ceiling on the second floor level.

The living room, called the parlor when the house was built, was even worse than the entrance hall. Ragged wallpaper hung from the walls and ceiling and jigsaw puzzles were stacked waist high across the entire width of the front part of the room.

"I guess he occupied himself by doing puzzles," Bonnie murmured. "This place is worse than I imagined. I have never been inside before. I can see why Ellen didn't want to include it on the preview list when it was first offered. She said it would only interest a buyer who wanted land."

What had been the music room brought tears to Maxi's eyes. A grand piano standing in the middle of dirt and debris looked pathetic. The library had books that were covered in mildew and mold. Maxi could feel her allergies being alerted. She sneezed.

The dining room was huge and had a beautiful beamed ceiling and a chandelier that was covered in dust and cobwebs. The plaster was gone from most of the ceiling. The bay window dimmed the morning sun coming through a thick skim of dirt on the windowpanes. A shoulder-high, narrow shelf topped the wainscoting that surrounded the room.

The old fashioned kitchen appeared to be the site of a fire that had scorched the wainscoting and left the ceiling blackened. The old-fashioned wood and coal range looked like it had been used for cooking; it had probably heated the kitchen as well, and was most likely what had caused a fire.

"It looks as though this is where he lived in the winter, doesn't it?" Maxi mused, looking at the old kitchen table and chairs, wondering what the man's life must have been like.

Retracing her steps to the central entrance hall, the curving stairs seemed to be solid as Maxi walked up to the second floor. She admired the curving mahogany banister and the beautifully carved spindles.

On the second level, things were even worse. There was more water damage, causing gaping holes in the ceiling. Nevertheless, Maxi continued to roam through the second floor rooms cluttered with old furniture, rugs, scattered rumpled mildewed clothing, fallen plaster and years of accumulated dirt. The one and only bathroom housed a claw foot tub that was filthy and couldn't have been used in many years. The commode was filthy, too, but posed a mystery as it looked as though it had been used even though there was no running water in the house. In the next bedroom a huge metal tub was set under a hole in the ceiling that went all the way to open sky. It was full of rainwater; a bucket next to it indicated that probably a bucket full was used to flush the toilet. *Mystery solved*, Maxi thought

"How long has it been vacant?" Maxi couldn't believe anyone had lived here for years.

"Only a month. The man used only the kitchen range for heat in the winter, so he spent all his time in there. With the bathroom directly overhead, some of the heat went through a floor vent to the bathroom and he slept in the bedroom next door, which also got some of the heat. I know, it is unbelievable, but that is what I have been told by the listing agent whose information came from the neighbors who brought his groceries, drinking water and cooked meals. They also brought wood and coal for him in the wintertime."

"The neighbors must have been wonderful to do all that." Maxi was amazed. "What are they asking for it?"

Bonnie looked at her as through she were crazy. "$50,000. It is considered to be beyond repair, so it is mostly land value and the buyer would have the cost of demolition. The county only wants to get the taxes owed on it. There are no relatives to inherit. There are 100 acres of land that consists of open meadows and woodland. As far as land value is concerned, it is a real bargain. It joins the State Forest land, too. The state land starts at the top of the rise where the meadow gives way to trees. The meadow goes all the way to the river and there is woodland there, too. Of course, it is off the beaten path and wouldn't appeal to a large number of buyers."

"Bonnie, I want to have a contractor look at it. Do you have to be here or could I have the key and make my own arrangements?" Maxi was totally oblivious to the objections Bonnie raised.

"Maxi, you can't be serious! This is way beyond your ability to handle. It's a money trap. Remember that old movie Money Trap?"

"I know. But something is compelling me to check out whether or not it's structurally sound.

Don't ask me why? I don't know. But what harm can come of checking into it?" Maxi gave a shrug of her shoulders. "And I really love the area. Maybe I'll consider building a new house here."

"Okay," Bonnie replied, somewhat mollified. "I'll let you have the key for today. I have to have it back tomorrow morning though or the listing agent will have my hide. Not that anyone has been rushing to see it. But you never know, a fool comes along every once in a while." Bonnie gave her friend an affectionate squeeze on her shoulder. With a backward look as they walked to the car, Maxi heard her muttering, "And no way is this place DSS."

Maxi, caught off guard, exploded with a loud guffaw. DSS was part of her new vocabulary meaning decent, safe and sanitary and no one could be relocated into anything less, even if they wanted a certain place. It had to meet standards.

"Bonnie, I never realized that you were a comedian."

"Well, just be careful, Maxi. A place in this condition is unsafe. If you got hurt there wouldn't be any insurance coverage," Bonnie admonished as she handed Maxi the key.

Later, back at her house, Maxi began calling contractors. It wasn't until her fifth call that she found someone at home.

Sam Jackson had a good reputation in the community and she trusted him to give her reliable information. In a city the size of Forest Hills, everyone knew everyone else and most of their private lives as well. Maxi had used Sam on several occasions when she was a Realtor and had clients who wanted an estimate of work needed on a property.

Sam suggested that he pick her up and a half-hour later they were on their way. "How are you doing, Maxi", he asked as she climbed into the cab of his pickup with Jackson Construction written on the doors.

"Better. Thanks, Sam, for doing this on such short notice," Maxi replied.

"That's okay. I had a free afternoon and who better to butter-up than the relocation specialist who may have lots of remodeling work to be done in the next couple of years," Sam joked.

"I must get estimates from no less than three contractors for each job. But you will certainly be on the list," Maxi replied, getting just a bit miffed at the recurrent theme of her job in relation to other's employment interests.

Ten minutes later they sat in the turnaround in front of the house. "You've got to be kidding!" Sam stared at the dilapidated structure in amazement. "You want to remodel this?"

"Come on, Sam. I just want you to walk through it with me and tell me if it is structurally sound. If it is, the rest can be restored."

"Jim would say you are out of your friggin mind," Sam sputtered as he reluctantly got out of the pickup. "God, what a mess. It would be cheaper to tear it down and start over. It is a beautiful location, though," he admitted, looking around at the meadow and woodland. As they crossed the rotted porch he added, "And it was once a grand old Victorian lady. It's really huge! "

An hour later, with much jotting down of notes on a legal pad, Jim said, "The foundation is sound. The ceilings in the rooms are square which tells me that the basic structure is not damaged, but Lord, Maxi, it would mean tearing out everything from the roof to the bare outside walls, which are plank by the way. A completely new roof is needed and I think probably all new siding. Since it hasn't been painted for so long, it looks as though it's done for. Inside, it would require new wiring, plumbing, a heating system, plus redoing all the ceilings. As far as the walls, the horsehair plaster that was used back in the mid 1800's has withstood all the dampness. A closer inspection might find some loose, but for the most part it seems in good condition, and of course when there is heat in here it could crack and fall off, too. Only time would tell about that. Maxi, it would cost more than building new.

"But it is structurally sound." It was a statement rather than a question. "And Sam, just look at the woodwork, the carving and detail. It had to have been built well or it would have fallen down with this kind of neglect," Maxi replied.

"Well, you have my opinion and that is all you asked of me. It is your choice to make. But the location is great and I have some great plans for new houses that I would like to show you. " S a m made one last appeal for a more reasonable course to follow. Sam was shaking his head as he walked back to the pickup.

Back at her house, Maxi got out and reached back into the truck to shake Sam's hand. "Thanks Sam. I appreciate your taking the time. Send me a bill. And I probably will listen to my better judgment, and your good advice, and leave it alone. I don't know; it was just something I had to do and don't ask me why." Maxi laughed at herself as she closed the truck door and started for her house.

Sam was only half a block down the street when a terrible explosion rocked his truck. Reflexively, he jammed on the brakes so hard that the engine stalled. Turning to look around the neighborhood, he saw Maxi's house had black billows of smoke coming from the collapsed roof followed by flames. He grabbed his cell phone and stabbed out 911 as he ran back toward what had been Maxi's house.

Chapter 4

Maxi was lying on the ground about twenty feet from the burning house. Fear shot through Sam as he reached her and started to drag her away from the fire. He knew it was better not to move her, but he was afraid of another explosion and the heat from the flames was so intense he felt it singe his hair and eyebrows. He braced her head and neck as best he could and gently laid her down near the street. He felt for a pulse in her neck and felt a faint beat. Even though it was a warm afternoon, he went to his truck and found a jacket, debating whether to cover her with it or tuck it under her head. She was probably in shock and he hoped it was nothing worse. For shock did you elevate the head or the feet? For the life of him he couldn't remember. A woman, with a young face and a crown of pure white curls, came with a blanket and pillow for Maxi. She was crying softly.

"What in the world happened?" she asked in a wavering voice.

"I don't know what caused it; but it was an explosion," Sam replied.

The entire neighborhood was converging around them. Within a few minutes the police arrived, along with fire trucks, the ambulance and paramedics.

Sam moved aside as the paramedics knelt beside Maxi and began their assessment. Talking into their phones attached to their shoulder straps, they began conveying information to the hospital emergency room. Sam stayed nearby but was glad to let the professionals take over.

"Everyone, please get back. We don't know yet what happened and there could be another explosion." The police were urging everyone back into the street away from the burning house.

"I think we should evacuate the area until we know what happened here. If there are gas leaks, other houses could be in danger." Mark Fields, the chief of police said to Fire Chief Dan Carter.

"I agree," Dan replied. "We don't know what we are dealing with here. It was some kind of explosion, but what caused it? Was it a bomb, a gas leak? We just don't know until we get the blaze under control. Let's just hope that none of the other houses are going to blow. Thank God these are really big lots and the homes are far apart." Dan left to give more orders to his men.

Mark turned toward the crowd gathered in the street, saying to the policeman standing next to him, "We want the area evacuated immediately. There could be danger of more explosions. Knock on doors in case there were residents inside their homes".

With the crowd already gathered, it was hard to believe that anyone could still be inside, but it was his job to be certain. He watched as two of his squad started herding people back and telling them to get in their cars and go to the town square until they could be certain it was safe for them to return. Streets were already blocked off to prevent curiosity seekers from entering the area, and he noted that two of his men were going down the street knocking on doors, one on each side of the street. He sighed, "God, what a mess" and hoped that Maxi wasn't seriously hurt. He guessed Sam had gone along in the ambulance with her, as his truck still was crosswise in the street.

Sam waited in the emergency room until Jake Reese arrived. As the Executive Director of the flood project and Maxi's boss, Sam thought Jake should know what had happened, and had called him. Jake had said he would be there in thirty minutes. Sam knew he lived in another town and it would take that long to drive the distance if he left immediately.

Later, Jake sat in the waiting room while Maxi was X-rayed and thoroughly checked out in the emergency room. Sam had left after extracting a promise from Jake that he would call him if there were anything more he could do. After she was admitted, Jake sat quietly in a chair in the corner of her room. It was now 8 o'clock in the evening and still she showed no sign of waking.

"God, please let this be an accident, not a deliberate act." Jake's thoughts worried him. There was opposition to the dike-levee, but he hoped not to the extent of harming anyone. And why pick on Maxi? He would be a better target if, in fact, it was deliberate.

Dr. Woods came into the room and checked Maxi's pulse and lifted her eyelids to shine a light into her eyes. He looked up at Jake and said, "No sign of waking yet. She has a bad concussion and a lot of bruises, but no broken bones or internal injuries that we can detect. Thank goodness she hadn't yet entered the house when the explosion occurred or she would be dead."

"Yes, it was so close. It's really frightening how quickly things can happen. Do you have any idea how long it will be before she wakes up?" Jake asked his long time friend Steve Woods. Jake stood up and crossed the room to stand next to the doctor.

"No. It could be any time or it could be days. Nature takes its own time. I'll check on her again before I leave for the night. I suggest that you go home, too, Jake. We have a good nursing staff and they will check on her frequently, and if she wakes or there are any other changes the monitor will record the change and the nurses will be here immediately."

"I suppose you're right; I should go home. I'll leave my phone number in case anyone needs to reach me," Jake said reluctantly and walked with the doctor out the door.

"You know that her house is completely demolished, don't you?" Jake asked.

"Yes, I heard that. It will be a terrible blow to her when she realizes what happened. It has only been a month since her husband died. This could put her into a deep depression." Steve added, "We will

just have to wait and see. It can't be predicted.
She'll have support from her friends in Forest
Hills and hopefully that will help. It's too bad
that her son lives in California and her daughter
in New York. It makes it difficult for them and for
her. They can't leave their jobs for long and I know
they will be very concerned, especially since their
dad's recent death."

Chapter 5

It was a sunny autumn morning. Maxi stared through the windows of the sunroom in the Forest Hills rehab facility, not seeing the beautiful color of the trees and the deep blue sky. Two nurses had walked her from her room to the sunroom as they did every day, and she went to physical therapy without protest. But to those caring for her, it seemed as though nothing penetrated her thoughts. She didn't notice anything around her, just sat staring vacantly. It seemed to others that she felt there was nothing to care about any more, that living took too much energy. She had been this way since she woke up in the hospital three weeks ago.

"Good Morning, Maxi. I have someone here to see you," Jake said as he came into the room. It had been a week since he had been there. He was extremely busy now with work, but beyond that he found it too draining to try to talk to her. But today was different. He had something that might bring her out of her depression. Watching her closely, he placed the small black kitten in her lap.

It took a few moments for her to focus her attention. Then she cried, "Beau!" She hugged him while tears poured down her cheeks, the first sign of emotion since the accident.

"He had been hiding in the debris from your house." Jake grinned as he told her of the crew cleaning up the wreckage from the explosion, finding the kitten and bringing it to his office.

"He had been hiding for a week before the cleanup crew discovered him, and he has been at the vet's for two weeks. I didn't want to tell you until I knew he was going to be all right. He was in terrible shape, nearly starved and terribly dehydrated. He must have found some food and water somewhere or he would have died in that length of time. It has taken this long before the vet declared him healthy again," Jake explained. "Then, I had to get permission to bring him in to you. I had to convince the administrator that the kitten could help with your recovery."

For the first time in the three weeks since that terrible day, Maxi managed a rough, hoarse laugh as she hugged the wiggling, squirming little cat. He was all over her, rubbing under her chin and turning around and around on her lap, then returning to lick her face again and again. His purr was amazingly loud for such a small kitten.

Jake knew the reunion was a success. Now was the hard part, talking to her about her job. He waited patiently until Maxi and the kitten both settled down with Beau curling into a ball to sleep in her lap.

"Maxi, we need to talk. We have to move on with the relocation. The project is underway with the first acquisition happening soon, probably the beginning of next week. You know we have to get the people relocated within three months of taking their property. You also know we have to go through channels to get approval from the Army Corps of Engineers for each relocation before we can tell the people how much relocation money they will be eligible to receive. We just can't wait any longer." Jake was being as kind as possible, going into details that he knew she was aware of. He really hated to do this. Her injuries had healed; but he was sure she would not able to do it, mentally or physically. Sometimes he hated being an administrator.

Maxi's joy burst like a punctured balloon. The awful void loomed in her inner vision again. What was she going to do? Fear grabbed her and she doubled over holding the kitten to her stomach. Then the panic subsided and gradually her natural optimistic and stubborn will began to assert itself. She straightened up and looked at Jake. He was waiting patiently for her to pull herself together enough to talk about it. She took a deep breath.

"Jake, I can do it. I have to do it somehow."

"Maxi, we have no choice; it will just be too much for you. You are barely walking. Think of the inspections necessary, and that is after all the paperwork to get approval. We are just getting started. The pressure to keep ahead of construction is going to be considerable and we can't justify adding staff to help you," Jake argued.

"I won't need anyone to help me. I'll be ready, Jake. I have to for my own mental health. Just give me some time to buy a car and find a place to live." Maxi's thoughts were flying, trying to come up with possible ways to accomplish it.

"Give me this afternoon to see what I can work out," she pleaded. "I will need a couple days to work on getting my strength back and to get into an apartment, but if you hired someone new it would be a month before they would be ready to do anything even under the best of circumstance. Anyone new would have to get the training from the Federal people. They only give that a few times a year."

"Okay, I won't put anything into motion until we talk again this evening. I'll stop by on my way home after five. That is all I can promise". Jake stood to leave and clasp her shoulder in a gesture of understanding and friendship as he walked to the door. Before he left, he turned and said, "You do know that the fire inspector said the explosion was caused deliberately, don't you?"

"No, I didn't. I guess I haven't been communicating much since it happened. Do they know who did it? And why?"

"They don't know who did it; but it was deliberate. The fire inspector said a gas burner was turned on but not ignited and a candle was lighted in the kitchen. It would have taken a while for the gas to build up enough to cause the explosion," Jake explained.

"But how is that possible? It was a new stove and had automatic starters. I hadn't even used the stove that morning, and there were no candles lit in the kitchen." Maxi was puzzled.

"Dan Carter explained that even those kinds of burners can be turned fast enough to skip the automatic igniting and the gas would be on but not lighted. At least no other houses were involved. When the entire area was ordered evacuated, it was thought there might be a gas line leaking," Jake continued. "It now seems that your house was deliberately selected by someone who wanted to destroy it and possibly kill you."

"So it was intentionally directed at me!" Maxi shuddered. "Why? Because of the project?"

"It looks that way. I'm sorry to lay this on you now, but you need to think of the consequences of continuing with the job," Jake advised before heading out the door. "I'll see you about 5:30."

Maxi got back to her room under her own power. She was exhausted by the time she got there and waited a moment to catch her breath and for her heart to stop pounding before reaching for the phone. It was picked up on the first ring. Maxi had taken a chance that Bonnie would still be at home and not at the office this early in the morning. "Hi Bonnie, it's Maxi."

"Well hello! It is good to hear from you. How are you doing?" Bonnie asked, her voice showing the pleasure at hearing from her friend.

"I'm doing better. Bonnie, can you find me an apartment or even a room to rent immediately?"

"I think I can find something if it is to be temporary," Bonnie replied. 'It will take a little longer if it is to be permanent".

"Temporary is best for now," Maxi said. "But I must be allowed to have a cat. Jake was just here and brought Beau. He was found in the wreckage of my house and he is here with me now."

"Are you ready to leave the rehab unit?" Bonnie asked. She had heard rumors that Maxi was still in really bad shape. Even though she had been especially busy since the day she and Maxi had looked at the old Sterner place, she felt guilty for not having stopped by to see her.

"Yes. I'm still a little weak, but I have to find a place to live and get a new car." Maxi smiled grimly at her understatement. She would overcome it.

"Okay, let me do some checking for you and I'll call you back this afternoon. Do you feel up to looking at anything today?" Bonnie was all business and her mind was clicking off possibilities.

"Yes. I'm going to call Bob at the BMW dealership and see if he can bring a car around for me this morning, "Maxi replied.

"Fine. I'll get back to you by early afternoon. That should give you time for the car thing."

Maxi hung up and headed for the bathroom. She hadn't even taken a shower by herself yet but she would do it now, and where were her clothes? It hit her suddenly that all her things had been destroyed in the fire. She had nothing to wear except what she had on when she was brought here. What had she worn from the hospital to the rehab unit? She looked in the closet and saw two sweat suits hanging there, one deep pink and one medium blue. The one she had on was yellow. She vaguely remembered Lorene helping her put one on and a pair of tennis shoes. She found them with a pair of socks stuffed inside. There was a comb and a few toilet articles, too.

Fifteen minutes later she sat down shakily on the bed, and then decided it would be best to lie down for a few minutes.

"Lunch time," a cheery voice called, waking Maxi from a sound sleep. "I had a hard time finding you when you weren't in the sunroom. You must be feeling better to walk back here by yourself." Jill, the aide who had been Maxi's special nurse since she had been in extended care, set the lunch tray on the bed table and looked at Maxi in amazement. This was the woman who didn't respond to anything except to walk when two of them urged her, and did what was necessary in physical therapy only when prompted. She had been worried when she went to the sunroom and found it vacant.

"Yes, I am feeling much better. Thanks Jill," Maxi eyed the lunch tray with apprehension. When the domed lid was lifted off the plate, a slice of meatloaf, mashed potatoes and green beans were revealed. Beau came to investigate the odor of food. Maxi had forgotten him in her exhausted sleep. She picked him up and hugged him. "We must eat and get strong, Beau."

"This is the kitten you lost during the fire at your place?" Jill grinned from ear to ear as she bent to stroke the small black kitten. She had been one of the advocates for Jake to bring the kitten into the facility. She was an animal lover herself and realized how much a pet could mean to its owner. It looked to her as though the kitten was a success.

Taking the saucer from under her cup of tea, Maxi broke up small pieces of meatloaf and set it on the bed for the kitten. He ate quickly, inspiring her to eat, too. She evidently hadn't been eating much, as she realized how loose the sweat suit was. She determined she would eat every bite. Her motivation was working overtime, she thought, and smiled.

Jill left them to their lunch with a feeling of satisfaction. She hadn't known Maxi before she became her patient, but she quickly became fond of her and had tried hard to bring her out of the depression she had been suffering. She could hardly wait to tell old Hawks, the administrator. He had only reluctantly agreed to the pet and gave them one day to see if it helped.

It was 12:30 when Maxi and Beau finished eating and she hadn't called about a car. Maybe the best thing would be to lease until she was stronger and could better decide what she wanted to buy. A phone call to the BMW dealership insured that Bob would indeed bring a car around and all the paperwork within the hour. She hadn't specified any particular model. It really didn't matter.

Next, she called her bank and requested a checkbook with her current balance recorded and was promised that a messenger would deliver it immediately. It was so strange not to have anything, none of the things that were used daily. It was almost as if her identity were wiped out. She mused that living in a community like Forest Hills where everybody knew everyone definitely had its merits. In a large city she wouldn't get this kind of service.

By the time Bonnie called that afternoon, Maxi had a car and her checkbook. It had a larger balance than she had expected. Her paychecks had been taken to the bank to be deposited during her illness. Roger, the bank manager, had also sent a note with the checkbook that she was to call the insurance office to make arrangements for the payment of the insurance on her home and all the cars. He confirmed what Jake had told her, that it had been ruled an act of arson and the arsonist had not yet been found. Maxi still didn't know if they had any leads.

"I have three apartments that are possibilities for you and they are available as we speak." Bonnie told her. "Are you able to look at them this afternoon?"

"Yes. But will you come pick me up, Bonnie. I have a leased car now but I am feeling a little shaky and I don't trust myself to drive just yet." Maxi had to concede that she wasn't really ready to drive the highway and city streets.

"I'll be there in 15 minutes," Bonnie assured her.

Beau was shut in the bathroom with food, water and a litter box, and Maxi was ready and waiting when Bonnie arrived.

By the time Jake came in a little after 5 o'clock as he had promised, Maxi was ready for him. Exhausted but energized at the same time, she told him the accomplishments of the afternoon.

"You did what!" Jake exploded in disbelief.

"YES!" It came out as an exclamation, full of pride at her accomplishments. "I have a car and an apartment. It's not much more than an expanded motel room but it will do nicely for Beau and me until I can find a house. It's furnished, so I don't even have to think about furniture, and it is only three blocks from the office."

Jake could hardly believe his ears or his eyes. This was a totally different person than he seen this morning before giving her cat back to her. It was incredible. "I can't believe you accomplished all this in one day."

"Tomorrow I will go shopping for clothes," Maxi said. "And I want to thank you and the Board for continuing to pay me and depositing it in my account. I had the bank bring me a checkbook with my current balance in it. I feel as though the bank account was the only thing not destroyed."

"The Board felt it was the least they could do since it seems that the explosion might be due to your employment." Jake replied.

"I admit that I can't believe how weak I am in a matter of three weeks, but I will soon build myself up. I plan on being at the office Monday morning. That gives me two days to get back on my feet. I may only be able to work half days the first week, but that will be better than trying to train someone new," Maxi looked at Jake anxiously, hoping that what she had just outlined would be enough to keep her job.

"Maxi, I am absolutely stunned!" Jake looked at her in amazement. "We will certainly give you a little time to get back to full time, and yes, it will be much better than starting someone from scratch. I don't even expect you to be able to handle half days yet. Just come in when you can this next week and stay until you are tired, then go home. Even with your determination it will take a little time."

"Dinner," Sally, the evening aide said, as she came through the door bearing a tray. "I hear you are making a miraculous recovery. We are all so thrilled about it, even if it means you may not be with us much longer." She continued chattering away as she went about putting the tray on the bed table and removing the domed lids.

"Thank you, Sally. I feel like I have come back from the dead. And I am also dead tired," Maxi smiled as she eyed the meal. The food wasn't really all that bad considering it was hospital food, and she found she had worked up an appetite from the afternoon's activity as well as from her better state of mind.

"Okay. I'll leave you to eat and get a good night's rest," Jake rose from the chair where he had been sitting. "Is there anything I can do for you over the weekend?"

"No, I don't think so. All I plan to do tomorrow is shop for some things to wear to the office and get settled in my apartment." Her doctor hadn't approved any of her plans, but she intended to go ahead with them anyway even if he objected. She would sign herself out of the rehab unit if necessary.

As soon as she finished as much of her meal as she could manage, she brushed her teeth, put on the hospital nightgown and crawled into bed, totally exhausted. Her adrenaline high had kept her going and now she was coming down, feeling drained. But it was a pleasant feeling, tiredness from activity, not depression. She probably would be a little stiff and sore in the morning, but that was fine and something she could deal with. Tomorrow's plans faded as she fell into a deep natural asleep instead of the drug-induced sleep she had been in for the past three weeks.

Chapter 6

Jill's cheery "Good morning" woke her. She felt like she was coming from a long distance as she struggled to find her way through clouds of sleep.

"Good morning," she croaked. "Wow, I think I died. I turned out the light last night at 6 o'clock." Looking at the clock that showed it was now 8:00, she realized she had slept 14 hours without waking or hardly stirring all night.

She ate her breakfast, not really hungry, but determined to get her strength back as quickly as possible. As she became more fully awake, she thought of all she had to do and realized that the first should be a call to her children. She knew they had been with her after the explosion. She had heard them talking and knew they had made the arrangements for her admission to the rehabilitation unit when she was discharged from the hospital, but she hadn't responded. They must be really worried by now, she thought.

She dialed Lorene's number first. Although it was only 9 o'clock on Saturday morning, she answered on the second ring.

"Hi, it's Mom."

"Mom! Are you all right? We've all been so worried. I have called the nurse's station every day and they keep telling me there is no change. It is so wonderful to hear your voice!" The jumbled words came pouring out. Lorene hardly knew what she was saying, but she knew her mother's voice. It had been three weeks since she and Michael had been there and saw her settled into the rehab unit.

"I'm fine. I have a very, very small apartment that I plan to move into today or tomorrow. I have leased a car and plan on going back to work Monday. I just have to get a few things to wear to work. I am going shopping today", Maxi said. "I am so glad to be able to give you some good news. There has been enough bad news lately."

"Just to talk to you is good news, Mom". Lorene was nearly in tears. "I'm so relieved. But do you think you should try to go back to work this soon?" She was also wondering what had brought her out of her depression. This seemed like a miracle.

"What has happened, Mom? I just checked day before yesterday and the nurse said you couldn't talk on the phone and there was no change in your condition."

"My boss was here early yesterday morning. He brought me a surprise. I have Beau back!" Maxi's voice wavered with emotion. "I guess it was the jolt I needed. Especially when he also told me that the Project had reached a point where they were going to hire a replacement for me. They have deadlines and construction schedules to meet. All of a sudden, I knew I had to pull myself together. I need this job."

"But Mom, you don't need a job. Dad left you more than well off; you're rich! Why don't you take it easy and do some traveling? Come here for a few weeks. I know Michael would like you to spend some time with him, too. We have talked it over and think maybe you can find a small apartment near one of us, and visit the other whenever you want." Lorene was concerned that her mother was trying to do too much, too soon. "You have had too many shocks in the past three months. You need time to recover." Lorene continued.

"Thank you for asking me to stay with you, but I don't need time to know what I want to do. I want to go back to work and finish this job. I need to feel needed, right now; and I know I can help these people as they settle into new homes. Maybe when it is over, I will want to take some time off, but not just now. Working will help me recover. It is not just a job for a paycheck. It is more than that; it is helping people in distress," Maxi reassured her daughter. "I will be all right, honey. If I sit around too much I will dwell on my losses and that won't be good for me. I need to build a new life. I can do it and I'll call often to let you know how things are going."

"Well, if you find it's too much, promise you will resign," Lorene insisted. "When you have holidays or vacation time, I want you to come here. It is only a five-hour drive and you have done it many times. We always want you. You know that, don't you?"

"Yes, honey, I know that," Maxi replied gratefully, "and I promise. And, I will call your brother later. It is still too early, California time; if I were to call him at 6:30 in the morning, it would scare him to death."

"Okay. Bye, Mom. Take care and know that I love you and I am so glad you are feeling better!" Lorene was relieved but still worried.

"Bye. I love you. I want you and Jack to enjoy yourselves and relax today, after all, it's Saturday. I know you have been worried about me, so it's time for you to have some fun".

Maxi realized as she hung up the phone that just making the call had tired her. She got back into bed to rest a few minutes before taking a shower and getting dressed. She would call Michael at lunchtime and then head for the mall to find some clothes, just the minimum for now to be properly dressed for work. It was hard starting from scratch. All she had now were the three sweat suits that Lorene had gotten for her when she left the hospital. She didn't even have underwear.

It was 11:30 when she woke again. Feeling rested, she headed for the shower. Ten minutes later, dressed in a clean sweat suit minus the none-existent bra and panties, she called Michael, and had nearly a repeat of her talk with Lorene earlier. Having reassured him, she thought about her shopping that afternoon and decided it would be best if she had someone go with her. Maybe Sue would be able to go along.

She dialed her best friend, who answered on the third ring. "Hi Sue. It's Maxi."

"Maxi! It's so good to hear from you. How are you?" Maxi could hear the surprise in Sue's voice.

"I'm really much better. In fact, that's why I'm calling you. I want to go to the mall. I need some clothes to wear to work. I am still a little shaky, and don't know if I'm up to doing it alone. Can you go with me?"

"Of course I can. I can't believe that you are really able to go at all; are you sure you're up to it?" Sue looked at her watch and calculated it would take her a half hour to shower and get dressed for shopping. "I have been working in the yard all morning so I need to shower first. How soon do you want to leave?"

"Just come over whenever you're ready," Maxi was relieved to have her friend accompany her.

By 4:30, after many stops to sit and rest, Maxi and Sue had completed a wardrobe suitable for the office, plus eight sets of underwear, a nightgown, and a robe and slippers to wear in the morning and evening at home. She now owned three pantsuits with blazer jackets and two blouses for each, two pair of casual slacks and four tops to go with them, as well as a turtleneck sweater and a matching cardigan. She also had three pair of shoes: two pair of low-healed dress pumps, one black and one tan; and a pair of black flats to wear with the slacks. A hobo shoulder bag in soft black leather completed her shopping.

She also now owned a cosmetic case containing all the necessary cosmetics demonstrated by the clerk at the cosmetic counter, shampoo, conditioner, setting lotion, a hair dryer and curling brush.

"I can't think of any other necessities," Maxi said as she sat down on a bench, exhausted. "I'll get coats and more winter clothing in a couple weeks."

"Just one more thing if you feel up to it," Sue said.

"What?"

"A hairdo! Your hair is a mess," Sue replied "There is a beauty salon just across the corridor. I don't know how good they are, but it's convenient. Let's try it."

"Let's get a pick-me-up first. After all this shopping, I need something." Maxi glanced at the salon rather mistrustfully. She was proud of her hair. It had suffered in the explosion and then neglect during her convalescence, but even so, she rather hated to trust an unknown beautician.

"Okay. It's a deal. There is a restaurant next to the beauty salon."

A club sandwich and coffee restored her somewhat and they started across the corridor toward the salon. Fortunately, they had no one waiting and Maxi was in the chair before she had time to think.

The beautician studied Maxi's hair with a critical eye. "Have you been sick?" She asked as she pulled her fingers through the dark auburn strands.

"Yes, I guess you could say that," Maxi replied with a rueful grin at Sue.

"Since the ends are split and dry, I think you should have a conditioning treatment first and then we will see about the cut. You have a nice natural wave and the color is good, only a few gray hairs that highlighting would blend in beautifully. Okay?" The beautician looked at her questioningly.

"Okay," Maxi was too tired to debate and it sounded as though it would be all right.

An hour later, Maxi was looking at herself in the mirror hardly believing the result. Her hair was shorter, just below her jaw line and curved under into her neck, a modified, shortened pageboy without bangs. It had a wonderful auburn luster.

The natural wave was just enough to lend movement to the hairdo and keep it manageable.

"I love it!" Maxi and Sue exclaimed in unison.

"And it will be easy to care for," the beautician said, pleased with their reaction.

As they left the mall and headed for the car, Maxi said, "Thank you for thinking of the haircut, Sue. I was so tired I wouldn't have considered it myself. And it does make me feel so much better. Why is it that women always feel better when their hair looks good?"

"I guess it is a girl thing," Sue said with a grin at her friend. "You do look fabulous. The makeup that the sales girl put on is great, too. You look like a new person, except a little tired. It's time to go back to your room and get some rest."

"I'll vote for that," Maxi said with a sigh as she sank into the passenger seat of Sue's car.

She dozed during the half hour drive to the Extended Care Unit. Sue helped her to her room with her packages and saw her to bed. Beau had greeted them as they opened the bathroom door to check on him, and then jumped onto the bed where he now curled up next to Maxi.

Sue checked the litter box, scooped the dirty litter into a plastic bag, tied it, and dropped it into the wastebasket. She put food into Beau's dish from the bag sitting in the corner, and fresh water into another bowl next to the food. Jake had provided everything when he brought the kitten in yesterday. *Thank goodness for Jake and Beau.*

Sue left feeling sure that Maxi was motivated to get on with her life. Even if she found the job was too much for her, at least now she could go on to something else.

Sue called Maxi Sunday morning, saying that she and Rob would be there to help her get settled in her new apartment whenever she was ready to go.

"I'll be ready in half an hour if that works for you," Maxi replied.

"That's fine. We'll see you in half an hour."

Since Maxi was wearing a sweat suit instead of getting dressed in her new finery, she had only her purchases from the day before and her two sweat suits in the closet to take with her. But she knew she had to get discharged from the facility. Her doctor had reluctantly agreed to release her, but told her that he felt it was too soon. She pushed the buzzer beside her bed to summon the nurse to tell her she was leaving in a half hour. She had already signed all the necessary forms regarding her bill and discharge instructions.

By five o'clock Maxi was situated in her tiny apartment. She had had dinner with Sue and Rob after they had carried in her belongings and hung her clothing in the closet. She and Sue had made the bed with linens furnished with the apartment. Her tiny refrigerator was stocked with milk, bread, butter, orange juice and eggs. The cupboards now held an assortment of cereals, crackers and soups.

"So Beau, how do you like your new home?" Maxi stretched out on the bed with Beau in the curve of her arm. Within minutes she was sound asleep.

Chapter 7

Monday morning arrived more quickly than Maxi had anticipated. When her alarm woke her at 7:30, she opened her eyes and groaned. Her whole body ached. With sheer force of will she got out of bed and shuffled toward the bathroom. Two hours later she was at the top of the flight of stairs leading to the offices of the Flood Protection Authority. She was winded by then and unhappy with being late on her first day back.

Dressed in a bright red pantsuit that she hoped would help keep her going, Maxi stopped in the open doorway of Jake's office. "Good morning, Jake. I'm sorry to be late on my first morning back."

"Good morning, Maxi." Jake whirled his chair around from his computer as he greeted her. "Wow. You look fantastic. I can hardly believe my eyes."

"It's wonderful what clothes, makeup and a hairdo can do," Maxi replied.

By noon, Maxi gave in and called it a day. Since Jake was out of the office, she left a note on his desk, so he would know she was okay, just tired.

By the end of her first week, Maxi had labored her way through the first five Comparison Schedules. It was a little like doing a market analysis for a new listing when she worked in real estate. She had to enter information on the house being taken and compare it with three similar properties that were available now, which meant checking to be sure that they weren't already sold. The information consisted of the type of house, type of construction, square feet of living space, number of bathrooms, bedrooms, eat-in kitchen or kitchen with formal dining room, and so on. Maxi took her time and was thorough because she knew her results would be checked closely by Brad, her contact at the Army Corps of Engineers, before giving an okay for her to proceed. And the people would want to know exactly how any additional money, or lack thereof, was calculated. It was possible to add $22,500 to the acquisition price that they were paid for the home being taken, plus the moving expenses, which required quotes from three different companies.

This Maxi discovered was rather redundant as the Pennsylvania Utility Commission controlled the prices that moving companies could charge. But the relocation code said there had to be three.

By the end of the second week, Maxi had made initial contact with the first five families and had encountered a wide range of circumstances.

First was the 96-year-old widow, Helen McGuire, who had lived in the same house all her life, and had just been told by her doctor two days before that she had breast cancer. She was already scheduled for surgery. But she was stoic, saying, "This house is getting to be too much for me, anyway. Now I'll have help getting another place, plus help with moving. I feel so much better about it all now that you have been here, and explained to me how it works and how much you'll help me.

"I didn't tell that man and the attorney who told me how much I would be paid for this place, but I had an appraisal done last spring. That appraiser told me less than I have been offered now, so I feel I am getting a good deal all the way around. Even if the dike wasn't going to happen, I would have put the house on the market and sold it. But, I tell you, as I got into it and got to thinking about it, there would have been an awful lot of work and a lot for me to see to. I don't have any children or even relatives who live here." Helen then added with a beautiful smile, "So you are an angel in disguise. You are helping so much, I can't begin to thank you."

The second family was a young husband and wife, Robert and Barbara Quincy, and their two children. The man did all the talking. He was belligerent and said emphatically that they objected to being forced from their home. With some gentle probing, Maxi soon learned that they had been looking for a newer, bigger home for over three years, but couldn't afford the prices. When they heard how the relocation worked and that they would have help with moving expenses and the work involved, he mellowed somewhat and Maxi noticed his wife was smiling. Their two children, a boy Stevie, and a girl, Jenny, were pleasant, well-behaved.

The next appointment turned out to be a likeable middle-aged couple, Frank and Marjorie Winkle, who said quite frankly said they were looking forward to moving, provided they would not be financially set back, as they were tired of worrying about floods and were facing retirement in a few years.

It was the fourth visit on her list that troubled her. Walter North was a very angry man. He triggered anger in her that she couldn't afford to feel. He was a widower, 70 years old, who refused to let her into the house. She walked away from the door, saying that when he was ready to hear what the relocation program could do for him, he was to call her office. Maxi was relying on his neighbors to help him understand what her job was. She would wait a reasonable time in hope that he would call her; if he didn't then she would make another attempt to talk with him.

By late Friday she approached the last house she had scheduled for the week. The yard was littered with broken toys, bicycles, and odds and ends of torn and dirty clothing that appeared to have been there for a long time. Why clothing would be littering the yard she hadn't a clue. As she neared the front door, three dogs came tearing around the corner of the house, led by a huge black and tan German shepherd. They weren't barking, and that made them seem even more menacing. The German shepherd blocked her way to the door, showing his teeth and growling. She stopped dead in her tracks, heart pounding, and spoke to the dogs in a quiet voice, "Hello, guys. Nice to see you. Are you going to let me in the house?"

Looking into the bared teeth of the snarling German shepherd, flanked by a collie of equal size and a small beagle, she felt more than a flash of fear. The beagle was the only friendly face in the crowd. She stood still, hoping to be rescued by the owner who was probably watching with amusement from the window. She hadn't been able to make a contact by phone. No one had answered during numerous attempts. Maxi had wanted to do this visit two days ago and had put it off hoping to make phone contact first and make an appointment.

She surveyed the three facing her. The black and tan dog looked less threatening now. His teeth were no longer showing, but he continued to watch her warily. When she moved he growled low in his throat. The collie was quiet, seeming to wait for a command from his partner, but the beagle looked downright friendly with his tail wagging. He did something with his ears that seemed to lower them and it looked like he was grinning at her. *Rather fanciful thinking, my girl.*

"Maybe you think this situation is funny, Beagle, but I am getting tired of standing here." Maxi took a tentative step toward the rickety steps leading to a small stoop and the front door. The dogs stayed with her, but didn't seem to be making more threatening moves. The German shepherd had stopped growling, but continued to keep pace with her.

"Good dogs. I am not here to cause trouble. Be nice, now." Maxi kept edging up one step at a time, escorted by the trio. She watched them in her peripheral vision, having heard that to make eye contact with an animal was to challenge it, and the last thing she wanted to do was challenge these three. Whether it was true or not, she wasn't taking any chances. At last she was at the still closed door. She pressed the doorbell but couldn't hear it ring. She wondered if it was working. She knocked twice and waited. She knocked again three times and finally heard movement inside. A woman barely opened the door, looking out through a three-inch opening.

"Whatcha want?"

"My name is Maxine Taylor. I am from the Flood Protection Authority. I need to talk to you." Maxi gave the woman her most winning smile and asked, "May I come in, please?"

Holding the door only partially open, the woman reluctantly stepped back then opened the door wider. The dogs bolted through and Maxi quickly stepped inside before the woman changed her mind.

She looked as though she would slam it shut at any moment.

"You're not from the welfare office, are you?"

"No. I'm Maxine Taylor. I need to talk to you about your house being taken for the flood protection project. I can explain it to you better if we can sit down and talk about it."

"You're the first person to come all the way to the door. The others stopped when they saw the dogs," the woman said with what seemed grudging admiration. She led the way to a sagging, threadbare sofa indicating that Maxi should sit there while she took the only chair, which was in equally bad shape. Both were upholstered in the latest fashion of dog hair, and Maxi sat gingerly on the edge of the sofa, hoping the dogs wouldn't object. She didn't relish the possibility of being dog food.

Maxi looked more closely at the woman now. She was extremely obese and was still in her nightgown even though it was mid-afternoon. Her frowzy carrot-colored hair looked like it hadn't seen a comb or brush in days, much less a shampoo. The obvious dye job had been awhile, too, as three inches of dark roots showed. Maxi guessed she was in her mid-thirties, but looked an old fifty.

Wanting to take a deep breath to steady her nerves, Maxi decided against it; the odor of the place was causing her to swallow repeatedly to keep from gagging. She chose instead to breathe shallowly through parted lips. While the dogs kept close watch, Maxi began to explain why she was there.

"Has your landlord told you that you will have to move because this house is being taken for the flood protection project?"

"I got a letter from him saying I would have to move, but I didn't pay it no mind. He's always threatening to put us out, though I can't imagine who else would rent such a hole?" The woman did not appear upset. In fact she showed no emotion, only resignation or maybe it was depression, Maxi thought.

"This time, it is true. This house is being taken for the flood protection project. My job is to help you find another home. So I need to ask you some questions regarding your needs, such as how many there are in your family and so forth." Maxi waited for some response.

A barely discernable nod gave her permission. "Your name is Evelyn Andrews?" She again nodded. "How many children do you have?"

"I got five kids. Their dad left us two years ago, Christmas Eve. He went out for cigarettes and never came back." This information was delivered in a flat monotone as though it had been recited many times to uninterested people.

"How awful for you." Maxi's sympathy was evident in her tone as she leaned toward the woman. "Tell me, how have you managed? How old are the children?"

At the indication of sympathy, the floodgates opened and the information came pouring out. How the youngest child, 7-year-old Jessica, had grieved so badly that her growth was stunted and she flunked out of second grade. The oldest, 12-year-old Jeffery was getting into fights at school and all of them were making poor grades except the second oldest, 11-year-old Tammy, who was getting good grades and helped her mother by doing the grocery shopping and cooking meals for the family. The two middle children, Johnny and Jerry, eight-year-old twins, were getting along but not getting the grades that they had achieved before their father deserted them. Evelyn said they were getting welfare checks and food stamps, and they survived on that.

"There is a new low-income housing unit nearing completion. Would you be interested in living there?" Maxi didn't want to push too hard so soon. "How 'bout I check with them, and get back to you, if there are still vacancies. I understand that there are more applications than the available apartments, but let me check for you."

"I don't want no part of low-income housing. Those people have all their regulations and we just won't fit in." Evelyn's jaw set stubbornly.

"Let's not be hasty. I'll look into it and come back next week and we'll talk some more," Maxi said, detecting stubborn pride that indicated she didn't want welfare programs or perhaps had been treated badly.

"I'll phone you before I come. I couldn't get you this week. Do I have your right number?" Maxi was hopeful that if she called, the dogs would be either in the house or tied up. She didn't look forward to meeting them outside again.

Evelyn indicated the number given was correct, but then added, "I don't answer the phone, and it was cut off yesterday, anyway. I can't pay for it."

"Oh. Well, do you want me to just show up when I have more about the housing?"

"Yea, that'd be all right. I'm always here anyway, never go no place." And seeing Maxi glance nervously at the dogs, added, "They'll be okay now that you have been here once, if you don't do anything suspicious."

Maxi wasn't sure what the dogs would interpret as suspicious, but nodded anyway, happy to make her escape.

Getting into her car, she wondered where the children were. School should be out for the day by now. She made a mental note to contact the manager of the new housing unit the first thing Monday morning. If he could see her, she would go to his office and start the necessary paperwork. Evelyn and her family should have priority as they were being displaced and certainly the family's circumstances warranted space in the new building.

It was only 4 o'clock. She decided to go back to the office and make some notes of things she needed to do first thing Monday. It had been a physically and emotionally draining week. She wondered if many of the people would be as needy as the last family. Going into her office, she saw an envelope lying in the center of her desk. There was nothing written on the outside and she opened it, absentmindedly, still thinking of the people she had seen during the week.

The large black type seemed to jump off the page and she gasped for breath as though she had been punched in the stomach, causing her to sit down hard in her desk chair. It had been typed on a computer in large letters.

You should have learned your lesson!!!!!! You should know by now how if feels to have your home taken away, bitch. Quit or face the consequences. Tell the rest of them assholes, they are in trouble too if this doesn't stop!!!!!!!!!!!!!!

Jake, on his way to his office, glanced into Maxi's office. Seeing her upset, he came in, "What's wrong? What happened?"

Maxi handed him the note without comment. She was speechless and shaking from head to toe.

"Where did this come from?" He demanded, his tone sharp with rage.

"It was on my desk when I came in just now. Someone was in here, and put it there. How could anyone be so bold as to think they could just walk in here and put this on my desk, and no one would see them?" Maxi's voice rose in pitch and trembled as the reality hit her that someone so vengeful had been right here in her office, during working hours.

Jake was out the door like a shot and heading for the front office to question Sarah, the receptionist, about who had been in that afternoon, or if she had been asked to put the letter on Maxi's desk.

"No one came in this afternoon. It has been very quiet. Why?" Sarah asked, mystified as to what was causing Jake's obvious anger.

Maxi was right on Jake's heels. "The back way. It has to be the back door. Someone just walked in the back door, down the hall and into my office without being seen."

"You're probably right. I have been out since two o'clock and all the other offices were empty when I left," Jake conceded, as he headed back to his office where he telephoned Mark.

It was close to six o'clock when Maxi left for home. She wasn't hungry, but decided she should stop for dinner even if she didn't feel she could eat. At the Gathering Place she ordered a bowl of clam chowder, and realized as she finished it, that she felt better, although she was still shaken. Reading the note and knowing that someone was bold enough to come into the building was enough to shake anyone, she thought, above and beyond the fact that the tone of the note suggested a violent, mentally disturbed person.

The explosion, which had demolished her home, was foremost in her mind. What might someone in that state of mind do next? Maxi shuddered at the thought as she opened the door to her temporary home and was greeted by Beau. She picked him up and snuggled him into her neck, "What are we going to do?" She felt frightened, confused and terribly weary.

Getting a permanent home was a personal priority, Maxi realized. She had been living in a kind of limbo with her job taking all her energy. She had come a long way the last two weeks, she realized, and congratulated herself by a mental pat on the back.

The house that she had looked at with Bonnie was suddenly in her thoughts again. I need to get on with my life and not live in fear, she thought to herself. Hugging Beau to her chest, she picked up her telephone and dialed Bonnie's home number.

"Hi Bonnie, its Maxi Taylor," she didn't bother with any of the usual polite ways to begin a conversation

"Well hello, Maxi. How are you? How are things going with work?" Bonnie inquired, happy to hear from her.

"I'm getting back into things quite nicely, thanks. I wanted to thank you for helping me find a temporary place to live, and now I need to move on and find a permanent home. Thanks for showing me the Sterner Property. Is it still available?"

"Of course, it is still available! Only a fool would buy it except to tear it down and have the location to work with," Bonnie replied, hoping to dissuade Maxi from making a foolish mistake. She was reading the signs of a serious buyer quite well.

"Bonnie, that's a terrible thing for a Realtor to say!" Maxi chided, teasingly.

"Well, you are a friend and I see buyer signs that you are on the verge of making a big mistake unless you are thinking of demolishing it and building a new house," Bonnie answered with spirit.

"Thanks for your concern, Bonnie. I really do appreciate it. Before we go any further, I want to talk to Sam Jackson again. I'll get back to you in a few minutes. Bye." Her fatigue of a few minutes ago forgotten, Maxi hung up the phone and looked up Sam's number. He answered on the second ring.

"Hi Sam, it's Maxi Taylor. I want to thank you for your help the day my house exploded. I apologize for not thanking you sooner. I have been busy getting back into the groove at work. Also, I understand that you saw that Bonnie got the key back to the Sterner house and I want to thank you for that, too."

"Well, hello, Maxi. It's good to hear from you and to know that you are back to work. It's the best thing for you. Keep your mind occupied," Sam was genuinely pleased to hear from her.

"Sam, I know it is the end of September and late to start a major remodeling job, but how busy are you right now?"

"I just finished building a new house this week and have only minor jobs lined up at the moment. Why? If you want to build a new house, there is still time to get it under roof to work on in cold weather," Sam's mind was already calculating the necessary scheduling of subcontractors and the likelihood of their availability.

"No, I wasn't thinking of a new house. I'm thinking of buying the old Sterner property and renovating it. I would like you to do it if you can start immediately," Maxi was getting excited about the possibility that it just might happen.

"Maxi, you're crazy. That place should be demolished. If you like the location it could be a lovely spot for a new house. I have several house plans that I would like to show you," Sam tried to reason with her; he honestly thought a renovation was a huge mistake.

"I don't want a new house, Sam. Can you do it or not?" Maxi was firm.

"Yes, I could do it. I could start making up a schedule tomorrow." Sam knew when he met a brick wall and, being a businessman, wanted the job.

"Great! That is absolutely fabulous! I would rather have you do it than someone else. I know you will do a good job as you have done renovations before and know a lot about preserving the special aspects of the architectural design, inside and out." Maxi was ecstatic.

"I think the roof is the first priority, don't you? Once the roof is repaired, the plumbing, wiring and heating can be done pretty much all at the same time. In that location, there is probably a well and a septic system. We might have to do all new systems there, too. What do you think?"

"I think I can get a crew on the roof by Tuesday, but you can't do anything until you own it," Jake replied, getting pulled into Maxi's enthusiasm. "Then, a week later, I may be able to get a plumbing and heating contractor and electricians working. Possibly I can get a well driller in to look at the well situation and get started on the state requirements for the septic this coming week."

"Sam, that is absolutely wonderful. I'll call Bonnie and get the paper work done for the purchase over the weekend. I hope we can close on Monday since I won't need a bank loan and the bank is selling the property. Everyone should be available to do it." Maxi hadn't felt this excited in years. She completely forgot the threat she had received that afternoon. "I have the insurance money to pay you for your work and it is only tied up a month at a time in CDs. Will that work for your expenses?"

"Yes, that will work just fine for me. Are you really sure about this? A new house would be better for you." Sam made one last appeal.

"Yes, I know, but somehow I have been bitten by the restoration bug. This project is more than giving me a house. I really can't explain it, but I need to do this." Maxi realized how true it was. Building a new house would be nice, but saving the

Sterner house meant more to her; she was saving part of her past. And she had an emotional need right now.

"Thanks a lot, Sam. I really appreciate it and I look forward to working with you. Would it be a good idea to go out to the place tomorrow and do some planning?"

"Yes, I can do that. How about I take you to breakfast and then we will go on to the property from there? I'll pick you up about eight?"

"Great. See you in the morning, Sam." Maxi hung up the phone and immediately dialed Bonnie's number.

"Bonnie. I want to do the Sales Agreement to buy the Sterner property. Can we do it now? I can meet you at the office in a half hour."

"Yes, I can do it," Bonnie said, "but I have to get dinner on the table for the family. It's all ready and everyone's home so it won't take long, but let's make it an hour instead of a half-hour. That way I'll have time to eat, too."

"Sure, fine! I'll be there." Maxi took a deep breath as she hung up the phone.

Taking stock of her finances, she knew she had enough to buy the property from her checking account. The renovations would be financed with the money in the CDs she had established with the $800,000 insurance money from her old house. She had thought far enough ahead two weeks ago, when she was getting her life back together, that she should not put all the money into long term CD's, but keep it accessible to purchase another home so she had put it into monthly accounts. Everything was working out, and she felt rejuvenated and ready for anything.

At eight o'clock she was seated across the desk from Bonnie filling out the Sales Agreement.

"I have never sold a property that closed in two days." Bonnie said. "I am also having trouble believing you are really doing this. Why the rush?"

"It is late in the year and I want to be able to move in by Christmas," Maxi replied. "I know everything won't be finished by then, but part of it should be livable. Three months in that small apartment is long enough, even though I am glad to have it for now."

"Fortunately, the bank has done all the preliminary work hoping for an early sale. There are no relatives so it is the property of the bank. The title search has been done and the property was surveyed. The only thing still to be done is have the well and septic checked. We can't do that and close on Monday, no way." Bonnie clicked off all the items required by law to be done before closing on a sale.

"I'll sign a waiver in regard to the septic and well. I plan to have new systems put in. The existing ones are so old that it will probably be necessary, at least the septic, which is probably an old fashioned cesspool. I wouldn't take a chance on the old one in any event," Maxi explained. "So the only thing is to set an appointment for Monday with the bank people and their attorney. Right?"

"Yes, it would seem so. Actually, I'll call them first thing tomorrow morning". Bonnie was aware that Maxi was hoping to get started on the work by Tuesday, and they couldn't do that until all the paperwork was signed and the bank had their money in hand.

"You sure do get rolling when you make a decision," Bonnie remarked, smiling at Maxi as they finished up the Sales Agreement.

"I've never before done anything like I've had to do in getting back to work and now buying this house to renovate. I haven't been this excited by anything in a long time," Maxi admitted. "This is going to be very good for me. I just know it."

With the house key in her pocket, Maxi got into her car and started home. She didn't notice the black sedan following her. The driver parked across the street from her apartment and contemplated what he had witnessed this evening. He didn't know what all had transpired at the real estate office, but he knew that the desired results of the letter he had left that afternoon had not happened. His boss would not be happy. He had hoped to scare Maxi out of town.

Chapter 8

"Good morning," Maxi hopped into the pickup when Sam stopped in front of her apartment. She had been up since 6 a.m., anxious to get going.

"Good morning," Sam replied, taking in Maxi's fresh appearance. He liked her good looks, not much makeup and shining dark auburn hair. "You look great! Bright-eyed and bushy-tailed this morning."

"Yes, I haven't felt this good in a long time!" Maxi was bubbling with excitement.

They had breakfast at The Gathering Place, where many locals met in the morning. Maxi felt really hungry for the first time since her husband's death. She ordered bacon, scrambled eggs, whole-wheat toast, coffee and orange juice. She thoroughly enjoyed the meal as well as the many interruptions by fellow customers glad to see her up and about again. It was 9:15 by the time they parked at the old Sterner house. *Soon to be my house*, Maxi thought with satisfaction.

"I'm hoping to be able to move in before Christmas," she said to Sam as they went up the steps to the porch.

"Christmas?" Sam stumbled on the steps, nearly falling. "And just how am I to get this place livable in less than three months? It's impossible, Maxi."

"I don't expect it to be completed, just the kitchen, a master bedroom and bath," Maxi hoped she sounded reasonably sensible. "The roof will be replaced and the heating, plumbing, wiring will be done by then. I have to get out of that tiny efficiency apartment. I can live here while the rest of the work goes on. In fact, I think it will be perfect. I can see what takes place every day."

Sam cringed. To him that meant everyday she would change her mind about something or add something to be done. "Can you live with plaster dust, paint smell, dirt and grime getting into everything?" Sam was hopeful that he could dissuade her and clearly didn't think she would enjoy that very much.

"Sure I can. I'll be at work all day. I could even live without a kitchen. That is what I am doing now. I eat at restaurants. So, if necessary, I'll need only a bedroom and bath. Did I tell you I will probably have ownership by Monday afternoon? So that means you can really start on the roof as soon as you can get the crew lined up."

"I'll spend Monday getting the roofing materials ordered to be delivered Tuesday morning and lining up the different work crews. Did you know that the present roof is slate? If it had been anything else it would probably be completely deteriorated and it would be impossible to restore this place," Sam remarked. "I am thinking of replacing it with cedar shingles. Will that be all right?"

"Yes, I think that would be much better than trying to replace it with slate, and cedar shakes will last a long time. Not as long as slate, but better than asphalt shingles, and I like the look of cedar shakes. It will go with the period architecture, too, don't you think?"

Maxi's cell phone rang. It was Bonnie.

"I can have the closing this afternoon if you still want to sign waivers for the septic and well."

"That's wonderful. How did you manage to get the bankers to stay on a Saturday afternoon?"

"Because this is one that will be done in a half hour since you have the cash. The bank is as eager as you to close. You will need to get to your bank this morning, though, and get a certified check for $50,000. Closing costs are minimal, just the state and local transfer tax and the attorney fees, which include the recording fee for the deed. Is one o'clock OK?" Bonnie was talking fast as a result of being in high gear the past hour.

"Fine with me, and I can get to the bank before noon." Maxi's heart rate jumped a few notches.

An hour later she and Sam had finished a preliminary tour of the house. Maxi was at the bank a little after 11. By two o'clock she was the sole owner of the Sterner property.

Letting herself into her apartment, she picked up Beau and gave him a hug, saying, "We are going shopping for a folding chair, a cooler, ice and a tuna sub. Then we are going to have a picnic in our new backyard. I'll share the tuna with you."

After loading her new chair and cooler, Maxi headed for the grocery store where she purchased a sandwich, drinks and a bag of ice. Maxi then added apples and grapes. Her eyes fell upon Bavarian éclairs. She gave in to the impulse and bought two, plus two Hershey bars.

"*That ought to keep us going for a few hours,*" Maxi thought to herself as she headed back to the car. Beau was peering out the windshield anxiously waiting for her return.

For the second time that day, she parked in front of what was now her house. Happiness welled in her as she got out and looked around with the proud eyes of ownership. In her mind's eye she saw the house magnificently restored to the gleaming elegance of true 1800's Victorian architecture. She pictured soft gold siding with the fancy trim painted light mauve, and dark mauve detailing the window sash and cream outlining the window panes. The fish scale siding in the gables would also be soft gold with maybe a fifth color somewhere. She remembered seeing Victorian ladies in San Francisco but couldn't remember the colors used, or how many. She recalled there were several to show off the Victorian features. "I need to do some research before deciding for sure about the colors." Maxi spoke to Beau. "What do you think? Do you like your new home, or it will be in a few months. I'm starving. Let's set up our chair under that beautiful old chestnut tree and have some lunch."

Beau was very interested in the tuna sandwich and ate about a fourth of the tuna, but nothing else tempted him. It was a lovely autumn afternoon, warm and sunny, with the trees beginning to change color. Red and gold showed among the dark green foliage and the darker hue of the evergreens. The meadow was still filled with wildflowers: golden rod, Queen Anne's lace and purple asters. The air was fragrant with the scent of the flowers and leaves beginning to dry. There hadn't been a hard frost yet. The buzz of bees collecting nectar hummed in the warm sunlight.

"Just listen to the birds singing, Beau. I think they are meadowlarks." With the kitten in her arms she started out across the meadow. "We have to find a name for this place. It may in time be a bed and breakfast. How about calling it Meadowlark Lane? Hmmm, I think I like that." Beau just purred and squirmed to jump down. Maxi released him. "Okay, but don't run away or I'll never find you." He began chasing the little cream colored butterflies fluttering about.

She walked about for a half hour, wanting to explore the boundaries, but knew that the kitten couldn't handle that kind of walking through the tall grass and flowers. She doubted that he could be still long enough for her to carry him. He wouldn't be heavy, but he was at the active stage and couldn't stand to be held for a long period of time. She turned and started back toward the house and her car, calling Beau who immediately began following her. *Who said that cats don't come when called?*

She noticed that someone was standing next to her car. Her heart gave a thump. As she drew closer she recognized the man who had spoken to her the day she found her purse down by the river.

"Hello! I hear you are going to be my neighbor," Jeff Knowles said in greeting.

"Word travels fast. How did you know that? I just bought the place this morning."

Maxi was wary, but didn't want to let it show. Why had she left her cell phone in the car? It would be difficult to get it now. Thoughts of who had caused the explosion in her house and then sent her the note yesterday were foremost in her mind. She didn't know this man, knew nothing about him. Could he be the one? He looked friendly and did not seem threatening, but who knew?

"I saw the contractor's pickup here this morning. I thought something was up so I called Bonnie and asked her if I was getting a new neighbor?"

"You know Bonnie?"

"Yes, she sold me my place two years ago. I am your closest neighbor. I also talked with Mark

Fields this morning. We were having coffee when you came in with Sam this morning for breakfast."

"You know Mark and Sam, too? I'm afraid that I don't remember your name." Maxi was beginning to relax a little, letting go of some of her suspicions.

"My name is Jeff Knowles, and it's a small world," Jeff said with a smile and brought up his arm. Maxi saw for the first time that he was holding a basket and the top of a bottle peeked out.

"I brought a bottle of Dom to welcome you. I think you are going to be a terrific neighbor, and I admit I wanted to give you a favorable impression." Jeff gave her his most disarming and charming grin. As he had hoped, it worked. He could see a smile begin on Maxi's expressive face. He wondered if she knew what an open book she was. He found it a refreshing trait.

"That's quite a welcome. Just how close is your house? Are you living in my pocket? Should I be careful what I wear if I come out on the porch to enjoy the early summer mornings while I have my coffee?" Said only half in jest, she hoped he couldn't see her every move whenever she was out. She liked her privacy and didn't relish being spied upon.

"I can see your porch from my kitchen window and no, I won't be spying on you."

Is he a mind reader, too? Somewhat taken back, Maxi wasn't sure she liked this bit of information. It depended on what kind of neighbor Jeff turned out to be.

"In fact," Jeff continued "I called Mark after I talked to Bonnie this morning. At breakfast he told me what had happened to your house and that you had received a threatening note at work yesterday." At her look of surprise and what he interpreted as chagrin about being a matter of discussion, he went on, "I was concerned about you living out here in this rather isolated location, even though you can't possibly move in for a long time yet. Mark is concerned, too. He asked me to keep an eye on the place until they find whoever is stalking you."

"I am not sure I like being watched or checked up on," Maxi said candidly. "Even by an attractive man who just happens to be my neighbor. If you can see this house, then I should be able to see yours. Where is it?" she asked, turning around in a circle and seeing nothing but the meadow and trees bordering it.

"Just over the rise, look between the trees."

Maxi could make out a bit of roof and a couple windows that reflected the late afternoon sun. She hadn't realized it was there before, as the trees mostly hid it. In winter it would probably be much more visible.

"So, you do find me attractive," Jeff grinned cheekily, clearly pleased by the thought. "I'm glad because the feeling is mutual." He turned slightly and picked up the basket he had placed on the ground beside him and put it on the hood of her car. Lifting the lid, he produced two Champagne glasses and a red and white checked cloth. Spreading it over the ground next to the chaise, he placed the glasses on it. Next there appeared a loaf of French bread, cheese and pears.

"Please join me for some refreshments," he said with a slight bow. "We could call it 4 o'clock tea without the tea, and have champagne instead. It's too bad we only have one chair, but I don't mind sitting on the ground." He motioned for her to sit while he opened the bottle with only a slight pop.

Maxi observed that he knew the correct way to open champagne as she lowered herself to the chair. Beau jumped from her arms to go exploring among the tall grass. Despite her initial misgivings, Maxi was beginning to enjoy herself.

"I hope you like champagne," he said, handing her both flutes to hold while he poured the wine.

"I love champagne." Maxi handed his flute back to him and sipped from hers. "I must say this is an unexpected welcome. But I would appreciate knowing more about you. You seem to know so much about me. What do you do? Why did you move here two years ago?"

"That's fair. I'm a writer. I moved here because I wanted a quiet, secluded place to do my work. I used to visit my aunt and uncle here when I was a kid and really liked the area. Maybe you knew them, Martha and Fred Cunningham."

"Of course, I knew them. They visited back and forth with my parents. Are they still living in the same house?"

"No. Martha died three years ago and Fred only lasted a year without her. I think he literally died of a broken heart; he missed her so very much."

"I'm sorry. I remember they seemed very close and were nice people."

"Yes, they were wonderful, and I had such a great time during the summers that I spent here.

They were more like parents to me than my own. They never had children, which I am sure you know, and they left their property to me. My wife died of cancer about the same time and I needed a change of scene. So I decided to move here but didn't want to live in town. So I sold that house and bought the place where I live now. It was really meant to be a summer cottage. I remodeled it, put in insulation, a heating system and new kitchen and bath. I am very happy with it."

They talked for an hour. The sun was going down when Maxi got up, saying that in another hour it would be dark. Beau had jumped into her lap sometime during their conversation and had been sleeping contentedly. He protested with a little meow at being disturbed.

Jeff folded the chair to put into her car, but Maxi stopped him. "I think I will leave it here rather than haul it back and forth. I have no place for it where I am living now anyway; it's no bigger than a closet," she said, smiling. "I can't wait to get this place livable. I am feeling too cramped in that small room."

Opening the front door, Maxi took the chair from him and put it just inside, and then locked the door again, saying coyly as she turned the key, "I would invite you in, but the place is a mess."

Jeff rocked with laughter. "You can say that again. I was inside the kitchen a few times when I brought groceries to James. I think you are planning on restoring rather than demolition and building new?"

"Yes. I love old Victorian houses and I remember this one when it was a grand place. My mother brought me here to visit when I was 10 years old and I loved it then." Maxi smiled fondly at the dilapidated structure.

"I admire your courage. It's a big undertaking." He paused, and then added, "I also want you to know, that I knew your husband. He was a great guy; I admired his investigative novels very much."

"You knew Jim? How is it that we never met before?"

"I first met him when he gave a lecture on writing fiction at Forest Hills University. Then we started meeting for breakfast about once a week. He was my mentor. As a new writer I needed all the help I could get. And he provided it."

"I still don't know why he never mentioned you," Maxi was puzzled.

"It was strictly a working relationship. Did he fill you in on all his lectures at the university?"

"No. I knew when he was giving them but not much more," Maxi admitted.

Seeing her back to her car where she had deposited the kitten earlier, Jeff held the open door and said, "I really enjoyed meeting you and look forward to getting to know you better."

"Me, too. Thank you for 4 o'clock tea. It was fun." Maxi said as she pulled the door closed. With a wave of her hand, she drove off unaware of the broad smile on her face as she reflected how attractive he was.

Jeff watched her drive away, spun around once and threw his fist in the air, "YES!"

Fifteen minutes later, he was on the phone with Mark.

"Do you think she knows that you knew her husband?" Mark asked.

"She does now. I didn't think it would be a good idea for her to find out from some other source. She didn't act as though she knew me from Adam, and was wary when she first saw me. Not that I blame her, after what she has experienced lately. In fact, she would be a fool if she weren't suspicious of strangers. I am glad that she is."

"It certainly is a piece of luck that she is going to be your neighbor!" Mark was somewhat relieved at the development. "I have men watching her during the day and when she is in her apartment, but I don't have the manpower to do it for long."

"I think I will take Major for a walk this evening so he will know that we are looking after that house as well as our own. With the contractors working, though, it will be more difficult during the day. I'll walk over while work is going on and take Major with me. I'll try to keep track of who is working there. I know the contractor and he seems to be a good man. What do you think of him?"

"Sam's a good guy. He's one of the best contractors, reliable and trustworthy. I trust him completely," Mark replied.

"Good. I'll keep in touch with you. By the way, she says she plans to move in before Christmas."

"Might be good, might not. Just keep me in the loop in that area." Mark said goodnight and hung up.

Immediately his phone rang again. "What do you mean discussing me with other people!" Fury literally leaped out of the phone and into Mark's ear. He grinned.

"And hello to you, too, Maxi."

"Don't get cute with me! I know you discussed me with Jeff Knowles today, and you have no business talking about my private business to anybody."

"I didn't tell him anything that all the town doesn't know. We were having breakfast and saw you come into the restaurant and Jeff mentioned that he had met you once. That's all. He put all the rest together himself. Well, except that I did tell him of the note you got yesterday."

"Well, just so you know that I don't like being the subject of talk," Maxi sputtered a bit more, then asked, "I take it you know this guy pretty well. Is he okay? I mean, I can trust him as a neighbor?"

"Yes, I know him quite well. As a matter of fact, he knew your late husband and they had great respect for each other."

"I know that he knew Jim. He told me today," Maxi was still surprised. She knew that she and Jim had drifted apart a little since the kids were on their own, but didn't realize that he knew people that she didn't or didn't mention to her. She tried to remember if he had mentioned Jeff.

"Well, they were both writers so I guess they had some common ground," Mark replied. "You can trust him, Maxi, and I am glad that you are not trusting of everyone until we get to the bottom of your house explosion and that note yesterday. I have another call coming in so I have to go. I'll keep in touch, Maxi."

Maxi mulled over the information about Jim and Jeff knowing each other. Shrugging her shoulders, she headed for the bathroom to get ready for bed.

Sunday was spent at her newly acquired house, making sketches and wandering from room to room. She pictured how it would all look when the restoration was complete.

"Maybe someday I'll want to run a Bed and Breakfast Inn," she mused. The house was certainly large enough. There were now five bedrooms on the second floor, but one of them might have to be sacrificed for another needed bathroom. Even better, maybe two bathrooms could be made from it. That would make four bedrooms, each with a private bath.

On the first floor she planned a bed and bath suite, which she would use. At least, that is what she wanted finished first so she could move in soon. Maybe Christmas was pushing it, but at least it was something to aim for. She made a note to start checking wallpaper books and get paint samples.

Chapter 9

All the next week Maxi worked furiously. By law everyone had three months before they had to vacate, but she was finding that once accustomed to the idea, most were ready to move quickly.

Evelyn and her brood of five were to move into the housing project this week. While still leery of the others in the complex, Evelyn was beginning to look forward to the move. She had found homes for the three dogs. The children cried briefly over losing their pets, but were eager to move. They had nice rooms, large enough to give them some privacy. The youngest girl had a room of her own, the twins shared another with the 11 year-old boy, and the oldest girl was in heaven thinking of having her own room, "All to myself," she exalted. Evelyn had already been approached to be a school crossing guard (at Maxi's suggestion to a school board member) and that gave her a reason to get dressed and be outside at least twice a day. She had improved her appearance and didn't seem quite so withdrawn.

Helen, the 96-year-old widow, had her surgery and came through fine. She had at least two more days in the hospital. She was anxious to get settled into her new apartment before she started chemotherapy. Maxi had gotten a moving company to move all the items that Helen wanted to keep. She had helped Helen label them before she entered the hospital. Her apartment was in a retirement assisted living center, where she would have the help she needed as she recuperated and went through the chemotherapy. She was keeping her bright yellow VW Beetle. "For when I feel like going somewhere," she chuckled. She was indomitable and Maxi admired her immensely. It was a shame that she had never had children and subsequently no grandchildren.

Maxi had arranged for an auctioneer to take the rest of the items from the house and include them in his next in-house auction. He had a good reputation and Helen trusted him to treat her fairly. He even took what Maxi thought of as "junk," the kind of things one accumulates but seems to have no value.

"You would be surprised what people will buy," Harley had said with a smile. "I'll box things together and sell the entire box like a grab bag, a mystery box. People like to be surprised, and a lot of collectors come to auctions hoping for a 'find'." He grinned as he completed his tour of the house and before leaving lifted Helen's hand to his lips in a courtly gesture, saying, "I'll do good by you, ma'am. Don't you fret, now, hear?"

Helen had smiled when she said, "I know you will be fair with me, Harley, and I thank you for it."

Maxi had left Helen that day amid the items packed and those she was still using until her move to the apartment. Marveling at the resiliency of the lady, Maxi thought she could teach some of these young people a lot. She thanked God that there was a unit available for her on such short notice. Of course, Maxi had pulled some strings to get Helen at the top of the list for the apartment. Her furniture and items that she had requested along with her clothing would be in the apartment awaiting her release from the hospital.

At the end of each day Maxi was exhausted and after stopping at a neighborhood restaurant for dinner, went home to shower and fall into bed. By the weekend, four of the first families that she had to relocate were a fate accompli plus three more that she had started to process a week later.

The 70-year-old widower was still being difficult. It had gotten to the point that Maxi said a prayer for him, *Please, God, help this man find a home. I've done all I can for him. I don't want him to be placed somewhere that he doesn't want to be, so I'm putting him into your hands."*

It was almost a miracle. Two days later, when she had all but given up hope that he would find a house and move willingly, he walked into her office. He wasn't smiling, but she had the impression that something had changed.

"I guess you have ta look at the place I move to." It wasn't a question but a blunt statement.

"Yes, I do. You have found a place?" Maxi was almost jumping for joy.

"Yea, I looked at it last night. It'll do, but it ain't like what I'm leavin, mind you, and I still don't like this whole thing. But everbody has moved already and I don't like staying there with all them empty houses around me. No telling who might take a mind ta take up livin in 'em."

"This is wonderful news, Mr. North. Where is the house?" Looking at her schedule, Maxi's mind was working to fit in an inspection for him that day. Time was important. Deciding she could postpone one of the visits until seven that evening, she asked, "Can we go at four this afternoon?"

"As fast as you want people to move, I thought you could go now?"

"I'm sorry, but I have a full schedule today. But I don't want to put you off until tomorrow, so I'll reschedule my four o'clock appointment." Maxi always had to keep a firm control on her responses to this obnoxious man. She tried to summon up sympathy for him, but Helen kept popping into her thoughts. *He doesn't know how lucky he is!*

He grunted what Maxi took as an agreement, and left without further comment. Maxi sent up a prayer; *thank you, God!*

Maxi worked steadily all day, taking a half-hour break at noon for a sandwich in a nearby park where she enjoyed the sunshine of the late autumn day before hurrying on to her next appointment. By four o'clock she was back at the office, expecting to have Mr. North waiting impatiently for her. He wasn't there. Feeling frustrated, she was wondering what to do when he walked in at 4:15.

She decided not to mention that he was late, thinking it was his way of showing control over his situation, and instead gathered up her clipboard and purse. "I'll drive and bring you back here to get your car after I check out the property," Maxi started toward the door, then turned and asked, "The real estate agent will be meeting us there?"

"He said he would. I'll drive myself."

"Okay. If that is what you want. You'll have to lead the way."

Grumbling at the inefficiency of the government, he led the way to the parking lot. Ten minutes later they were outside the city limits in an area dominated by Amish farmers. The house was a brick ranch. After completing her inspection and checking off the items on her clipboard, she determined it met the necessary standards. It certainly met all the DSS conditions and was a much better built house than the one he was leaving.

The Amish farmer from next door came over when he saw them emerge from the house to the driveway.

"You be our new neighbor?" He inquired politely.

"I guess so, if I get permission from this here one," he replied, jerking his head in Maxi's direction.

Gosh, he is so obnoxious! "The property meets all requirements and if this is where you choose to live, then you have my blessing, Mr. North." Turning to the Amish man, she asked, "So you are to be Mr. North's neighbor?"

"That I am. Sorry I didn't introduce myself; the name is Jakob Spinner. We will be good neighbors to Mr. North. We look out for each other here."

"I'm sure you do, and Mr. North will be fortunate to have such good neighbors." Maxi suspected that Mr. North would supply transportation and telephone service to his Amish neighbors, at a price, of course. It was a well-known fact that the Amish hired people to drive them when they needed transportation to stores and doctor appointments. They would use a telephone if it were on someone else's property or a phone booth.

Maxi thought that North probably had already figured out how much he could charge for his services and probably get free garden produce in the summer as well, maybe even some home cooking and baking. She gave him grudging marks of admiration, considering he had worked the system to get a place where he could make a little money. She was sure he would put his almost new van to good use. And after all, what was the harm? He would be providing a needed service, and even though she knew he would never admit it, Maxi suspected he was already anticipating the move.

Maxi discussed the necessary items with the realtor. Ed Brown was from a different county and they had never met. Maxi was concerned when Ed told her the list price.

"Maybe we need to sit down and talk about this, Mr. North. You won't have enough from your house that was taken, even with the relocation money allotted, to get you into this house at the asking price." Maxi's hopes plummeted.

"I think the owner will take the amount Mr. North is receiving. He has relocated and the house has been vacant for six months. He wants to sell. Since I have your approval, I will write up an offer, and we will see what he says," Ed replied.

When discussion of the financial details began, the Amish man prudently left. Noting this, Ed said, "Actually, I have shown the place to many people. But they didn't want to be surrounded by the Amish, so I think this may be a deal that will make everybody happy. Just the way we like it. Right?" He winked at Maxi as if they were in a conspiracy.

She didn't like it, or him, but wasn't about to quash the deal.

"Okay by me. Mr. North, do you want to make a formal offer on this property?"

"Of course I do. I wouldn't ha brung you all the way out here if I didn't, now would I?"

"Then you will have to go with Ed and sign a formal offer. I'd get the paper work started right now, if I were you," and she looked at each in turn with 'you' meaning each of them. She was not surprised when Ed quickly said that he had papers in his car ready for North's signature. She left them and returned to the city. Maxi was tired enough to call it a day, but still had the 7 o'clock appointment.

Later, as she got ready for bed, Maxi's thoughts turned to North. *Thank you, Lord, for your help. I think we will be working together a lot before this job is finished.*

Exhausted but too wired to sleep, she lay in the dark with Beau's warm body snuggled against her side and let her thoughts wander. As usual they turned to the house she had bought and a warm feeling encompassed her, helping her fall asleep.

The following days blurred into one another with her job keeping her running all day and sometimes overflowing into evenings and weekends when she needed to meet with someone who worked and couldn't see her during her normal work day. And, of course, there were the monthly board meetings where she was required to attend and give a written status report; sometimes the meetings lasted until nearly 11 p.m.

Her free weekends were occupied with her new house. By the end of October the roof had been completed, also, the well and septic. She had met with Sam to determine where the new bathrooms on the second floor should go, as well as the laundry room, powder room and master bath on the first floor. The kitchen layout also had been completed and the plumber was installing the new plumbing throughout the house.

The heating system was working, installation having been started as soon as the new roof was on. It was getting chilly at night now and some days as well. She was beginning to think she might not be able to move before Christmas, but hadn't given up hope and thought of it as her Christmas present, hoping that Santa could deliver.

By the first of November, the master bedroom and bath were taking shape with the plumbing finished in those rooms. Fortunately the horsehair plaster walls were in fine shape and only needed a little patching here and there. But all the ceilings had to be completely redone.

Maxi almost forgot about the loss of her house and the note she had received. But Mark and Jeff still remembered, and kept watch over Maxi, unknown to her.

"What worries me the most are the appointments she goes on by herself," Mark said to Jeff as the two shared breakfast at The Gathering Place.

"Yes, I've thought about that, too," Jeff replied. "I've been keeping up with the restoration of her house, too, and it looks as though she may be able to move into the downstairs bedroom suite before Christmas."

"We'll have to think about telling her about the seriousness of her situation. She still doesn't have a clue that Jim's death wasn't accidental and the destruction of her house was probably connected to that as a way of destroying any evidence that Jim may have kept in the house. Hopefully, whoever is responsible will think that is true and let her alone," Mark frowned at his plate of bacon and eggs, his appetite suddenly leaving him.

"I wish I had some idea where Jim had hidden the tape he told me about when he called me on his cell phone just before his accident." Jeff, too, had a sudden loss of appetite. "It's not just Maxi's safety, but Jim was my friend, and he trusted me to follow through on his investigation."

"We're definitely going to have to talk to Maxi. She may have an idea of where Jim would have put something like a video tape for safekeeping."

"I think it would have been just before he started home that afternoon. But Jim didn't say where he had been." Jeff pushed a forkful of pancakes around the syrup on his plate.

"You two look like you have the weight of the world on your shoulders."

The unexpected remark had Mark and Jeff looking up in surprise at the man standing over their table.

"Mark is just trying to help me out with a sticky situation I've gotten myself into with my novel. He is my source for police investigations," Jeff replied, smiling in spite of his irritation.

"Yes, you'd be surprised at the tricks and turns he gets his characters into. It's true, that fiction is stranger than truth."

Mark tried to hide his dislike of the man who continued to hulk over their table.

"So how is the landfill business these days, Dick?" Mark had never liked the man and now that he knew that Jim had been doing an investigation into his business, Mark not only disliked him personally, he now considered him to be a suspect in a murder.

"So, so. It doesn't vary much. People keep adding to their disposables every day. You'd be amazed at how much garbage people generate daily. Jeff, you should write a novel about that," Dick Sheppard smirked.

"People think all kinds of things can be compacted and dumped to be covered over. You really should give it some serious thought. If you need inside information or an on-site look, just let me know." With a wave of his hand Dick headed out of the restaurant joking and waving at others on his way.

"Actually, Dick, I was wondering more about your strip mining operation," Mark called him back to their table.

"That keeps going on as usual. I'm just opening up another area, as the one that I had been working is now closed and reclaimed with trees," Dick responded as he turned back and headed out of the restaurant.

Jeff and Mark looked at each other. "The gall of that man," Mark exploded.

"That sounded like a threat to me," Jeff responded. "The remark about an onsite look, I mean. I don't like to be threatened. It has always been against my principals; it sort of felt like I was challenged to a duel: 'Meet me at dawn at Sheppard's Meadow'".

"It sure did. We have got to do something about this and sooner rather than later. I'm convinced the man is a murderer. We just have to prove it."

Chapter 10

It was Saturday morning, the week before Thanksgiving and Maxi was at the house by 8 o'clock. She sat in the car for a while, bemused, just looking at her house. The exterior painting was done. She got out of the car and slowly approached the front porch.

"It's beautiful!" she breathed the phrase as if she was too overcome to say anything out loud. The house gleamed. The soft gold tones of the main structure took on a special glow in the early morning sun. It picked out the highlights of the light mauve trim around the cream edged windows. The fish scale shingles on the many gables were painted gold. The carved bargeboards, the finials and pendants in the gable peaks were all dark mauve. The second floor railings on the many tiny porches and the Brevelier room's veranda with its turned wood columns supporting the witch-hat roof were all painted cream.

"It is totally lovely," Maxi said out loud to herself as she stood in the dew-wet grass looking up at it before going inside.

"I totally agree," a male voice spoke from behind her. Maxi jumped and spun around. She hadn't heard Sam's truck, being so engrossed in admiring her newly painted house.

"Oh, Sam, you startled me. I didn't hear your truck." Maxi spun back toward the house, "I just love it."

"You have a good eye for color and I suppose you did some research, too." Sam had stood quietly after he got out of his truck, admiring the woman so engrossed in her house, that she didn't know that he was there. He had been divorced for three years and so far had not had any inclination to begin a new relationship. But that had been before Maxi. He felt awkward and clumsy, like he was 16 again. *Man, you have got to get hold of yourself. She isn't interested in you that way. She sees you as her contractor and nothing else. Remember she is recently widowed and has had a lot of trauma with her house exploding and everything. Forget it!*

Moving to stand beside her, he gazed at the house, seeing it through her eyes. It was indeed magnificent. Architecturally, it was a perfect Victorian. He had thought he preferred new construction and didn't really care for all this fancy stuff, but now he, too, was caught up in the restoration coming alive before his eyes. He had restored buildings before and done a fine job, but never got really pulled into it like he was on this house. *Is it the house or Maxi,* he mused.

"We've been lucky with the weather holding like it has, not too cold or too wet to do the painting. Seth did a fine job."

"Yes, he did," Maxi replied, still in awe at the transformation.

"Have you been inside yet today?" Sam asked.

"No, I was too taken with the metamorphoses to move another step," Maxi grinned at him. "I have been so busy that I haven't been here since last Sunday and they had just started the painting the middle of the week before that. Is there something I need to do inside?"

"The fifth bedroom upstairs has been divided into two bathrooms and the nursery off the master bedroom is now plumbed to be a bathroom. With the original bath there are now the four bedrooms with four adjoining baths as you wanted. The rough plumbing is finished. I thought you might want to see how it came together."

Maxi could hardly wait to see this new development and practically ran up the stairway. What had been a doorway to the fifth bedroom had been closed off and now studs were in place to make a niche open to the large square hallway that surrounded the open stairway. "That is a nice touch," Maxi commented on the treatment of the closed off doorway. "I want a recessed light at the top so I can use it as a nightlight as well as showing off whatever I decide to put into it. It is positioned perfectly for this upstairs balcony." She looked around the square space that was surrounded by a railing providing a hallway to each of the four bedrooms.

The huge chandelier that had been suspended from the ceiling to light the curving stairway and hallway at night had been taken down to be cleaned and repaired. The repairs weren't finished yet, but the owner of the antique restoration shop had assured Maxi that it would look like new when he was finished with it.

Maxi walked through what was changed from the original three rooms across the front of the house.

Now the center room was divided into two bathrooms. Each remaining bedroom had direct access to a bath. It worked perfectly.

The original bath was now accessed from the back bedroom. At the other side of the hallway were the former master bedroom and an adjoining bath that had been a nursery when the house had been built.

"It has worked out beautifully. I can picture the bathroom fixtures now. The baths are all large enough to be comfortably fitted with a Jacuzzi and separate shower, double lavatories and space between for a bench or chair to sit on. Besides, the most necessary item, the commode, is in it's own private niche," Sam said as he showed her around. Maxi was thrilled with the layout. Even though it was only rough plumbing at this point with flooring torn up to install it, she could visualize it perfectly.

Each bedroom had a fireplace. The fireplace that had been in the room divided for the bathrooms was impossible to incorporate into either of the bathrooms so it had to be removed. The space required for the chimney was needed. She knew that tearing it out had been difficult. The walls were now filled in with wallboard and ceramic tile would go over it. The roof had been done before the decision to remove the fireplace so it had been sealed off at the attic floor level.

If I later decided to finish the attic, maybe it could be opened there and a gas log fireplace built using the existing chimney. The attic would make a lovely apartment.

"Sam, could rough plumbing and new wiring be run to the attic in case I want to finish it later?"

"I can check it out before walls are too far along, but I think it probably could be done."

"Please, I don't know that I will ever do anything with the attic, but it is a nice idea. There is such lovely space up there. I am glad we included heat up there, too. Of course, I want to be able to shut it off for now."

"What do you plan to do with all this space? Open a hotel?" Sam teased.

"I might do that." Maxi grinned back at him. "The job I have now won't last forever, probably only another year."

"Yea, you're right about that." Sam said.

Maxi noted that he was looking at her in what appeared to be a very strange way. She wondered what the look meant, but didn't ask; and Sam suddenly got busy checking out the rolled up drawings while he wondered if he might have a place in her future.

"I better get busy too, I have a lot of wallpaper books in the car that I want to bring in and see what I like." Maxi hurried down the stairs and went to her car, returning with several large, heavy wallpaper books.

It was close to 10 o'clock when a knock sounded at the kitchen door interrupting her absorption with the wallpaper. When Maxi opened it she found Jeff standing there with a thermos, a donut box and his dog at his side. "Isn't it time for a coffee break?"

Standing back and holding the door open, Maxi invited him in. "You are always arriving with drinks and food. Is it a good neighbor policy?"

"You bet. I want to be the best neighbor you've ever had. Is it okay if Major comes in, too? He wants to see your house." Jeff gave her his engaging grin as he indicated the German shepherd sitting at his side and looking at Maxi with what she interpreted to be an expectant expression. It was the first time that Jeff had brought the dog along.

"Please come in, Major."

"Come on boy, the lady has invited you to come in. He is very well trained. We keep an eye on the place when you are away or at work, especially at night. We usually take a walk around the house about midnight." Jeff gave the dog an affectionate look.

He's a big dog for a big man, Maxi thought, but said, "I can understand that he would detect someone when you were on the grounds but from the distance of your house, how would he know if someone is here or not?" Maxi was a little doubtful of the dog having abilities that advanced.

"Believe it or not, but Major does have keen hearing and an even more sensitive sense of smell. We walk around your house at night before I turn in, and Major is getting used to what is normal. He won't hear much from inside our house, but when he is outside, he will know if something is different. He goes in and out on his own through the doggie door during the night. I have the back yard fenced but he will come and wake me if anything suspicious is going on." Jeff gave her an appraising look. *Did she believe him?*

"Well, I admit I don't know much about the ability of dogs. I do know they use them to search out people in earthquakes, cave-ins and such. So maybe Major can do all that."

"Major, shake hands with Maxi," Jeff ordered the dog and he immediately sat and held out his paw, looking at Maxi with big, soulful brown eyes.

"He does look like a great dog." Maxi looked at the handsome animal holding out his paw as he kept his eyes on her, "I'm pleased to make your acquaintance, Major. I have a cat called Beau. He isn't with me today because he gets lost in all this space and I'm afraid he will get into a hole and not be able to get out. But when I can bring him, will you promise not to chase him?"

"He won't chase the cat if I tell him not to. Now that you know each other, are you hungry? I have coffee in the thermos and donuts in the box." Jeff looked around the room, "But no place to put them."

"Just a second." Maxi went into another room and returned with a folding table that she set up in the center of the kitchen. Then she returned and brought two folding chairs and set them at the table. "Never let it be said that food was turned away for lack of dining facilities."

"Ah, a resourceful woman. I like that." Jeff leered at her with a grin splitting his face and wiggled his eyebrows suggestively. Maxi could not help laughing. What was it about this man?

Sam appeared in the doorway with drawings held open in front of him. "Maxi, I need to have you look at this to see if it's how you want it..." Sam stuttered to a stop as he saw Jeff and the table with a thermos and donuts on it.

Jeff was in the process of lifting out two mugs that he had put in the large box of donuts. Sam froze, and the two men eyed each other like two dogs sizing each other up and bristling a little.

Maxi leaped into the awkwardness that was growing momentarily, "Jeff, this is Sam, my contractor. Sam, this is Jeff, my neighbor."

"Hi. We've met." Jeff recovered first. "Join us for a coffee break. I brought plenty."

Sam accepted with a nod of thanks.

Maxi reached to receive her mug of steaming black coffee as Sam moved toward the table where Jeff was filling a second mug. Jeff held it out to Sam. "I know that Maxi likes hers black, and so do I, so there is no cream or sugar."

"That's fine." Sam took the cup while silently noting that they seemed awfully easy with each other.

"But you don't have a cup now," Maxi protested, ready to hand hers back to him.

"Sure I do. I'll use the cup on top of the thermos." Jeff replied as he poured coffee for himself. "It is getting colder in the mornings now. A cup of hot coffee is pretty good. Actually coffee is good regardless of the weather." Jeff felt the tension coming from Sam, and realized that he was invading what Sam thought of as his territory. *He is romantically interested in Maxi, and I don't think she has a clue.*

They all sipped and ate donuts. Gradually the air cleared and talk about the renovations took over.

"The exterior painting is really great. Who chose the colors?" Jeff asked.

"I did. It's not authentic to what was used when the house was built, but it's what I like," Maxi replied. "I understand the historical society is a little miffed at me for not asking them for recommendations. I was told the other day that they could have analyzed the clapboards that had to be removed and probably have told me what the original colors were."

"Was that important to you?" Jeff asked.

"No, not really. I suppose it should have been. But the paint and colors now are so superior to what was available in 1866 that I just went with my own choice. And I like it," she added, a trifle defensively.

"I think it looks great," Sam joined in. "We did stay with the same style wood siding as was removed, to keep the historic integrity. The Society would have had fits if we had used something different and surely would have died of massive heart failure if we had put on vinyl," he added, as they all laughed at the thought.

"Heaven forbid!" Maxi managed through chuckles, then added seriously, "I do want to keep it as near the original as possible, and it is on the historic register. I guess with the cedar shake roofing and the colors, I am lucky they haven't taken it off."

"They are really happy that you have bought the place and are restoring it, so I don't think they will object too much," Jeff told them.

"Don't tell me, you know the people on the Historical Society Board too." Maxi was beginning to think this man knew more people in town than she did, and he had only lived here two years.

"I know some of them from spending summers here; my aunt and uncle were board members. In fact,

Lester Maynard bought their house when I wanted to sell. It was built around the same time as this one."

Sam got to his feet as he said, "I have to be on my way. I have another appointment at 10:30."

He was reluctant to leave while Jeff was still there, but he didn't have a choice. He grabbed his coat and started out the door, as he reminded Maxi to set the thermostat lower when she left, "There is no reason to keep it this warm when there is no one here. Set it about 50 and whoever gets here first in the mornings can turn it up. We'll go over the blueprints later, Maxi."

"I'll do that, and thanks for coming out on a Saturday, Sam." Maxi stood in the doorway to shut the door behind him.

"It is getting much cooler these days." Maxi was filling the momentary silence that fell with just the two of them there.

"Sure is," Jeff started gathering up the donut box and empty mugs. "I'll take these home and wash them since you don't have running water yet."

Maxi watched Jeff and Major disappear over the rise. She mused that Jeff made her feel attractive and she was a little uneasy with it. *And what was going on between Sam and Jeff. I wonder if they have had some kind of trouble? They seemed to know each other, but at the same time weren't too friendly. Well, I guess I don't have to worry about that. Let them work it out.*

She spent the rest of the morning pouring over the wallpaper books that she had moved from the floor and spread out over the folding table. She settled on two possible choices. She would put it aside for now and look at them again tomorrow. A little time usually helped her make decisions like this. She wandered around the house, planning colors and anticipating how it was going to look when it was finished. A happy glow stayed with her all the way home that afternoon.

Chapter 11

The days flew by. The relocation work was in full swing and Maxi was doing comparison schedules, arranging appointments to inspect the relocation houses, and starting the process all over again with new people. It was going well most of the time. As word traveled among the people, Maxi found that her welcome was usually assured. There were still some who wanted to be hard-nosed about the situation, usually looking to squeeze more money out of the project.

Yesterday, she had met with a widow whose daughter lived with her in her bungalow. Shirley seemed nervous and upset. As Maxi talked with her and explained how she would be helping her get moved into a new place and that she would receive relocation money plus moving expenses, she began to look quite pleased.

"I have looked at a new double-wide in the Greentree Mobile Home Park," Shirley said. "Chet Holmes has been helpful. I think I can afford it, with the relocation money. My nieces and nephews have said they will help me move my furniture. Is it true what I have heard, that you will pay me if we do it ourselves instead of a moving company?"

Maxi explained the moving money, based on the number of rooms of furniture, would be paid to her if she moved herself rather than having a moving company and Shirley seemed very pleased. "Actually, if you have young people helping I would prefer to pay you rather than a moving company."

The daughter, Janet, sat with a scowl on her fat face from the moment Maxi had entered the home. Now, she spoke up, "You can sound like you are God's gift to these people who are being pushed out of their homes, but we all know that what is happening here is a disgrace. My mother is 65 and is worrying herself sick over this. You should be ashamed!" Her voice was as ugly as her facial expression.

"I know it is hard on people and especially hard on the older ones," Maxi sympathized, although she didn't see Shirley showing any great degree of distress since she had explained how the relocation part of the project would help her.

"My dad bought this home brand new with the idea that Mom would have a place for her old age. And you people are taking it right out from under her with no respect for her age or health or anything," Janet complained angrily.

Maxi could see the distress beginning to show on Shirley's face again as she listened to her daughter and her hands began to shake. Maxi opened her mouth to reassure Janet that her mother would be fine. She didn't have a chance to say a word as Janet continued.

"You're going to have older people dying from all this."

"You're mother will be fine. She has a lot of spirit and..."

"I am a realist and I know what this is doing to her," Janet cut in. "All your do-good attitude is just a cover to make it all seem like you're doing everybody a big favor."

"Janet, I am a realist, too, and this house is going to be taken." Maxi's voice accompanied a stern, steady gaze. "It's a fact! So live with it. Your mom was doing just fine this morning until you started your tirade, then she started getting nervous and upset. You can either help her or hinder her. For myself, I intend to make this move as easy for her as possible. Are you going to help her or make it harder on her? It's your choice." Maxi challenged, with a stern look at Janet. As she said this, she noticed Shirley visibly straighten in her chair and a look of satisfaction come over her face. She has wanted to talk to her daughter like that and was afraid to. *I'm with you, Shirley. We'll get this spoiled 40-year-old brat off your back.*

"And what about me?" Janet whined, changing tactics. "I have my own separate entrance here and my own phone line, and I will have the expense of having that moved, too. I need my own place in the house we move to."

"Janet, be quiet," Shirley spoke sternly. "The double-wide will have a door directly outside from your room. Chet promised me that. You will have your own bedroom and bath and I know that you can afford to have a phone put in. I like the Greentree Park much better than here. It is a beautiful park with winding streets and shade trees and all the homes are new. I know several people who live there, too." She said the last for Maxi's benefit. Then continued, "I am tired of living in fear that a flood will take everything that I have, and I am looking forward to the move. As far as your Dad leaving me with a new home, the one I will be moving to is new, and this one is 25 years old now. It's going to need a new roof soon and there are other things that I have not been able to maintain. If we go through another flood the heating system will be shot.

"The only thing I won't have is ownership of the land, and I don't give a hoot about that. I will have less tax to pay and I can still plant flowers if I want. And the grass is mowed and snow removal is done by the park employees."

But Janet had hit her stride and had her own agenda. She was not to be detoured. "I pay rent here," Janet went on, "so that makes me a tenant. I should get what other tenants get, plus moving money."

"Okay", Maxi hit her stride now too. "I need to have receipts and cancelled checks showing how much rent you pay to substantiate your claim. You can receive moving money for your part of the home but that will have to be deducted from what your mother receives, since it is based on the number of rooms of furniture to be moved. I can't approve more than that."

"Will the phone line be put in? And I know that tenants can receive up to $5,050. I deserve that, too."

"Janet, stop it!" Now Shirley looked ashamed of her daughter. "You don't pay me rent, you pay for some groceries and that is all. I won't sit here and let you go on like this."

"I will check out the phone line. Everything I do has to be approved by the Corps." Maxi couldn't help but notice, as she began gathering up her papers to leave, that the prospect of taking some of the moving expense reimbursement from her mother didn't bother Janet at all.

As she moved behind Shirley's chair, she put her hand on her shoulder and assured her, "You will be fine, Shirley, and I am glad your nieces and nephews are willing to help you all they can," Maxi said as she gave a challenging look toward Janet. *Too bad your daughter isn't as helpful. You would be better off if she lived by herself.* "Janet, maybe you would be happier if you had an apartment of your own."

"Mother can't possibly manage without me," Janet's whine sounded professional, like she had lots of practice.

More likely, you can't get along without her. You are a freeloader of the first degree.

Shirley stood up next to Maxi and looked at her daughter. "Yes, that is an excellent idea, an apartment of your own. Then you can live as you please." Shirley was pleased at the idea.

"Would I be eligible for the $5,050 that I have heard tenants get?" Janet looked a little hopeful at the idea of getting money.

"I'll look into it, if you get receipts for me." Maxi knew that receipts could be done and backdated. If they produced them, she wouldn't be inclined to check into that too deeply, for Shirley's sake. She was sure that Janet would think of this solution. *Shirley would be better off without her, Maxi thought.*

It was two days after her confrontation with Shirley and Janet, when Maxi came back to her office to see an envelope on the middle of her desk. *Oh, no. Not again,* her mind going instantly to the last time she had come in and found the envelope, with the threat, on her desk. But this one had the return address from a local attorney. She was being taken to court, and by Janet of all people.

"Oh, damnation. Poor Shirley. This brat of a daughter just won't help her at all." Maxi knew that Shirley would be dragged into this as well, if Janet had her way. She took the letter immediately to Jake. He looked at the letter in Maxi's hand as if he too suspected it was another threat.

"No, it isn't that kind of letter. I'm being taken to court," Maxi handed the letter to him.

"What's going on?"

Maxi explained what had happened at Shirley's. "Shirley was really happy with the situation. It's her daughter. She thinks she can get a lot more and make some money herself, all in the name of helping her 'poor' mother. She'll make her a nervous wreck, that's what she'll do."

Maxi was getting agitated at the thought of it. She liked Shirley and detested Janet. She was nervous about appearing in court. She had never been taken to court before, and she felt that her integrity was being questioned. *I realize that is not the situation at all and I don't doubt my decisions. I just don't trust the attorney.*

"I'll give Thomas a call," Jake said. "And I'll have him get started on this; maybe a letter from him will end the matter before it goes any further. If it doesn't, Thomas will be there in court. He will ask you to give your version and you will be backed up by the statistics and approval of the Corps and myself. I will want to look over the file before I call Thomas, though. He will probably want some background and maybe want you to FAX the file to him."

It didn't go to court. The next morning Jake called her into his office. "Thomas talked with the attorney and it is agreed that we will have a grievance hearing here. If that doesn't satisfy her, then it will go before a judge. I want you to cite the articles in the law to back up your case."

There had been a couple of protests of the acquisition price, but no objection to the relocation money until now. *Well, Maxi thought, this is America and it is good that they have a right to do it.*

Shirley and Janet arrived promptly for their grievance hearing. Shirley was looking unhappy, but Janet had an air of triumph as she gave Maxi an "I am to be reckoned with" look. The rental receipts were produced, and the outcome of the hearing was that when Janet found a place of her own, she would receive the $5,050. Shirley's monetary help would remain as Maxi had calculated, since Shirley was happy with the help she would get, minus the moving money for the room that Janet occupied.

That evening, with the loneliness of her life and without Jim to share their thoughts as they talked about the events of the day, Maxi's emotions caught up with her. She lay in bed crying and miserable. Beau huddled in her face trying to nuzzle his way into her neck, giving licks to her chin and pawing at her shoulder. Finally exhausted, she began stroking the cat, then as she snuggled him into the curve of her body, she fell asleep.

Still depressed the next morning, she entered her office without her usual energy. Thinking of calling Sue and asking her if she would like to have lunch, she reached for the phone. Just as she touched it, it rang.

"Hello. Flood Protection Authority. Maxine Taylor speaking."

"Hi Maxi. Sam here. How are you this morning?"

"Hi Sam. Is there a problem at the house?"

"Nothing new that we haven't discussed. I just wondered if you had any plans for this evening."

"Not after 5 o'clock. Why?"

"How about having dinner with me?" After a long pause without a reply, Sam thought he had probably overstepped himself. "Are you still there, Maxi?"

"Yes. You caught me off guard. I'm just surprised."

"Well, if it makes you uncomfortable, that's all right. Maybe some other time."

"No, that is, I would like to go to dinner with you. Where should I meet you?" Maxi stammered in her confusion.

"I'll pick you up at work, if that's all right. Or at your apartment, if you would rather go home first."

"Here is fine. I'll just leave my car in the parking lot and pick it up after dinner." Somehow that seemed safer, not so much like a date, just dinner with a friend.

"Okay. See you at five."

Hanging up, she sat down suddenly, and stared at the phone. Butterflies danced in her stomach. *It's not a date; it's not a date. He probably wants to talk over some of the plans for the house. It's not a date.*

Maxi realized that her social life had deteriorated since Jim's death. Most all their friends had been couples and now she was the odd one. Women she had thought her friends seemed less friendly now, as though as a widow she might have designs on their husbands. Little did they know that not one of them appealed to her in the slightest, but she always ended up feeling very uncomfortable. After a few such occasions, Maxi made excuses by saying that work took all her time and she had no energy by evening. She could literally feel the relief of the wife who had issued the invitation and could almost hear her saying, 'Well I tried, and it is her decision.' She realized that with the exception of her work she felt totally inadequate in trying to make a life for herself. There was the occasional lunch with Sue, but other than that she hadn't tried to do anything other than make plans for the renovation of her house. *I'm sure that is why Sam called so there would be a chance to go over some of the details.*

Feeling a little more comfortable with this thought, Maxi settled down to work. The day went quickly and before she had time to think more about it, it was 5 o'clock.

"Hi." Sam stood in her doorway grinning at her. "Finished for the day?"

"Hello! Yes, just putting files away and making notes for tomorrow. I'll only be a minute."

"I made reservations at The Mountain Top Inn. Is that all right? They have good food and don't require fancy dress."

"That's perfect. I haven't been there since Jim's ..." Her voice trailed off as she realized she was about to say, since Jim's death. Not a very good response.

"If it is difficult for you I'll cancel, and we'll go somewhere else." Sam gave her a worried look. *Gee, he hoped he hadn't blown it.*

"No. That's fine. I just have to get used to going to places where we used to go. It's unavoidable in a town this size. I'm glad I'm not going alone." Maxi stood up and reached for her coat, putting it on before Sam could move around the desk to hold it for her. Somehow that seemed too intimate.

Dinner was good and Sam soon made it clear that he did not want to talk about the renovations on her house.

"I'm a little awkward with this, so bear with me. I haven't asked a woman to dinner since Diane left me three years ago, so I'm rusty." He gave a self-deprecating laugh.

Maxi smiled her sympathy, "I knew you were divorced, but didn't know how long. Was it a difficult time for you or did you initiate it?"

"No, I was taken completely by surprise. I went home after work one day and she was gone. Just left a note. I was a mess for months. I had known she wasn't happy, but I thought we could work it out. I thought it was the 'empty nest' syndrome. I guess she stayed until the kids were both in

162

college and then decided it was time for her to do what she wanted."

"That must be a terrible adjustment. A loss is a loss and yours was as unexpected as my loss of Jim, just different circumstances. Perhaps yours was worse. You must have felt rejected along with all the other feelings."

"I was devastated. I had thought we would have many years together, do some traveling and other things we had talked about for years, but hadn't been able to do. But I am over it now, and realize that we had different goals.

"Diane went back to college and is married again. She seems much happier than I had seen her for years. We have a good relationship, and see each other for the kid's birthdays and holidays."

"That's remarkable! I always thought that divorced people hated each other and fought over the kids, each trying to get them on their side."

"That does happen to some people, but we agreed early on that we wouldn't do that to them. Perhaps it made it easier because they were pretty much on their own. I give her credit for staying in a situation that caused her unhappiness until the kids were old enough to deal with it, better than they would have in their teens."

That set the tone for the evening. Both were relaxed and talked of likes and dislikes and loneliness and how they dealt with that.

"I have buried my self in my new job and the renovating of the house. Both have been so rewarding that it has helped enormously." Maxi realized this fact as she said it, and was surprised. "I hadn't realized that's what I've been doing."

"I did the same thing. Survival instincts kick in when we need them, I guess. I didn't realize it until later, either."

Later, when Sam dropped her off to get her car at the parking lot, she turned to him and said, "It was a nice relaxing, enjoyable evening, Sam. Thank you."

"My pleasure. I'd like to do it again, soon."

"Me too," Maxi replied. She smiled all the way back to her apartment where Beau met her with a scolding meow.

"I know it has been a long, lonesome day for you. Soon we will be in our own house and you will have more room to roam. I may even have a kitty door put in for you, once I know you won't roam too far and get into trouble. I guess I better talk to the vet soon about keeping you a nice house cat and not a roaming Tom."

Chapter 12

Mark and Jeff were having their weekly breakfast meeting at The Gathering Place. It was the Wednesday before Christmas, and the restaurant was crowded with the regular customers. Sandy always kept a small table for two in the corner for Mark who came in every morning at 7:00 and no one ever sat there until after 8 o'clock. That table was Mark's territory.

"Well," Mark called out, "There's my sometimes breakfast buddy! Come on over, and tell me what's new."

Jeff sauntered over, speaking to several people on the way before he returned Mark's greeting. "Hello to you, too, you old fart; what're you up to today?"

"Nothing much, maybe arresting a few ax murders, drug lords, and just cleaning up the town a little. How bout you? What're you writing these days? You're probably here to pick my brain again. Get a freebee."

"How'd you know? As a matter of fact, I have run into this problem with a story I'm working on. Maybe you can help." Jeff then lowered his voice so the others around them couldn't hear. It didn't matter much. The noise of the many conversations going on simultaneously made a good cover.

"When is she going to move?" Mark hunched his shoulders over his plate of bacon and eggs and took another bite.

"I have a feeling that she is going to be moving this weekend. The bedroom and bath on the first floor are complete. The kitchen isn't finished yet, but she is getting antsy in that little apartment." Jeff stopped speaking when the waitress put his usual stack of pancakes in front of him.

"Don't you two ever get tired of the same thing for breakfast?" Sandy couldn't resist jibbing as she put a fresh pot of coffee on the table between them.

"I've tried to tell the Chief that all that bacon and eggs will clog up his arteries, but he won't listen," Jeff replied as he loaded up his pancakes with butter and syrup.

"Can't see that all that flour, butter and syrup is any better for you?" Mark shot back.

"Well, far be it from me to discourage regulars, especially good tippers like you two." Sandy grinned good-naturedly at both of them and left them to their breakfast.

Both men ate in silence for a minute after Sandy left, and then resumed their discussion. "I sure wish we had a lead on whoever totaled her house and left the note in her office," Mark said between bites. "But we haven't a clue. Mrs. Cotter described the man she saw coming from Maxi's house the morning of the explosion, but we haven't found anyone yet that fits the description. No one else saw anything suspicious."

"I worry about her moving and living out so far, but maybe that is safer than in town," Jeff said. "I'll do what I can to keep an eye on things, but it would be very easy for someone to get in without my knowing. My dog is good, but he can't be alert to everything out of the ordinary."

"I think it's time we have a long talk with her and tell her everything." Mark scowled at Jeff as if to say 'don't tell me I'm wrong.'

167

"How do you want to do it?" Jeff asked, getting the message. "In your office, her apartment, or wait until she moves and go there?"

"She will definitely be at the house Saturday morning, won't she? You say she spends every weekend there? Even if she hasn't decided to stay overnight yet, she will be there as usual, won't she? She hasn't indicated that she will be doing anything else?"

"No, she hasn't said anything to me about other plans, so I expect she will be. Sometimes she goes to pick up wallpaper or paint or something before going to the house. You could come to my place and when we see her car you can go over and talk to her then."

"I think we should both go. You've built up a pretty good relationship with her and I think it will help to have you there. I think you should also tell her what Jim told you about his investigation, the video he said he made and the meeting that was to take place with your FBI buddy. We both know that is the motive behind the threats to her." Mark was still scowling, something he did when he was worried.

"You think she should know everything?" Jeff sounded skeptical.

"Yes. That is the only way we can convince her of the seriousness of the situation. She's too intelligent to be fooled, and I think she feels that the threat to her is over now. Nothing has happened since the note on her desk. From what she said to me last week she has convinced herself that it is someone upset with the dike-levee project, and has now gotten it out of his system. She said she thinks the note was just to scare her and it won't happen again."

"All right. Meet me at my house Saturday morning. She is usually at her place by 8:30 on Saturdays".

"I'll be there right after breakfast, and we can go over what we are going to tell her." Mark pushed his chair back and put fifteen dollars on the table, saying more loudly, "Breakfast is on me today. You pay next time."

"Sure, till next time, Chief." Jeff followed him from the restaurant to the parking lot where they separated, going to their own cars.

It was only a little after eight Saturday morning when Maxi unloaded her clothing from the car; a second trip took care of Beau's litter, litter box, and food. It only took her a half hour to bring in everything and put it away. *There is something to be said about losing everything. I'm glad that I haven't bought anything more. I can't believe that this is everything I own!*

She went directly to the thermostat in the bedroom and turned it up to 70 degrees. The bedroom was on its own heating zone and it didn't take long for the room to warm up.

A knock on the kitchen door cut into her musings. It was too early for Jeff, who always showed up between 9:30 and 10.00 every Saturday.

"Good morning, Jeff. You're early! And Mark, what brings you here so early in the morning?"

"Good morning, Maxi. How is the remodeling coming? The outside looks great!" Mark stepped into the kitchen, looking around at the newly spackled walls ready for cabinets and appliances. "Looks like you may be moving soon. Didn't you say you wanted to move as soon as the bedroom, bath and kitchen were completed?"

"I have already moved, Mark. Just now. I don't have many personal belongings. I can get along without a kitchen as I have been in that mini apartment." Maxi moved to show them the bedroom, which was bare of furniture.

"It looks a little stark. You going to use a sleeping bag?" Mark grinned at her as he walked toward the door, which he thought probably led to the bathroom.

"Bedroom furniture will be delivered momentarily," Maxi assured him. "Sam is going to come this morning and re-hang the interior shutters. I will think about drapes or curtains later."

"It looks great, Maxi. I didn't think it was possible to do this much since you bought the place."

"You are not here to see the house, Mark. I've known you since kindergarten and I can see you have a mission. Do you have some information on who destroyed my house?" Maxi gave him a direct look that told him to stop fooling around and come out with whatever had prompted the visit. She led the way back to the kitchen and the makeshift table. She had added two more folding chairs since Jeff was there last. She used the table for conference talks with the contractors and often needed more chairs.

Seating himself in one of the chairs while Jeff sat next to him, Mark indicated the other chair across the table. "Please sit down, Maxi. We need to talk."

Concern creased her forehead. Maxi sat on the edge of her chair, her eyes never leaving Mark's. "Why do I get the feeling that I'm not going to like what I'm about to hear?"

"There is no easy way to get into this, so I am just going to go ahead and say what I have to say. Just remember that Jeff and I are your friends. I am not just the 'law,' so to speak."

Maxi sat silently staring from one to the other until Mark took a deep breath and said, "I don't think the explosion that blew up your house and the note left in your office are a result of your work for the project".

As she opened her mouth to protest and ask another question, Mark held up his hand, palm toward her. "Jeff is going to tell you something that will shock you; you may find it hard to believe, but it is true, I assure you. Jeff..." He looked at Jeff, giving a nod of his head for him to begin his tale.

"This is a little complicated to tell, so bear with me, Maxi." Jeff took a deep breath and continued, "I think you knew that Jim was basing his new novel around strip mining. He felt he had a wealth of information locally, since it has been done in the mountains for years, and now is the center of a lot of environmental controversy.

"At Maxi's nod, Jeff continued. "You also know that Jim could talk to anyone and as a result gained invaluable information on all kinds of subjects." Again Maxi nodded, but didn't speak.

"Jim traveled to several strip mining operations and talked to men who worked them. It was at one that was finished and ready to be reclaimed where he talked to Elmer, the supervisor, and scheduled a lunch meeting with him for the next day. Jim wanted to know how the land was to be reclaimed. He had an uncanny way of getting people to bare their souls and that is exactly what Elmer did.

He was angry, and concerned that there was illegal dumping going on. He told Jim that he had been ordered to hold off on getting the bulldozers in to start leveling the ground and putting in topsoil.

"He lived along the highway that leads to the site and became suspicious when a fleet of trucks went by his house in the middle of the night. After two nights of this, he decided to investigate and followed the trucks. He didn't turn on his headlights, as he said he felt that he shouldn't let them know he was following them. They drove to the site and dumped their loads.

"The next morning he decided to check it out in daylight. He detected a strong chemical smell and saw drums of something that he couldn't identify, and some of them were marked as hazardous waste. He went home and called his boss to report what he had found. He said he told his boss that he was sure that somebody was trespassing and doing it illegally without the company's knowledge. His boss told him it was okay, that a deal had been worked out to fill in some of the land before topsoil was added and not to worry about it.

"Jim told me what I have just told you". Jeff paused, and then continued, "He felt he should notify the environmental agency but wanted more proof first. I told him he should be careful as if was as big as he thought, he could be in danger.

"Jim had known, when he confided in me, that I had been with the FBI until my wife's illness when I resigned to take care of her. I told him that I still had contacts. I suggested he meet with my former boss. Jim agreed, but said he was going back to the area and stay at the motel where he had stayed before. He hoped to have some kind of proof by the time of our meeting. We settled on a time and place.

"Before we could meet, Jim called me again. He said, the night before he had taken a camcorder he bought with a nighttime long distance lens and waited for the trucks. By this time he knew the territory quite well, and he drove to a tower that had been built to oversee the entire area; he had a perfect view. About an hour later he spotted Elmer's pickup coming around the bend. Elmer parked and waited. About midnight the trucks began arriving. Jim said he had a perfect view and captured the name on the garbage trucks, "Sheppard's Waste Removal.

"He saw Elmer stop the first truck. He and the driver talked, and then the driver phoned someone on his cell phone. Jim was too far away to hear what was said, but after he put the phone back in his pocket, Jim watched as he reached under his jacket and pulled out a pistol. Jim said he watched in horror as Elmer was shot point blank in the head. The driver loaded his body into the cab of the truck, and proceeded onto the site, where he stopped and pulled Elmer's body from the cab, and dragged it to the open pit area and dropped it. Then he motioned to the drivers of the trucks to dump their loads.

"Jim got all this on tape. He said he felt physically sick having witnessed Elmer's murder. But having the name of the company on the side of the trucks and everything that happened on tape kept him quiet. He realized his own life would be in jeopardy if he were to be discovered. There were ten trucks that night before the bulldozer covered it all with earth.

"Jim said he scanned the morning newspaper expecting to find a report of Elmer's disappearance. He found nothing, no mention of Elmer at all. Surely Elmer's wife would have called someone when he didn't come home. Jim said he mulled over what he should do and finally decided to put the tape in a safe place. But first, he went to Elmer's house expecting to talk to Elmer's distraught wife. But there was no answer to his knock and it appeared that no one was about.

"On his way back to the motel, he stopped at a nearby gas station-grocery store and asked if anyone there knew Elmer, that he was a friend. He said he was worried when he didn't find him at home. He was told that Elmer was a widower and something of a loner. Nobody had seen him for several days, maybe a week. Before someone could put together the fact that he had called himself a 'friend', but didn't seem to know that he was a widower, Jim left.

"Later that day, Jim called me again and asked me to meet him that evening. He told me what I have just related to you. He didn't say where the tape was."

Mark picked up where Jeff left off. "We know that it was not an accident. Marks on the car showed that a bigger vehicle, probably an SUV, hit his bumper and also the driver's side of the car, forcing him over the cliff. They picked their spot well."

"So we have no idea where he hid the tape or where he was when he called me in the afternoon," Jeff concluded.

Maxi shot to her feet, knocking over her chair and stared at him in horror. "You're saying my husband's death was murder, not an accident? You're sitting there as calm as can be, and telling me that you have known all this and never told me?"

"Calm down. Take it easy." Jeff and Mark spoke in unison.

"Calm down, take it easy! What do you expect from me, for God's sake?" Maxi looked like a wild woman ready to claw their eyes out. Trembling, she clutched at the table to keep from falling to the floor. Both men circled opposite ends of the table to take hold of her arms and steady her, but she would have none of it. She fought them away and stumbled over the fallen chair. This time they caught her and kept their hold, leading her to the other chair where they got her to sit. Maxi's mind raced. *No, it couldn't be true. I would have known if Jim were working on something so dangerous.*

She started to say these things aloud, only half listening to what Jeff was saying. "Maxi, I know it is a shock. Jim told me that you knew nothing about his involvement, and he didn't want you to be involved in any way. He knew these people were dangerous. But that was then, this is now. Jim is dead, and we don't want the same thing to happen to you."

Maxi was still shaking her head in denial.

"Are you beginning to understand now? I know it is a lot to take in. Please bear with us. There is more that you need to know."

She nodded dumbly; her body almost folded itself back in the chair as though she was too weak or tired to sit straight. "What else is there for me to know?"

Mark took over. "When your house exploded, Jeff and his superior came to my office and told me what you have just heard from Jeff. They were sure that it wasn't an act of violence against the dike-levee project. They felt that the people responsible for Jim's death probably thought there might be records in the house. What better way to be sure that nothing turned up when you started going through Jim's papers and checking his computer? It was all taken care of in one big explosion. And what better way to cover it up than to use the project as the reason."

"Jim was a writer. How did he get involved with these people?" Maxi was still not convinced.

"It began innocently enough. He was getting background for a novel." Jeff waited for her next question as she tried to sort through all she had just been told.

"What about the note on my desk?" Her voice was barely more than a hoarse whisper.

"Just adding fuel to the idea that it was some demented idiot with a grudge against the project and you."

Pulling herself together, she straightened her posture. "So then, it is over. No house, no records, nothing to make me a threat any longer. It's over."

"I don't feel sure enough to let you go without protection," Mark stated firmly. "Jeff lives nearby but not close enough to keep you from harm. We have discussed a couple of alternatives. One, we can have your house wired so Jeff can keep surveillance."

"I'm not having my privacy invaded. NO BUGS!" At the look exchanged between the men, she added, "NO BUGS, do you hear me? I won't have it."

"I am not looking to invade your privacy. I just want to know if someone tries to break in so I can stop whatever they have planned", Jeff was getting a little hot under the collar, too. Damn, she was pigheaded and stubborn.

"Well, you will just have to forget it. I can take care of myself, thank you very much. I don't think you took very good care of Jim. He's dead. Remember!"

That set Jeff and Mark back on their heels, she noted with satisfaction. *I'm not having any of their protection. If what they say is true then any motive for harm to me is over and done with. If it isn't true, then the worst is that some idiot may continue to harass me because of my job.*

Shaken by her observation regarding their protection of Jim, Jeff and Mark had nothing to say in response. Instead they sat and looked guilty. If Maxi hadn't been so upset herself, she would have taken pity on them. But she was still too angry to feel any other emotion. Standing up she said, "I think that will be all for today, gentlemen. Goodbye."

"There is one more thing you should know before you kick us out". Jeff continued to sit and looked at the chair across the table, indicating that Maxi should sit back down.

"Okay, one more minute then out you go," Maxi sat on the edge of her chair, convinced that anything they might add would not change her mind one iota.

"Just before Jim's accident when he called me on his cell phone, he said he had put the tape in a safe place. We haven't found it. We have no idea where it is, and the note you received may mean that our suspects haven't found it either, and think that you know something about it."

Now it was Maxi's turn to feel stunned. "You think I know where he might have put it?"

"It's a possibility that those behind his murder think you know if they searched his car and found nothing." Mark stated bluntly. "We just don't know. When we searched it, there was nothing except some personal items which were turned over to you."

"And now even those things are gone." Tears threatened and Maxi's voice quavered.

"I'm sorry, Maxi," Jeff spoke quietly. "But you are so damm stubborn that there wasn't any other way except to tell you all of it. When Jim last talked to me on the phone, I had the feeling that he had hidden the film somewhere other than in the car or his house. It hasn't been found. Do you have any idea where he might have put it? Do you have a vacation home, cabin in the mountains, anywhere you can think of that he might have put it?"

"No. I don't know of anyplace other than the house. He worked from home, didn't have an office any other place."

"Now you can see why it is necessary to protect you. We don't want you harmed, too, and we need your help to find Jim's killers."

"I am still not having my house bugged. So forget it." Maxi stood and walked to the kitchen door, opening it. She continued standing there with head bowed, refusing to have eye contact with either of them.

"Okay then, but I will call a security company to put in an alarm system for you. I'll let you know when they will be here." Mark stood stubbornly in place and looked as though he wouldn't budge until she agreed.

"Okay. That I can agree to." Maxi inclined her head toward the open door.

Without saying a word they filed out. On the way to Mark's waiting patrol car, Jeff jammed his hands into his pockets as he vented his frustration, "Damn. Mark, what are we going to do about her?"

"Nothing. There is nothing that we can do as far as putting any surveillance devices in her house. You know as well as I do that we can't without her permission."

"Not legally, anyway. But what if I did it on my own without telling anyone?"

"Forget it, Jeff. That doesn't make it any less illegal. She could have you put in jail. Then you could really keep an eye on her from there, couldn't you? No, we have to find another way."

Chapter 13

Maxi stood rooted to the floor just inside the door after closing it behind the two men. She was shaken with the information they had just told her. *It can't be true. I would have known if Jim were involved in something like that. He wouldn't have kept it from me. He wouldn't! Then why do I know in my gut that it is true?*

A car door slammed. Looking out the window, she saw Sam pull something from the back of his pickup and start toward the house with it. *The refinished interior shutters for the bedroom. I forgot.*

"Hi, Maxi. I have the shutters for your bedroom." Sam proceeded directly to the bedroom. "You getting furniture delivered today?"

"Yes. It should be here any time now." Maxi had trouble pulling her thoughts back into the morning's original plans. She still felt disassociated.

Somehow, the morning passed in a relatively normal fashion. Sam didn't seem to notice anything strange in Maxi's behavior, and that was a relief to her.

By noon, with her furniture delivered and placed, her bedroom was really looking like she had pictured it. The shutters blended perfectly with the beautiful dark oak trim around the windows. They were the original shutters, separate sets for the top and bottom windows, and they fit inside the casing so the beautiful carved corner pieces and molding were not hidden.

The deep color of the reds and blues in the oriental rugs looked warm and inviting on the wide planked pine floors. The solid cherry four-poster king size bed was waiting for her to make it up and the armoire on the wall opposite held a new 52 inch TV which Sam connected for her before he left. She had had a satellite dish installed, as there was no TV cable available. A triple dresser graced the wall between the two windows and a highboy chest fit into a niche in the short hallway to the walk-in closet. She plugged in the brass bedside lamps, adjusted the position of the nightstands and turned on the lights. Immediately the room looked cozy and inviting.

Before starting to make the bed, she turned on the gas log in the corner fireplace and everything seemed just right. At one side of the fireplace she had a huge, comfortable club chair upholstered in soft mauve floral chintz with matching ottoman and two soft pillows, one dark mauve and one dark green, for added comfort. A small table and a floor lamp beside it made it perfect for reading in the evenings.

A beautiful patchwork comforter of jewel tones in velvet and satin and a border of old-fashioned roses and ivy completed the bed-making. She looked around, pleased with the results. It looked great with the forest green walls that were muted by softer shades of green sponge painting. A 12-inch border matching the border on the comforter showed off the beautiful crown molding at the high 8-foot-ceiling. All the rich colors seemed right for the large room. She mused, *I may want cooler colors for a summer bedspread, but this is so cozy for the winter months. I'll hang pictures and add other accessories as I find the right things.*

Only one thing was missing. "Beau, where are you?" Maxi panicked, as she didn't remember seeing him since Sam left.

Going to the front door, she looked out and sighed with relief as Beau came bolting across the porch, meowing a complaint 'why did you shut me outside?' Once inside, he immediately headed for the warm bedroom where he jumped on the bed and made himself comfortable. Maxi smiled. *Now it looks complete.*

It was early afternoon before she left to go grocery shopping. The refrigerator was still not in place in the unfinished kitchen, and the microwave and coffee pot were on the folding table where she had sat with Mark and Jeff a few hours before.

On the way to town she realized she was famished and stopped at The Gathering Place for a sandwich and a bowl of soup. Sandy made her own soup. It was always delicious and was especially good on this cold, frosty day. Decorations reminded her that it was only four days until Christmas.

Her packages for her kids and their spouses had been mailed two weeks ago. Lorene and Jack had tried their best to entice her to come stay with them over Christmas. Even Michael and Eve had called from California trying to convince her to go to Lorene's. They were worried about her spending this Christmas alone. But she wanted to stay home. She gave her work as the reason, saying it was too difficult to get away long enough to make the trip worthwhile. Plus, she didn't like the idea of driving in the snow. So far there had only been a scattering of snow showers, but more was predicted for Christmas Day.

What she didn't tell them was that she was too tired to make the trip. Work had slowed, and she was planning on taking vacation time over the Christmas holiday, but she needed rest. She had been running at top speed since her return to work and every weekend was spent at the house with the hope of living here before Christmas. She was exhausted. Now that her one room was livable, she looked forward to relaxing in it. *Just to have some time alone will be heavenly. No schedules to keep, no demands, it will be wonderful. I'll see Sue and Rob at their Christmas Party and catch up with old friends who will also be there.*

She stopped at the post office on her way to the grocery store and retrieved her mail from the box she had kept there since the explosion that destroyed her house. There was a notice to pick up two packages, Christmas presents from her children. Back home again, she dumped the mail on the dresser and went back to the car for the rest of her groceries and the packages.

The refrigerator was humming away, and it felt good to fill it with food for the coming week. She had included a trip to the liquor store to stock up on wine; not that she drank much, but it would be nice to have a glass now and then as she relaxed for a few days. She pictured herself sitting in her club chair with her feet on the ottoman, a fire in the fireplace, sipping a glass of wine while watching a television show or reading a good book; she had stocked up on books, too, at the store.

Beau was still sleeping in the middle of her bed. It seemed he had been content while she was gone. He already had discovered the wide windowsills were a wonderful place to sit and look out. Sometimes there were birds in the bare branches of the lilac bush. The first time he had watched them, his teeth had started chattering in excitement and Maxi had laughed.

It was late afternoon before she got back to her mail; a stack of Christmas Cards, which she put on the little table beside the chair for later; a few bills and a letter from a bank in Smethport. *Why would I be getting mail from that bank?*

She opened it to find it was a notice that the lockbox six-month rental fee was due. Checking the envelope again revealed it was addressed to Mr. James Taylor, not Ms James Taylor as she had thought at first glance. It hit her in the chest like a sledgehammer blow. This may be what Mark and Jeff were searching for.

A minute later she was on the phone to Mark. All she said was that she needed to see him, immediately. He was at her door fifteen minutes later, looking worried. "What is it?"

"Come in, Mark, I've something to show you." Maxi went to the dresser and picked up the letter, handing it to Mark. He took it, glancing at it curiously, and then looked at Maxi.

At her nod, he opened the envelope and took out the renewal notice for the lockbox. He looked again at the address, as Maxi had done, and a low whistle escaped his pursed lips. "Is this what I think it is?"

"You tell me. Do you think this could be the safe place that Jim referred to when he called Jeff before the accident? It seems that date would correspond with the time that he called Jeff."

"It very well could be. Have you told Jeff?"

"No, I called you right away. It seemed the best thing to do. And I didn't want to say why I had called you over the phone. I guess your news this morning has made me a little paranoid."

"Good girl. And you were not being paranoid," Mark replied, adding, "I'll get the judge to issue a court order to have the bank open the lockbox for us. They won't let you have access without a lot of red tape requiring a death certificate, proof of your ID and probably a waiting period besides. It will be quickest and easiest to have Judge Wimple give us a court order up front. It'll probably be hard to get the bank manager to go in on a weekend, but I don't think we should wait until Monday."

"Okay. Whatever you think best. That's why I called you right away. Do you need me to do anything?" Maxi looked at him anxiously.

"You will have to go with me to the Judge's house." Mark raised his eyebrows at her, asking for her agreement. "Take some ID, your driver's license should do for that, and do you have a copy of Jim's death certificate handy? It might be a good idea to have that."

"I don't have a copy of the death certificate. I never asked for more after the original was destroyed in my house. Do you really think we will have to wait for that?"

"We'll check with the funeral director and see if he can give us a certified copy," Mark replied. "I'm not sure what to expect in this situation."

While Maxi was getting into her coat and gathering up her purse, Mark looked around the room. "Nice," he murmured nodding approvingly. "Of course, you realize that living in one room like this you will have to do all your entertaining in your bedroom," he added with a leer and wiggling of the eyebrows. He accomplished his purpose in making her laugh and relax a little. He was concerned about her pale complexion and nervous, twitchy movements. She had a lot of shocking information laid on her today and the bank letter to top it off. He didn't want her freaking out.

As soon as they were in the cruiser, he got Judge Wimple on the phone. "Hello Judge, Mark Fields here. What information do you need to issue a court order to open a lockbox of a deceased individual?" He asked without any preliminary niceties, getting right to the question.

"I need a copy of the death certificate, a copy of the probated will and ID of the beneficiary."

"They were all in the house when it was destroyed," Maxi said when Mark disconnected the call to the judge.

Mark then made two calls: one to the funeral home that had taken care of Jim's burial and one to Mary Beth, the prothonatary, at home. He asked Mary Beth to meet him at the court house, only explaining that he needed a copy of a document and that it was urgent.

A call to Jeff insured that he would meet them at the court house. After a quick stop at the funeral home, Maxi had a copy of the death certificate.

Mary Beth and Jeff were both waiting at the Court House when Maxi and Mark arrived fifteen minutes later. They all entered the prothonotary's office where Mary Beth booted up the computer and found the probated will. In a matter of minutes Mark was holding a printed copy in his hands.

"Are you a notary, too, Mary Beth?"

She was, and in a few more minutes she had an affidavit prepared for Maxi's signature verifying that she was Maxine Taylor. It was all signed and sealed when they left the Court House twenty minutes later on the way to Judge Wimple's residence. He was waiting for them and opened the door immediately on their arrival. Ten minutes later they had the court order and were on their way.

Within the hour they were in Smethport meeting the manager of the bank. A phone call to his home had assured them that he would come and open up for them. But he said if they didn't have the key, they would be unable to open the lockbox. Mark had the dispatcher at headquarters get Lenny on the radio and have him meet them at the bank. Lenny was the resident locksmith, among other things. His patrol car had been waiting when they arrived at the bank.

Five minutes later, Maxi, Jeff and Mark stood around the table staring down at a single key lying on the bottom of the metal box. There was nothing else inside. Disappointment was heavy in the air.

"Now what?" Maxi experienced such a feeling of failure and letdown after the hectic afternoon that she was near tears. She had pinned her hopes on solving the entire dilemma and being free of the fear that was plaguing her after her talk with Mark and Jeff that morning. She had just managed to convince herself that she was no longer in any danger. *So much for that hope!*

"I would guess that it is the key to another lockbox," Mark replied. "But where is it?" He went out to where the bank manager waited and showed him the key, asking if he thought it was another lockbox key. The bank manager said it looked like one, but shrugged his shoulders, telling them it wasn't one of theirs. It was evident that he wasn't happy being called out on a Saturday afternoon.

"Back to square one." Maxi turned to leave after picking up the key.

"I'll keep that." Mark had the key before she could react. "I don't want anyone to think that you have it. They may try to take it from you, if you get my meaning." He tilted his head toward the bank manager who was locking up the building again, indicating that he didn't want to say more while other ears could pick up anything.

So, Maxi said nothing and in a way was glad that she wouldn't be responsible for it. "I guess I'll just have to wait until I get another notice from somewhere else about a rental fee. That could be another six months to a year. Jim could have paid for a two-year period."

"I'll have two detectives start checking all the local banks and then spread out to surrounding towns if nothing shows up locally. We'll find it."

Mark dropped Maxi off at her house, admonishing her to lock up.

Jeff had followed in his car and went with Maxi into her house, wanting to be sure that she was all right and nobody was waiting for her. At a peek into her newly furnished bedroom he gave a low whistle, "Nice!"

"Yes, isn't it? I'm so happy with it and I am going to enjoy my vacation time just relaxing here." Maxi gave a sigh, "I just wish I didn't have all this other stuff to worry about. Couldn't you and Mark have waited until after the holidays?"

"I'm sorry, Maxi. We just felt that you had to be made aware of the circumstances, especially now that you are so far out in the country."

"Yea, I know. It just takes some getting used to. I'm definitely not going to tell my family or they will demand that I quit my job and go to one of their homes. I need to keep on with my work. I'd really go crazy, knowing what I know now, if I didn't have my job to keep my mind occupied. Don't you think whoever killed Jim wouldn't be worried any more after this much time has passed?"

"Possibly, but not until we find the tape and have them in prison will you really be safe," Jeff replied.

"Well, I've had enough for one day. I'm going to fix myself some soup, a sandwich, have a glass of wine and relax in my new chair. Then hopefully, sleep all night, maybe even until noon tomorrow." Maxi started toward the front door with the intent that Jeff should go home.

"Okay, I'll go, but you have to promise to call me if you can't sleep for worrying. I can be here to keep you company in a couple minutes." Jeff opened the door and stepped outside. "It's starting to snow!"

"Really?" Maxi stepped outside with him and looked at the lazy flakes drifting down. "How nice. It makes it seem more like Christmas. I'll call you tomorrow, Jeff, and thanks for everything." Maxi stepped back inside and closed the door. Jeff waited until he heard the deadbolt click into place before he turned toward his car.

Chapter 14

Mark phoned Jeff from the cruiser on his way back to headquarters. They discussed the absence of the tape and how they might find the lockbox for the key. "I was really hoping that this was it," Mark said.

"Yea, me too," Jeff replied, and added that he would keep a sharp eye on Maxi's house.

Twice during the night, Jeff and Major walked to Maxi's house, circling the outside for anything suspicious. Major didn't pick up any scent that alerted him that something was amiss. It started snowing harder at 2 a.m. At 5 a.m. after his second patrol, Jeff turned in to get a couple hours sleep. He slept soundly and woke at nine. Immediately he knew that the snow was considerable. The silence was too deep even for a winter morning. A look out the window confirmed his suspicions.

"Holy shit!"

Snow was coming down so heavily that it was obscuring anything more than fifteen feet away. In minutes, Jeff was dressed in ski gear. He checked his pockets for his compass, water bottle and flask containing whiskey. In a backpack, he put a first aid kit, and dehydrated food and ten pounds of dry dog food. He closed it, then on second thought, reopened it and put in a pair of jeans and knit shirt. I don't think I will be coming back right away, and I don't want to be in ski pants all day. "Okay, boy, we're ready."

Major followed him out onto the porch, looking curious, as though he wondered what Jeff was planning. Jeff told Major to heel. "I'll go first and break a trail. Stay close, now. This stuff is shoulder high on you."

"Of all times for her to decide to move here, this is the worst," he muttered, but admitted to himself that the weather report had not predicted such a storm. Only a light snow had been forecast on the 11 o'clock news last night.

Major watched Jeff step off the porch into the snow. He wanted to follow but was wary of jumping into it. Whining, and pacing back and forth on the porch, he finally took the plunge. Immediately it was shoulder high as he struggled after Jeff, whose tracks helped a little. He wasn't about to let his man out of his sight.

It took a half hour to get to Maxi's back door, four times as long as it took in good weather, with several checks on the compass. He pounded on the door and shouted, "Maxi, open up. It's me, Jeff."

Inside the house, Maxi rolled over, willing the pounding in her head to go away. It persisted and finally she was awake enough to realize that the pounding was at her door. Moving sluggishly, she rolled from the bed, groped for her slippers and robe, and staggered to the door. Opening it brought in a blast of cold snow that hit her in the face. Jeff and Major pushed past her into the warm foyer.

Jeff took one look at Maxi and knew she was sick. Her eyes were puffed, red and watery; her face was pale. The minute the cold air from outside hit her she started shivering uncontrollably.

Quickly closing the door, Jeff shed his boots; he grasped her shoulders to steer her toward her bedroom where it would be warmer. The minute he touched her, she cringed and he stepped back, dropping his hands. His immediate reaction was, *God, she is so mad at me for yesterday that she can't stand for me to touch her even to help her to a chair.*

A low moan preceded Maxi's words, "I hurt all over, even my skin hurts, and I have a headache to beat all headaches."

Hearing that, Jeff reached to help her into the chair, his touch gentle. He realized how relieved he was, that she hadn't cringed just because he touched her, but because she was hurting.

"What are you doing here, pounding on my door?" The words came haltingly between her chattering teeth as a chill shook her from had to toe.

"We came to see if you were all right. There is a terrible snowstorm going on out there. The snow is already over three feet deep. You should be back in bed, let me help you." Jeff stood next to her chair ready with assistance. She looked terrible.

"I think you have the flu. When did you start to feel so bad?"

Struggling to stand, she started toward the bed. Maxi said she felt ill after Mark dropped her off last evening. "At first I thought it was just the let down after the anticipation of finding the lockbox. I went straight to bed after I had some soup. I only got up once during the night. I remember not feeling very good, and I took some Tylenol. I was asleep when you started pounding on my door. I thought the pounding was part of the nightmare I was having," she said as she crawled back into bed.

Jeff covered her with all the bedcovers and looked for more. She was shaking with chills. He couldn't find any more blankets. She had probably only bought what she thought she needed for her bed right now. "I'll fix you a hot toddy to warm you up. Have you taken any other medication?"

"No, not since I took the Tylenol last night. I don't remember what time it was. I wish I had gotten that down comforter that I looked at."

"I'll start a fire in the fireplace before I fix you that hot toddy. We'll get the room warmer." Jeff turned on the gas to the fireplace and lit it with the lighter from the brass planter on the hearth. The blaze leaped to life immediately. He preferred a real log fire, but this gas log looked real and was certainly a lot quicker. He found the Tylenol in the bathroom and brought it to Maxi with a glass of water. He shook two capsules into his palm then waited for her to elbow her way to a half sitting position so she could take the medication.

Jeff went to see what he could find in the kitchen. He didn't expect it to be much with everything still so unfinished. He was pleasantly surprised to find an electric teakettle, a large electric fry pan that could be used for many things, a toaster and a coffee maker on the table where they had sat that morning. On the floor beside it was a large cardboard box that held a few dishes, tea bags, coffee, condiments, sugar, and flour.

The refrigerator was well stocked, too. Surprised at finding lemons in the fruit drawer, he decided to use fresh lemon juice for the toddy. He pulled the whiskey flask out of his backpack, found a large mug, dumped what he estimated was a good-sized shot of whiskey into it, added the juice of half a lemon and finished filling the cup with boiling water. He decided not to add sugar, remembering his grandmother's saying that sour lemonade would reduce a fever.

Within minutes he was back beside the bed, holding a steaming mug, "Here, I want you to drink this. It will help the fever and chills you are having." He held the cup for her, slipping one arm behind her shoulders to prop her up. "Be careful, it is steaming hot."

A small sip had Maxi puckering her mouth and nearly spitting it out. "What are you trying to do to me? Strangle me to death? Couldn't you at least put some sugar in it?"

"Well, I could, but I remember my grandma saying that sour lemonade would bring down a fever. If you can't drink it that way, I'll put some sugar in it. Should we try that?"

Handing the cup back to him, Maxi was shaking her head. "I sure as heck can't drink it that way."

Half an hour later, Maxi was giggling and the chills had let up, "I sure do feel better, Doc."

"Maybe I overdid the whiskey. I forgot you probably hadn't eaten since last night."

"Soup last night before getting into bed." She giggled again and snuggled down into the blankets.

"I'll check the cupboard, I mean box, and frig to see what I can fix us to eat."

He found plenty of salad stuff, chicken breasts, frozen skillet meals, frozen veggies, and the five and a half remaining lemons. What was she planning on making with all the lemons?

Going back to the bedroom to see what appealed to her appetite, he found her in a fetal position crying softly. "Hey, what's going on here?"

When she didn't respond, he tried to move her so he could see her face. She resisted that attempt, too. In frustration, he pulled back the covers and lay beside her, gathering her into his arms. After the first tensing of muscles in protest, she gave in and let him hold her. He didn't try to get her to talk, just held her until the tears quieted and she lay relaxed against him. Her body was still hot from fever despite the Tylenol and the lemon whiskey.

"Can you talk to me now?"

"Mmmmm," and a negative shake of her head was her only response.

He was encouraged when she didn't pull away. "You've had a lot happen to you in the last six or seven months. It's not surprising that you feel the need to cry, let it out and you'll feel better."

"I'm never go-go-going to feel better." Had she not sounded so miserable, Jeff would have been amused at her stuttering denial.

"Sure you are. You will get over the flu and feel better again and everything will get back in perspective."

"Nothing will ever bring back all the people that are gone."

"What do you mean?"

"My husband, my parents. My parents were only in their mid 60s, too young to die. And, Jim, he should have been with me another 30 years. Now, they're all gone and I couldn't do anything to stop it." The sobbing began again.

"Tell me about it."

"My parents both died only a year apart. Then Jim had the heart attack a year later. He was doing so well. Then he had the car accident and died."

"I knew that your parents were gone, but don't remember them. I knew Jim very well and liked him a lot. I miss him, too." Jeff felt inadequate. What could he say to help her?

Her sobbing increased, "I don't even have any pictures, no mementos. They were all blown up in my house. I hate the person who took everything away from me. I don't even have baby pictures of my children."

"But thank goodness you have your two kids."

"Yes. And now I live in fear that something is going to happen to them, too. I feel like I am a jinx; like I must have done something terribly wrong to be punished so."

"Sssshhhhh. You have done nothing wrong. You are a good person. What has happened to you is called 'life'. Some people seem to get through it without many bad things happening and others seem to get it all." Jeff's arms tightened around her.

"When my wife got cancer", Jeff continued, "I didn't want to believe it. She was always so vital, so full of life and laughter. She was too young to die. I denied it as long as I could, but then I watched her get sicker and sicker and felt so helpless. She helped me deal with it, rather than me helping her. She fought long and hard, but when all the treatments didn't work, she accepted it and helped me deal with it, too."

Maxi lay still, listening. His voice was soothing but his words touched something deep inside her. Through her fevered brain, his words penetrated and settled in her heart. It was like touching a kindred soul. He understood her pain, and she understood his. His words were a healing balm for her aching heart. She slept.

Jeff lay still, her even breathing told him she was in a deep sleep but he didn't move. It was hours later when he awoke and realized that her fever had broken and she was perspiring heavily. He slipped from the bed, trying not to disturb her but she woke immediately.

"Your fever has broken and you are wet with perspiration. I'm going to get you some dry clothes. Can you get to the bathroom and wash and change into them by yourself?" Jeff looked at her, uncertain if she was up to doing that, but he didn't want her lying in the sweat soaked sheets and nightgown.

"I think so. I feel better. Clean sheets are in the closet on the top shelf and a nightgown is in the top drawer of the chest," she sat up and swung her feet to the floor. She didn't even feel embarrassed by his presence and her appearance. His being there felt so right that she didn't question it.

After changing the bed, Jeff made tea and toast. He had heard the shower running as he was finishing the bed. He hadn't expected her to get into the shower. He wished he could go to see if she was all right, but didn't think she would appreciate his being that helpful. He made her some breakfast and coffee for himself.

"What time did you get here?" Maxi asked as she came from the bathroom, towel drying her hair.

Jeff thought she looked pale and shaky but also looked kind of sexy in her long flannel nightgown, covered from neck to toes. Perhaps a woman covered up was sexier than one in revealing underwear. He didn't mention his thoughts as he watched her sit down in the chair by the fireplace.

"It was almost 10 o'clock when Major and I came banging at your door. It took us thirty minutes to get here from my house because the snow was so deep. With the wind howling and blowing it in my face, it was hard to see; I was off track twice and had to backtrack. I had my compass, but had to keep scrubbing the snow and ice off it to see it."

Looking at the mantle clock, Maxi realized that she had slept for ten hours. "That was some drink you fixed for me. I think I remember crying and telling you all my troubles." She looked up at him through a curtain of hair hanging over her face as she continued to towel it. She wanted to keep her hair that way and not have to look at him.

"This is very embarrassing. I hardly know you and here you are taking care of me." Her voice was getting shaky, and she didn't want to break down in tears again. She straightened up and tossed her hair back, still avoiding his eyes.

"Don't be embarrassed, please. I'm glad that I was able to be here. After I laid all the information on you yesterday, it was the least I could do. I didn't know you were sick when I came this morning. I was concerned that you had heat and food, considering the storm."

"Well, thank you. I would have survived, but you made it much easier. I hate to admit it but I think I need to lie down again." As she got to her feet she staggered and would have fallen if he hadn't caught her.

Tucked in bed again with pillows behind her back, she sipped her tea and nibbled toast. Jeff pulled the club chair from the fireplace closer to the bed, sat down and drank his coffee.

"Do you need more Tylenol? How's your headache and other aches and pains?"

"My head still hurts and I feel as if I had been run over by a freight train. The shower helped, but a Tylenol would probably be a good idea, too." She sipped more tea and the toast was gone by the time he got back with orange juice and two Tylenol tablets.

"Can you sleep again? That's what you need."

"Probably in a little while, after the Tylenol takes effect. What about you? Are you planning on staying here?"

"Wild horses couldn't drag me away. Do you have a problem with that? Want me to leave?" He watched her closely, hoping that she didn't insist on his leaving.

"No. Not if you don't mind staying. It is kind of scary staying by myself when I feel so rotten and with the snow and all. Is it still storming?"

"Yes, it has tapered off but it's still coming down. I opened the door and looked while the water was heating for the tea. It looks to be about four feet deep. I would have a tough time getting through it if you kicked me out. 'Please don't kick me out in the storm'!" He sang the last words, hoping for a laugh. He was pleased when he accomplished that. She looked better, too, he thought.

"I vaguely remember telling you about the deaths of my parents and crying over the loss of pictures and such when my house exploded. Did I say anything too embarrassing?" She glanced shyly at him, keeping her chin down.

"Nothing you said should embarrass you. I'm glad you talked to me. I think you have needed to say it for a long time. It isn't healthy to keep everything inside. My great-grandmother had a saying that she got from her mother. "Grin and bear it." I don't believe that is the best policy. Not if you have someone to share your feelings with."

"Your great-grandmother sounds like an interesting woman."

"Yes, she was. I never knew her but heard all the stories when I was a kid. They said she was never sick until she had a massive stroke at age 86 and died at home within three days. Until then, she continued to work every day, taking care of her own house and her own needs."

"Tell me more about her."

"She was born in 1865, the year the Civil War ended. She was uneducated. She was sent to school when she was six years old but only stayed part of the day and came running home, saying she didn't like school and wasn't going to go. Her father said she had to learn something, and sent her to live with a wealthy family where she was trained to be a servant."

"Six years old? What in the world could she do at that age?

"She learned to polish silver, wash dishes, scrub vegetables. That sort of thing."

"A six-year old girl having to leave her family and go to work is unthinkable." Maxi was incredulous. "How awful. Did she talk about it? Did she finally get married and have her own house?"

"Not so unthinkable in those days. She was the middle child at that time with nine older brothers and sisters, four younger and another was on the way.

"Yes, she talked about it, according to grandma. She worked for the family until she was sixteen when a family friend came to visit, fell in love with her and married her within two months. He was quite well off, but much older. They had one child, my grandmother. He died twenty-five years later. My grandmother was twenty-four and my great-grandmother was only forty-two. She had a comfortable income from investments, owned a farm and seemed secure. Then the depression came and wiped out all her investments. She was left with the farm, a large house and a rental house that had been used for the tenant farmer."

Maxi was listening wide-eyed. "And then?"

"And then she married again but it didn't work out. The man was crazy, so she left him and moved back to the farmhouse with my grandmother, who was married by then. My grandpa did the farming. They had the additional income from the little rental house and some other land that was leased out, but too far away from the farm for my grandpa to farm it."

"That's a fascinating story. You should write it for a novel. Have you even thought of writing novels?"

"Yes. I've thought of it. Have you heard of the name Harry Patterson?"

"Yes, the author. I've read all his books." She looked more closely at him and recognition hit her.

"OmiGod! You're Harry Patterson? When I first met you I thought you looked familiar, like I should know you. Now I know! It was because I had seen your picture on the back cover of your books." Her voice squeaked. Jeff wasn't sure if it was surprise or disbelief.

"Yes, that's me." He gave a modest grin.

"All those secret service stories. But then you are an FBI agent," she grew pale as she remembered the events of Saturday.

"Not any more. I have contacts but am officially retired. That is how all this came about with your husband. We used to meet at least once a week, sometimes more often for breakfast or just coffee. We talked about writing and sometimes used each other as sounding boards. When he unintentionally got involved with the illegal dumping operation, he called me. We met at The Gathering Place and when he had told me all he had uncovered, I suggested that he talk to an old friend of mine that is still with the FBI. He hadn't known I was a retired FBI man, until then. It isn't something I broadcast."

"Couldn't he have just stayed out of it? Why did he have to continue trying to uncover the whole bit?" Maxi's cry came as she pulled back under the covers, hiding her head.

"I am going to tell you what Jim told me when he decided to do it. It might help you or it might not. But I'll chance it.

"He told me about having the heart attack a couple years ago. It caused him to rethink what his life meant. Had he made the world a better place, or had he just been passing through without making any real contributions?"

Maxi uncovered her head and began to protest, Jeff motioned for her to let him finish. "Beyond that he also was concerned about the environment and what the future held for his children and grandchildren. That's why he chose to write about strip mining and the resulting damage it caused. When he accidentally stumbled onto a real nightmare of pollution and murder, he felt a moral obligation to do something about it."

"I can understand that part, but I can't imagine him not talking to me about it, and letting the authorities take care of it."

"He knew you would want him out of it and not to be in danger. I think, and it is only my supposition, that he felt he didn't have long to live. Of course, that may be typical of heart attack survivors to feel vulnerable to another attack." Jeff hoped that what he had just told her would ease some of her heartache.

When she lay unmoving and silent, Jeff finally asked, "Can you eat anything? Want another hot toddy to help you sleep? What can I do for you?" He wished he knew what to do for her. He felt like the proverbial "fish", and she looked so fragile and needy with her feverish glow and red, puffed eyes. He wondered if her eyes always look like that when she was sick.

"I'll try to eat some soup. I got some canned yesterday. Any kind will do. Maybe some toast or crackers with it."

Before looking for soup, Jeff fixed her another hot toddy and took it to her to sip while he prepared the soup and crackers.

Later, sitting up in bed and feeling slightly dizzy but pain free after the hot drink, Maxi looked at Jeff over the soupspoon as she sipped, "I really can't believe you are Harry Patterson! And I'm not only sitting across from him, but in my bedroom of all places," she giggled, sounding like sixteen. Jeff was relieved to hear the giggle; it was probably the whiskey kicking in. In turn, he leered at her and she responded with a hoot of laughter.

The soup was eaten; the fire burned brightly, making the room cozy with the only light coming from the fire. Maxi was drowsy again. She looked flushed rather than pale as she had earlier.

"I know you told me about writing, but I didn't think about novels. Tell me how you came to write novels," Maxi requested, as she snuggled down into the depths of the comforter with only her eyes and the top of her head visible.

Chapter 15

Jeff settled back into the club chair, put his feet on the ottoman and leaned his head against the back of the chair.

"When my wife, Sally, got sick with cancer, I wanted to stay home and take care of her, so I asked for a leave of absence from work. I took her out as much as possible that summer, because she felt so confined in the house and she loved being outdoors. When we would come back home and all the housework was finished, and she was resting, I found I was fighting depression. I couldn't make her well, and the routine of housework did nothing to take my mind off what was down the road for us.

"I couldn't leave her alone even for short periods, so for sanity's sake I began writing short notes about cases I had worked on, and the notes grew into several pages and it all just sort of grew of its own accord into book length.

"I didn't plot a novel or the characters but used events and experiences from my work and my imagination did the rest. In other words, it just sort of grew on its own. Of course, I had to go back and do some rewriting so that it all flowed correctly and with continuity."

"That is so interesting, and wonderful too, that you could create something during a very difficult time in your life," Maxi was enthralled.

"It's my belief that when we are most troubled or sad, that is when we are most creative. I had a friend who wrote a whole book of poetry during such a time in his life. Someone asked him years later if he still wrote poetry and he replied, 'No, I am much too happy these days. I need to be sad or troubled to write poetry.'

But, I still write novels. I am not sad or depressed any longer but I found I had a talent for story telling and that there is a market for my kind of stories. I prefer writing to being an active FBI agent nowadays," he grinned at Maxi while looking faintly embarrassed at her amazed expression, obviously greatly impressed.

"It's a great life. I walk every morning, in all kinds of weather; and that is when I do a lot of the creative thinking, working through the plots and getting out of the corners I sometimes write myself into. The area around here is great for walking and thinking. My parents left me with a sizeable inheritance, and my aunt and uncle also, since they had no children. I didn't have to worry about finances in the beginning and now, of course, due to the success of my books, I could stop writing and live more than comfortably the rest of my life."

They talked late into the night. "You know," Maxi mused, "Jim used to say to me that there were some phrases that he just hated. They got to be popular and people just spouted them off without thinking of the meaning, and, therefore, they lost any meaning. Like, 'Have a nice day.' How many times a day do you hear that, and how often do you think it is heartfelt? 'To make a long story short' is another one. Why not just make it short or long to begin with?" Maxi was obviously enjoying herself now.

"Yea, I know what you mean. Like, 'let's do lunch?' and it never happens; it is just a way of trying to sound like you care when really you don't.

"Or, did this happen to you?" Maxi continued. "When your spouse dies, and people are saying, 'Just let me know if there is anything I can do.' And if you do mention something, they don't hear you. But the very worst was when well meaning church people started spouting, 'It's God's will.' That made me so angry that I wanted to spit on them. And another is 'This will make you a stronger person'.

"I hated that one, too. I didn't want to be stronger; I just wanted my wife back."

"After losing both parents, I did say to one person, 'If God makes me any stronger, he'll be out of a job'. You should have seen the look of shock on her face, like she expected me to be struck dead on the spot by a bolt of lightening. In fact, it probably disappointed her that it didn't happen."

"What gave you the most comfort?" Jeff hadn't talked this way to anyone before. No one else understood.

"One of Jim's friends simply said, 'I am so sorry. I'll miss him, too,' and gave me a hug that was really heartfelt. It was the most comfort I received from anyone except my kids. They were, and continue to be, simply wonderful. They were in shock, too, but we seemed to have a bond that helped us, help each other".

"I have a feeling that you and Jim were really good parents and that is why you feel so good about your kids now. He used to talk about you and your children. He really loved you; he was a real family man."

"Thank you," was all that Maxi could manage as her throat closed and tears welled in her eyes.

"You know, I really liked Jim's columns and the novels. I always felt he was one of the best columnists; he had a lot of insight regarding current happenings and moods of people." Jeff spoke remembering the many talks he and Jim had over coffee at the Coffee Shop. "I miss him too."

They fell silent, each lost in their own thoughts. Maxi finally nodded off to sleep, and Jeff sat sprawled in the chair until he slept too. Beau was snuggled close to Maxi's side, while Major slept beside Jeff's chair.

Chapter 16

Maxi was back in her office the day after New Year's. She felt fully recovered and ready to dig in and continue with her work. She was midway through a stack of files when a young man appeared in her doorway. She saw movement out of the corner of her eye or she wouldn't have known he was there. He didn't knock, just stood waiting for her to look at him. *How odd!* "Good morning. Is there something I can do for you?"

"I was wonderin' when we was goin to have to move?"

"What is your name and where do you live?" Maxi immediately had her list up on the computer waiting for the information she would need to answer his question.

"Sam Crosby. We live at 325 Chestnut St."

"Do you rent or own the property?" Maxi didn't see his name coming up but did note that address of the house was located in the next acquisition area.

"Well, we're buyin it from Sissy's uncle, but now he says we was only rentin, not buyin." He was getting agitated and stood directly in front of her desk. His jacket was open revealing a stained T-shirt that in his agitation he pulled up to reveal a bare belly. He then proceeded to nervously pick a piece of lint from his bellybutton.

Maxi had to keep her gaze averted so she wouldn't start laughing. She really felt sorry for him. He obviously was a few bricks short of a load and was little more than a teenager. "Do you have a written contract with the uncle stating that you are buying?"

"No. We'uns trusted him. He said he wanted us to have a nice home and he was goin' ta help us."

"How did you pay him? By check? Cash? Money Order?" Maxi knew before he answered what it would be.

"Cash money."

"Did he give you a receipt?"

"You mean a piece of paper saying we had paid him?" At Maxi's nod he continued. "No. My wife says we can't prove that we was buyin it; and so, we won't be able to get anything from you."

"I am afraid that your wife is right, about proving it." At his look of despair, Maxi said, "Let me do some checking on who the owner of that property is according to the records. Even if you are living there as tenants, there will be some help for you, and I'll help you find a rental that you can afford. There won't be anything happening for at least another week as far as the Authority purchasing the property; and you have three months after that before you have to move as an owner or a tenant."

After assuring, and reassuring, him that he would have help, he finally left and Maxi went to check on the name of the owner of the house. Sure enough it wasn't Sam Crosby. The name was probably the wife's uncle. *Some uncle!*

She talked with Ken about the situation. Ken said a letter had already gone out scheduling the appointment with the attorney to finalize the purchase. The owner hadn't contested the price and was anxious to close and get his money.

"I just bet he is. I really feel sorry for the kids who thought they were buying the property. I wish there was something we could do for them."

Jake had come in during the discussion and now said, "I'm afraid all we can do is help them find a rental. If there is no paper work to verify his claim our hands are tied."

Maxi heard her phone ringing and hurried to her office to answer it. It was Sam.

"Is there something wrong at the house?"

"No. Everything is coming along fine. I wanted to ask you to go dinner with me this evening?"

"Oh, thank you Sam but could I have a rain check? I am so overwhelmed with work trying to get going after the break over the holidays that I know I am going to just want to collapse when I am finished here." Maxi apologized.

"Okay, what about Saturday evening. Maybe dinner and a movie?" Sam wasn't easy to put off. He was determined.

"All right. That would be a wonderful break from my routine."

"I'll pick you up about 7. Is that okay with you?"

"Fine. Bye till Saturday, Sam."

As expected, the week was hectic with appointments, interviews and faxes to the Corps for authorizations. It seemed there were arguments with everyone -- administration, the Corps and, of course, the people who were being displaced. By the weekend she was totally exhausted.

Maxi slept in Saturday morning. It was nearly 11 o'clock when she managed to get her eyes open enough to see the clock. She hadn't made any plans for today except for Sam's invitation to dinner and a movie.

That evening, Maxi found Sam to be good company and was enjoying her dinner. She had expected to discuss the renovations of her house, but Sam said he refused to talk business on a date. The term 'date' set Maxi back a little and left her speechless. She hadn't considered it a 'date' but didn't say anything as Sam continued without pause, "I really admire you, Maxi. You have done so much to get on with your life since Jim's death. Most women would have retreated into as calm a lifestyle as possible, or maybe gone to live with their children."

"I almost did retreat. Remember? The three weeks after my house was destroyed, I didn't want to do anything. I know I worried Lorene and Mike, but at that time I didn't even think about it. In fact, I don't remember much at all about that time."

"Well, you did come out of it and came out fighting."

"Thank you Sam. But enough about me, what movie are we seeing tonight?" Maxi was getting uncomfortable with the way the conversation was going. She was glad that Sam had chosen a movie that was a comedy and not something heavy or disturbing with violence. By the time she was back at her house, it was nearly midnight.

Sam caught her off guard as she was unlocking her door and kissed her. She felt fission of nerves tingle through her body. It was the first such contact since Jim's death and it caused her to realize how much she missed him. Sam's kiss was pleasant but nothing more.

"Thank you Sam for the lovely evening. It was just what I needed. I have been so busy that I haven't even thought of going to the movies. I have always really liked movies and Jim and I went whenever there was one that appealed to us." Maxi quickly entered the house as she was talking and stood ready to close the door.

"I hope we can do it again soon. Goodnight, Maxi." Sam headed back to his car and thought about her staying so far out of town, and then to be in the middle of a snowstorm at that. He wasn't aware that Maxi had been sick or that Jeff had stayed with her.

The headlights of his car bounced off the piles of snow around a cleared parking space as he turned around and headed back to his own house. *I really like this woman. I hope she feels the same.* Sam knew she respected him professionally and felt comfortable talking about the renovations but beyond that he didn't have a clue.

Over the next few weeks Maxi worked furiously trying to keep on schedule. The properties being taken now were in the poor section. A lot of them were mobile homes and run down rentals. As Maxi made her visits to the homes, she was determined to see that better housing was available. The problem was that even though the housing was terrible, it was very low rent. She said a silent prayer of thanks for the relocation laws. *Thank goodness for the decent, safe and sanitary section.*

She worked the low income housing units until the managers shut their office doors when they saw her coming and the receptionist always said the manager was too busy to see her, perhaps tomorrow would be better. Maxi knew that tomorrow would be the same story. Trying to make an appointment was impossible. There were never any openings for appointments so she continued to show up unexpectedly.

Finally, she decided the only way to get her people registered in all the HUD units was to send a certified return receipt letter listing all the people that needed housing and qualified for the low income. She sent copies to the state legislators as well as the congressmen and senators for the district.

Miraculously, units opened up and within a week ten families were placed, including Sam Crosby and his wife. They were terribly disappointed in not owning their own home but settled into the one bedroom apartment without too much grumbling. Their living conditions far surpassed what they had in the house they thought they were buying. *But ownership,* she mused, *has it's own prestige.*

Then she had a 'first'; her first experience of being 'hit on'. Lorene had warned her to expect this to happen, but Maxi hadn't believed it would happen to her. She always stayed businesslike and matter of fact.

Bill Sanford lived in an expanded mobile home. He invited her inside like it was a mansion and proceeded to explain all the virtues of his home, what he had done with it since he lived there, and what he expected in the way of a replacement.

By way of excusing the housekeeping, he explained, "My wife just up and left a year ago without so much as a note left behind. I just never quite got the hang of housekeeping. I plan to find a housekeeper-cook soon," he snickered.

"You're a widow ain't you?" he continued. "I betcha you get lonely, just like I do. How about I take you to the Moose Club this Friday, and show you a good time." He grinned showing stained teeth from the cigarettes he evidently chain-smoked. The cigarette smell and the look of the ashtrays littering the room confirmed this, and left Maxi fighting to breathe.

She had put off spreading her papers out on the dirty table as long as she could. Lumps of unidentifiable stuff, some dried and some sticky, almost covered the surface. Finally, desperate to escape, she opened her briefcase on the table but kept the papers inside. *At least I can sanitize the outside of the briefcase.*

Instead of replying to his suggestive mannerisms and come-ons, Maxi explained the procedure to him as quickly as possible, and suggested he look at several properties currently on the market.

"I'm sure that you can make one of them into a home, just as you have this one." She knew her sarcasm went completely over his head, as she surveyed the clutter and dirt. Her head was beginning to thump and her vision blurred. *No, please, not a migraine. Not now.*

On the way back to her car, she traversed through a minefield of junk cars, old refrigerators, and washing machines and piles of stuff she didn't try to identify. She had seen junkyards looking better than this.

Despite a bad night fighting the migraine, she was in the office early the next morning. It was February 14th. At 9 o'clock Sarah came knocking on her open door bearing a huge Valentine bouquet of red and white roses for her from Michael and Eve. She went back to work with a smile on her face. In a few minutes the UPS guy knocked on her door. "Have a package for Maxine Taylor. Is that you?"

"Yes, Johnny, you know me by now. Who is sending me a package?" She looked at it a bit nervously; since getting the threatening letter she was cautious.

Taking the box, Maxi realized by the return address as well as the handwriting that it was from her daughter, Lorene. "It's from my daughter. Thank you, Johnny."

"Have a nice Valentine's Day Maxi; you deserve it." With a salute, Johnny turned back down the hallway.

Opening the box, Maxi found a beautiful, bright red suit. *Just the thing for when I need recharged or for courage when court appearances were demanded.*

It was to be a morning of interruptions Maxi concluded, when only ten minutes later, Bill Sanford stood in the doorway, coughing and waiting for her to notice him. Just as she looked up from her work, Bill noticed the flowers on her desk. "Oh, you got a Valentine." He looked deflated as he backed out of the doorway on the pretext of seeing Joe about something.

Hallelujah, Amen! Thank you God! And Michael and Lorene. Maxi was so relieved to be rid of him that she went to see Joe as soon as Bill left, wondering what excuse he had given for talking to Joe.

Joe was on his way out. Grinning he asked, "What did you do to that poor man. He was offering you an opportunity to live with him -- something about needing a housekeeper and cook. He was absolutely devastated. Why did you turn him down?"

Stopping in the doorway to Ken's office, Joe continued, "Hey, Ken. Our Maxi just turned down an offer from Sanford & Son. He wanted a cook and housekeeper and it seems he thinks she is already taken." Lounging in the doorway, Joe kept laughing and Ken joined in.

"You just missed a golden opportunity, Maxi." Ken chortled. "And I don't see anyone on your horizon or waiting in line."

"For your information, I'm not looking for anyone on my horizon, or anywhere else. You guys are a real piece of work; you know that? I thought you had more respect for me than that." If they had just been kidding her in good humor, she would have taken it in stride and gave back as good as she got, but there was a feeling of nastiness to their remarks and in their looks at each other.

Back in her office, Maxi plunked herself down in her chair and refused to hear anything they said the rest of the morning. She refused to go to lunch with them saying she preferred her own company, thank you very much. She knew lunch would only mean more of their wisecracks.

When she returned that afternoon from an appointment, her door was closed and a computer printed sign taped to it. SHUN MAXI. The hurt hit her in the chest like a fist. She knew immediately that it was a product of Ken and Joe's warped sense of humor. When the two of them got together they could get absolutely mean. She tore off the sign and went into her office closing the door. She punched the phone button for Sarah. "Sarah, I have my door closed, but if you need to speak to me please come in, and I'll take any calls".

It was mid afternoon before Jake opened the door a crack and stuck his head in. "Okay to come in?"

"Sure." Maxi was actually glad to see someone. She might have even welcomed Ken or Joe, but only if they apologized, she hastily amended the thought. It was lonely in the office; she didn't even have a window and was getting a little claustrophobic.

"Something wrong?" Jake sat in the chair in front of her desk.

"Just a couple of jackasses in the office. Nothing important."

"Ken and Joe?"

At her nod, he asked, "Anything I need to take care of?"

"No. They are just being mean." Because she needed to talk to someone, she told him what had happened about Bill Sanford and then the note on her door when she came back from an afternoon appointment.

"It has nothing to do with my work, so let it be. Ken hasn't been very cooperative lately. I have to go and get the information that I need from his files. If he protests my helping myself, then I may need help.

"I can't recall anything I did to upset him, except that I didn't side with him about his proposal for that increase in salary. I told him he didn't have any justification for the increase he wanted."

"I knew it was bugging him but not that he was taking it out on you. Why would he feel that way as far as you are concerned?" Jake leaned forward toward Maxi.

"Because I told him when he first mentioned it that he didn't stand a chance. He had signed a contract the same as I did."

"In that case, I don't think my saying anything in your behalf would help you right now. It might even make it worse. Can you live with it a few days and see if he simmers down?"

"Sure. I only need property information from his files. If he objects to my going into the files, then I'll let you know."

Maxi left work that evening in a real blue funk. She hated discord and usually got along with coworkers. When she arrived home and opened the door into the kitchen, she found that even the completed kitchen didn't raise her spirits. Usually the sight of her home cheered her and she had been especially proud of the way the kitchen had come together. It was a beautiful room and so convenient to work in. She hadn't cooked a meal for anyone yet, but she knew the layout would work perfectly.

At a knock on the door, Maxi frowned. *Please, no visitors tonight.* She opened it to find Jeff standing there with a basket in each hand and a wide grin on his face.

"Will you be my Valentine?"

"Sorry Jeff, I am in no mood for Valentines." She moved to close the door, but he was already too far into the doorway. Shrugging, she backed away and he came on into the kitchen. Some delicious odors were coming from one of the baskets he carried, and despite her bad mood she was intrigued and barely resisted lifting the red and white checked towel to see what was inside.

"Hey, that is no way to greet a bearer of good food." He placed both baskets on the island counter and turned to look more closely at her. She appeared pale and tired. "Bad day?"

"The worst. I don't even want to talk about it." In spite of herself she couldn't resist asking, "What is in there?" indicating the two baskets.

"A feast, that's what!" Jeff whisked off the towel and revealed a large covered tureen that he removed from the basket and placed on the counter. "Soup. Tomato Bisque." Then out came a fragrant loaf of French bread that gave off the aroma of garlic. The second basket revealed a huge platter covered in foil. Removing the foil with a flourish he revealed a golden brown roast chicken surrounded with vegetables: carrots, onions, small whole potatoes with the red skin still on in a butter/parsley sauce. Going to the stove, Jeff turned the oven temp to 250 and placed the entire platter in the oven, covered with the foil.

"One more trip to the car," he said, vanishing into the night and returning moments later with two boxes, one on top of the other. Out came a bottle of Dom, two champagne glasses, a bright red tablecloth and white napkins. From the other box he lifted a pie mounded with clouds of whipped cream pillowing whole strawberries, "Chocolate. Not very original, but I thought it was the best offered by the Bake Shoppe. And chocolate is a must on Valentine's Day, and strawberries, at least, that is what I was told." He cast a hopeful look in Maxi's direction.

"Still want me to leave? If I leave, all this does, too!"

"Blackmail. You are blackmailing me!" Maxi was laughing now. "But I'll let you stay. It smells heavenly and I'm suddenly starving." Maxi stood, amazed at the feast he had brought and a little ashamed of herself.

"I apologize for being in such a foul mood. It was a bad day at work, nothing to do with you." She started toward the china cabinet and got out two plates, cups and saucers, soup bowls and bread plates. "I'll start some coffee."

Jeff busied himself with spreading the red cloth over the round table in the bay window. When a knock sounded at the door he didn't move to open it but waited for Maxi to do it.

A surprised "What in the world?" came from her as she took the flower arrangement from the delivery boy, thanked him and turned to place it on the counter, plucking the card from the holder, saying "I already received flowers at work from Michael". There was no name just 'Happy Valentine's Day to a beautiful neighbor'.

"Oh, Jeff," was all she could say and tears welled from her eyes slipping down her cheeks. "Thank you."

"Hey, what's with the tears? I meant to cheer you up!"

"And you have, immensely. Don't you know women get teary when they are deeply moved as well as when they are sad?" A large square crocheted doily had been placed in the center of the table over the red cloth in readiness for the flowers, which she now put there. The arrangement of red roses and white baby's breath looked lovely and Jeff came with two fat, white candles that he placed on either side, struck a match and lit them.

"Please be seated, madam, and let me serve you." Maxi sat down, too amazed to say a word.

They sipped soup in silence for a few moments. "Jeff, you have no idea what this means to me. I came home in such a blue mood, that I don't think I even wanted to open a can of soup; now here we sit enjoying a delicious meal. I didn't know you could cook like this. If this is canned soup what did you do to it?"

"Just added a little fresh oregano and basil, and a fresh chopped tomato. There isn't much to roasting a chicken and steaming veggies." He raised his glass of champagne, "A toast." When she picked up her glass, he continued, "To a beautiful neighbor."

"To a thoughtful, wonderful neighbor," Maxi countered.

Later, in front of the fire in the bedroom and mellow with food and wine they talked quietly of this and that and nothing in particular.

"When are you going to have the living room finished and furnished? People will start to talk if you keep entertaining gentlemen in your boudoir."

"I don't care a fig if people talk or not," Maxi laughed. "But I do hope to have the dining room and living room finished before Easter. I want to have a family Easter. I am hoping that Michael and Eve, and Lorene and Jack can make arrangements to be here. I would like you to join us if you don't have other plans."

"I accept. There wouldn't be any other plans that could possibly keep me away. I am looking forward to meeting your family." Jeff said happily. Then looking at her closely asked, "Do you feel ready to talk about what happened today?"

"It's foolish, really. It started when this man that everyone calls Sanford, as in Sanford and Son, from the old TV sitcom – do you know that one?" At Jeff's nod she continued, "Well, he is one whose property is being taken and I have to help him find a new place. He has been hitting on me. His property's a junkyard and his home is an expanded single wide trailer that saw better days a decade ago. He has grandiose ideas of what he is giving up and what he should move into. He thinks I should welcome the chance to move in with him, mostly because he wants someone to cook and clean for him.

"I have kept him at arms length, but this morning he showed up at the office shortly after I received flowers from Michael and Eve. He looked at the flowers and mumbled, "Someone sent you a Valentine" then went on to Joe's office.

"I breathed a big sigh of relief that he thought I had a boyfriend, and hopefully would leave me alone. After he left, I went to Joe's office to see what he had to say to him, expecting to get a laugh. Instead Joe razzed me about turning him down, and making it sound like I had a grand opportunity.

I got a little upset when he went to Ken's office, told him the story and they both laughed and laughed, and really started being mean. I got huffy and went back to my office. Then I turned down an invitation to lunch with Joe and Ken, which would have been more of the same. When I came back from an appointment about 2 o'clock, there was a sign on my door, 'SHUN MAXI'. It hurt." Her voice quivered and she paused.

"I thought we all had a good working relationship and we did in the beginning. I don't know what I have done to ruin it." She had to pause again to hold back more tears.

"Just last week, Joe went with me to check out a relocation property and afterward he took me to see his cabin. It seemed curious at the time, but everything seemed fine. We stopped for lunch. I was a little nervous taking so much time, and running around on company time, but Joe didn't seem to think anything of it."

"Did Joe make advances at the cabin?" Jeff realized he felt a twinge of jealousy, but also thought he had an idea what had happened with Joe.

"Not really. I felt a little strange when we were touring the cabin, but he didn't say anything or touch me, if that is what you are asking. I had this strange feeling and kept wondering why we were there."

"Maxi is it possible he expected you to want to make use of the cabin before going back to work? You know, the sex starved widow?"

"Oh, that is ridiculous! He is only four years older than my son. He couldn't have had anything sexual in mind." Maxi looked incredulous that Jeff would even think of such a thing.

"I think you are too naive. You are a very attractive woman. So he is what, twenty-five years younger? So what! Age doesn't matter. Some men think they are doing widows a favor, and I have a feeling that you insulted him, unintentionally on your part; but whatever, he may have felt rejected. He probably hasn't a clue that you didn't realize what he was offering you -- or even if you did, that you weren't that kind of woman. He probably felt rejected."

Maxi thought about it and finally said, "It was after that when he seemed to change. He and Ken started having lunch together and every day they would come back in a terrible mood. Ken has been brooding because he had this grandiose plan about how he could get a substantial raise and Jake turned him down flat. He has been nursing his wounded ego ever since. Maybe you're right. They both have wounded egos and keep feeding each other's mood over lunch. It kind of makes sense."

"Why would Ken's raise affect how he felt about you?" Jeff frowned over that, not seeing a connection.

"Because I told him before he presented it to Jake that he didn't have a leg to stand on. That he had signed a contract agreeing to his salary when he was hired. I guess unfortunately for me, I was right. He is also bitter that the Board approved my trip to Houston for training. His ego is bruised. I don't know what I can do to make him feel okay again. I'm not very good at healing damaged egos. I am good at bolstering someone who has low self esteem and needs encouragement to use their talents."

"Whatever the reasons, they seem like immature, insecure men." Jake wished there were something he could do but had to admit that she would have to ride it out.

Chapter 17

Maxi had little time to worry about anything during the next few weeks, especially Joe and Ken's attitudes. She was on the phone every day, sometimes more than once, with her Washington contact Eleanor Fitzpatrick in the Federal Bureau of Transportation.

Maxi was head-over-heels in the middle of relocating businesses, two of which were restaurants, both owned by Italian families. It seemed she was constantly subjected to verbal abuse and demands by one or the other. She relied heavily on Eleanor to help her sort though the regulations and interpret them. Sometimes she was amazed at how much the business owners got to reestablish their businesses. In all cases, they were ending up with much better establishments. In truth, she was getting tired of the demands of the two owners.

When one demanded a grievance hearing, she was ready to spit nails. She prepared herself for the hearing and when her decisions were upheld, the owner and her daughter stormed out of the meeting shouting abuse. It was hard not to point out all the advantages they were gaining, but Maxi kept quiet. As it turned out the next time she stopped at the new location to inspect the ongoing work, and get an estimate of when the business move could be completed, she was pleasantly surprised at the warm reception she received.

"We're sorry about our behavior last week. It is hard on our nerves getting this all together, and feel that it is all going to work out all right, especially since we have taken on a large loan. We haven't had a payment like this for years, and frankly, it scares me." Maria said. She blushed at the memory of their last meeting.

"I know. Even with the help offered it is difficult to get it all done and know that your business won't suffer. Actually, I think your business will grow. You have more room here and can seat more people and it is a central location." Maxi gave the woman a hug. Both smiled as the tension was relieved. "You don't have a loan payment for six months, do you?"

"Yes, that's right and we should have rebuilt our business by that time." Marie then began showing her what had been accomplished since her last inspection. "We think we can open the business in three weeks."

"That's great. I am really happy for you. Have you scheduled advertising for the grand opening? I want to be one of your first customers."

However, as well as things were going with Marie, there were still problems with the other restaurant owner. The following day, Maxi received a call from one of the workers at the location of Serifini's new location.

"Maxi, if Antonio comes in demanding a new front door, you should know that he took a chain saw to it himself when he was in a rage. He was in a major snit because you turned him down for a new door yesterday.

"Thanks, Steve. And I never got this call!" Maxi replied. As she hung up the phone, she heard someone coming back the hallway toward her office. *I'll bet next week's pay that it is Antonio. All that stomping sounds angry and determined to me.*

Antonio stormed into her office. "Ya know that new door ya refused ta get for me? Well, now you'll-a have to. Someone broke in-a last night by-a sawin

248

the whole-a center out; that's a how rotten it was." He waited expectantly for her surprise.

"Was anything else damaged or stolen."

"No. Just-a the door. I have-a ta get it replaced today," he made it a demand as he added. "If anythin gets-a stolen, it'll be-a charged to-a you. It'll be-a your fault!"

"No, Antonio. It will be your fault. I happen to know that you used the chainsaw yourself on that door in a fit of rage." Maxi tried not to show her amusement at the expression on his face and continued, "I suggest that you get a new door today and pay for it yourself."

"You can't-a know nothin' of-a the kind. It wasn't me-a that done it. I'll have-a ya fired for not-a doin your job and costin me-a money if it ain't fixed today!" He leaned across her desk, stuck his face practically into hers.

His garlicky breath nearly caused her to choke, but she glared back at him. "Don't threaten me. I'll call the police and have you arrested." She didn't know if he had done anything yet to warrant that, but she wasn't going to let him know that she was uncertain how to handle this, or that she was the least bit intimidated.

"I'll get even, you bitch!"

Maxi stood up. "Get out of my office **NOW**," placing her hand on the phone, "or I'll call the police." She stared at him though slightly narrowed eyes, her mouth set in a grim line.

"What is going on here?" Jake's voice broke the tension.

"Antonio thinks he can get us to buy him a new door to replace the one he destroyed himself with his handy, dandy chainsaw. Unfortunately, he was seen doing it and I have been receiving calls ever since I got into work this morning. I was just waiting until he showed up with his request." Maxi never took her eyes off Antonio's. "You were just leaving, weren't you, Antonio, to go buy yourself a new door?"

"You-a ain't heard-a the last-a this!" He shook his fist in her face, then stepped back when Jake moved in front of him. Jake had been a linebacker for the Pittsburgh Steelers football team, and he still had a linebacker's build.

With one last glare, Antonio stormed out making even more noise than when he had arrived, stomping his feet with each step.

"What was that all about?" Jake asked, looking closely at Maxi as she shakily lowered herself to her chair.

"I received a call from one of Antonio's employees just before he showed up here. It seems in a fit of rage he took a chainsaw to the front door of the building that is going to be his new restaurant. It was his attempt to get us to pay for the door he wanted. I had turned down his request yesterday because the old door was sound and only needed a coat of paint."

"Be careful with him, Maxi. He is known to have a violent temper and doesn't always stop to think of the consequences. Maybe Joe should go with you when you do your periodic inspections."

"Thanks Jake, but I think I can handle it. I'll let you know if I get any more threats." She wasn't about to ask Joe for anything since the fiasco on Valentine's Day.

A voice spoke from the doorway, "Have any job openings? I just got fired."

"Steve! I didn't tell him how I knew about the door," Maxi apologized.

"I knew what would happen when I made the call. I was the only one who saw him do it." Steve was smiling. He didn't appear to be upset. "Actually, I am glad to be away from there; he's crazy."

"Can I do anything to help you get another job?" Maxi was concerned that she had caused him to be fired. "I'll vouch for your integrity and honesty." Maxi offered.

Jake spoke up. "I'll make some calls for you. There are contractors who will be glad to get you. I have seen your work and know you have a variety of skills in construction. Give me a phone number where you can be reached." Jake reached for a note pad on Maxi's desk and helped himself to a pen.

Steve gave him his number and they shook hands. "Thanks, Jake. I appreciate it. Maxi, don't worry; this has been the best thing. I couldn't have worked for that man much longer anyway."

"Thanks for your tip this morning, Steve." Maxi shook his hand. "I'm sure you will get a better job with Jake's help."

After Steve left, Jake turned back to Maxi, "I meant what I said about having Joe go with you."

"And I will let you know if I need him." Maxi had no desire to have Joe's help.

"Okay. I'll trust your judgment. Do you have a cell phone?"

"Yes," Maxi pulled it from her handbag.

"Be sure you have it with you when you make site inspections and all other appointments you have. Do you have 911 programmed in so that you only have to punch one button?" Jake was still nervous about the situation.

"I don't, but will do it now. I'll have the number ready to punch in before I go in for any inspections or any other appointments," Maxi promised. "I don't want to have any confrontations, or my head bashed in, Jake. I also have the office number in here and promise to call the office if there is any trouble."

"All right. I'll leave it to you." Jake put his arm around Maxi's shoulders and gave a squeeze before heading for the door. Pausing before he left, Jake turned back to Maxi, "The first property is to be demolished tomorrow morning. Did you know that?"

"Yes. It's Helen's, or was Helen's. She is the first person I met, the first relocation contact."

"Well, be careful when you are away from the office," Jake said as he went back to his own office.

The rest of the day was routine paperwork until the phone rang at 4 o'clock.

"Hello, Maxine Taylor."

"Hello Maxi, this is Helen. How are you?"

"I'm fine Helen, how about you?"

"I'm doing very well. I called to ask a favor of you."

"What can I do for you?"

"I just heard that my old house is to be demolished in the morning. If it is true, I would like to see it one last time. Will you take me?"

"Of course, I will be glad to pick you up. It will be very early. Are you sure you want to see your home destroyed, Helen?"

"Yes, I think so; but I will appreciate your company."

"I'll be there at 6:30, so we have plenty of time to find a parking place and see where we have to stand."

"Thank you, dear girl."

"See you in the morning. Bye."

Chapter 18

The next morning, February 28, 2001, was the red-letter day, the first demolition, signaling the real beginning of The Project. It was cold even for February. Maxi stood next to Helen, shivering, her breath making white puffs in the chilly air.

Maxi had not known what to expect from Helen, as she watched her life-long home being reduced to rubble. She hadn't really been paying that much attention to the crowd as her concern had been for the 96-year-old diminutive lady standing next to her. When Helen said it was like going to a funeral to say goodbye, and she was ready to leave, Maxi was relieved until they encountered John with his threats. He really did sound like he had been the one to cause the gas explosion that had completely destroyed her home.

Feeling briefly restored by Helen's flattering, but sincere, comments about her on their way back to Helen's apartment, Maxi was back to feeling like she was a total wreck by the time she got back to her office building. She headed straight to Jeff's office to tell him about what John had said to her. "He literally hissed at me, 'you'll get yours!' He really scared me."

Later, feeling somewhat more calm after having related to Jake and Mark what she thought of as John's threat, Maxi went to her office and checked her schedule. Her calendar was clear the rest of the day, just as she had told Jake and Mark. She caught up on paperwork. Before clearing her desk, she checked her next day's schedule.

She noted a 1 o'clock appointment at the Barton Trailer Park for the next afternoon. She made sure her cell phone was programmed with 911, Mark's number as well as the office number. The occupants of the park were not always hospitable and she wasn't looking forward to any more confrontations. Also the remarks made by John just this morning were still vivid.

It was just one o'clock the next day when Maxi reached the trailer park. She noted the small, littered and otherwise messy yards and dilapidated trailers. What a depressing place to live. Locating Lot #2, Maxi parked and got out. As she reached the trailer, she was surprised to find the door open. It was too cold for open doors. She knocked on the doorframe and called out, "Hello! Anybody home?"

Thinking she heard a sound, she stepped cautiously inside. She stared, disbelieving at the wreckage she saw. Cabinet doors were chopped to pieces as well as furniture, interior doors and light fixtures. Broken dishes littered the floor.

A thumping sound and what sounded like a groan had her heading back the hallway toward the bedrooms. As a precaution, she gripped her cell phone inside her shoulder bag.

"Oh my goodness," she gasped as she spied a woman lying on the floor of the back bedroom, holding a sneaker in her right hand thumping the floor with it. Kneeling beside her, Maxi noted the bruised and battered face. Her one good eye was open and whimpering sounds came from the puffed lips. Touching her tentatively, Maxi noticed that her skin felt cold and clammy. Probably she was in shock and with the door open the place was a refrigerator. "Sssh, you'll be okay now. I am calling for help."

She pulled out her cell phone and punched the button for 911. "I need an ambulance at the Barton

Trailer Park, Lot 2. This is Maxine Taylor from the Flood Protection Authority and I have just found a woman here who is badly injured."

Not waiting for any more questions, she left the phone line open but gave the woman her entire attention.

"Can you talk to me? The ambulance will be here in a couple minutes. You're freezing!" Maxi pulled blankets from the bed. "I'd put a pillow under your head but I don't think I should move you to do it."

"Thank God you came." The voice was weak and the words mumbled. Maxi had to lean close to hear.

"You'll be all right now. You'll soon be in the hospital. Don't try to talk any more now, save your strength."

Five minutes later, the police, paramedics and the ambulance arrived simultaneously. Maxi kept out of their way as they checked the woman over for back and neck injuries. They put a back brace on her as a precaution, then splinted her left arm and left leg both which appeared to be broken. While the paramedics worked, Maxi gave the police what few details she knew. When the ambulance pulled away a half hour later, Maxi followed it to the hospital. She would have to give the admissions office what information she could. It wasn't much and she couldn't be sure the woman was the name she had in her records. The owner was Bruce Boynton and she supposed the woman was his wife, Sally.

She called in to the office to tell Sarah where she was and why. "I don't have any other appointments this afternoon, so I'll stay at the hospital to answer what questions I can, and to see how bad Sally's injuries are. Is Ken there?"

"Yes. Do you want to talk to him?"

"Yes, I do."

A moment later Ken was calling on the phone. "What's happening?"

Maxi filled him in about finding Sally Boynten and told him that the trailer – which now belonged to the Authority – was a disaster and thought he would want to know. "I doubt that the door will stay closed let alone locked."

"Okay, I'll call someone to have it boarded up."

Three hours later, Sally was admitted to Intensive Care. She had a concussion, a broken jaw, a fractured cheekbone, a broken arm and her leg was broken in two places. She also had a bruised kidney, probably from being kicked, the doctor told Maxi. She hadn't been coherent enough for the police to get any information as to who had done this to her. They suspected it was her absentee husband. The police had found her purse in the trailer and her driver's license confirmed that she was Sally, even though her bruised and bandaged face didn't much resemble the photo ID.

Maxi returned to the office once she knew that Sally was receiving proper care and would have to be admitted. It would be several hours before all tests were completed and the admission process done.

Maxi headed straight for Ken's office. "How was Boynton when you settled on his property in Barton's Trailer Park this morning?"

"He was very pleasant, pleased at the amount he was paid. Why?" Ken replied gruffly, not looking up.

"Was his wife with him?"

"No. He said she was out of town." Ken looked up at her and noticed her agitation. He really hadn't paid much attention to Maxi's earlier call just noted that the trailer needed boarded up. He had pretty much blocked anything Maxi said.

"What's the matter? Did he give you a bad time?"

"No, not me, but he sure beat his wife. At least it is suspected that he did it and wrecked the trailer too. He was nowhere to be found. The police have an APB out on him." Maxi slumped in the chair as all the days' events hit her at once.

Jake came back the hallway returning from a meeting. He stopped in the doorway glad to see Maxi and Ken talking again, until noted her apparent agitation. "What's happened?"

Maxi filled both men in on the situation then said she was going to call it a day and head home.

"You look beat. Get a good night's rest and we'll see you in the morning," Jake told her.

Chapter 19

Jeff, with Major by his side, was waiting on her doorstep. Maxi wasn't particularly happy to see him. She was looking forward to getting into a hot shower, a warm, comfortable robe and relaxing with some hot soup in front of the fire. All the company she needed was Beau.

"Hi. Rough day? You're home early."

"Yea, so how come you are waiting for me since I am early?"

"Mark called me." Jeff gave a shrug of his shoulders that said without words, so what could I do?

"Oh, great! Nothing like being the subject of gossip."

"Maxi, he wasn't gossiping. He is worried about your safety and so am I." Jeff was not put off by her sour tone and waited patiently until she unlocked her door. He and Major followed her inside. Beau was waiting; and he didn't look any happier to see the big dog than Maxi was to see Jeff.

"I am not up for chit-chat. I'm taking a hot shower and I would like to be alone. What happened this afternoon has nothing to do with me so you aren't needed here? You can lock the door on your way out." Beau was right on her heels or he would have been shut out of the bedroom as Maxi slammed the door.

Later, warm from her shower and in a comfortable flannel robe and floppy slippers, she turned on the gas in the fireplace, immediately bringing a comforting blaze. A knock sounded on the closed bedroom door. With an exasperated sigh, she jerked it open to confront Jeff, "I thought I told you to go on home?"

"Yea, well I thought you needed company, in spite of your bad mood. I heated tomato bisque soup and grilled a couple cheese sandwiches. You want to eat at the table or in there?" He nodded toward the bedroom.

Maxi headed toward the bar having noticed the steaming soup bowls and plates with sandwiches. "Okay, I give up. I apologize for being in such a bad mood. I had a terrible day." She glanced at him through a veil of wet hair, but kept her head down as she spooned soup, "which, I suppose you know in detail already."

"Mind if I join you?" Not waiting for an answer Jeff took the other bar stool.

"Might as well, seeing as you fixed it." Maxi gave him a sheepish grin.

"That's more like it!" Jeff happily settled in to enjoy his meal. "You know, Mark is concerned for your safety. He said you had a confrontation with John Carlucci yesterday, and then this afternoon the situation with the battered woman. This afternoon's situation probably isn't connected in any way with you, but it does seem as if this guy is full of anger and he might decide you need a taste of what he gave his wife. As for John, Mark is checking on his whereabouts. "

"Yes. I was shaken by John's nastiness yesterday and went straight to Jake's office with it. He called Mark. But this afternoon was worse. Oh, Jeff. You should have seen that poor woman! If I hadn't made the appointment to go out there this afternoon, she would probably have died. The place was freezing, and she couldn't move. Neighbors don't seem to take care of each other out there."

"Well, you did go, and now she is being taken care of. I also heard that you had a tough time with Antonio. Actually that guy worries me more. He is unstable."

"And a crook! You should have seen him when I told him I knew he had carved up the door himself with his chain saw. He was livid!" In spite of her bravado, she shivered. Maxi was quiet for a while as she finished her soup.

"Is there any more soup? I have been too upset to eat much the last couple days. I didn't realize how hungry I was until I started to eat."

"Sure thing." Jeff got up to ladle more soup into both bowls. "Want another sandwich? Everything is still out, won't take a minute." He didn't wait for a response but started to put together two more cheese sandwiches and place them on the griddle. "Comfort food is good for you!"

Later, after cleaning up the dishes from their supper, they sat before the fire in the bedroom. "You know, I have never spent this much time with a woman in her bedroom, except for my late wife of course." Jeff grinned at her.

"Well, don't get any ideas." Maxi was too preoccupied to notice the look of resignation that passed over Jeff's face. He told himself that she was too newly widowed to be ready for anything more than friendship. But he was more than ready, and the thought caught him unaware that he was heading in that direction. Abruptly he stood up, and with an exaggerated weariness, said if she was all right, he would head home.

"Sure, I'm fine and that is partly due to you feeding me and listening to me vent my frustration." Maxi smiled up at him and got to her feet too.

"Okay. Be sure to lock your door behind me."

As he and Major walked home, his boots crunching on the frozen snow, he talked aloud to the dog. "I don't like leaving her alone but what else can I do?" Major whined in response and stayed close to his side.

Chapter 20

Maxi kept track of Sally Boynton's recovery. The healing was slow but steady. Three days after she was hospitalized, Maxi visited her after her workday was finished. Even though her jaw was wired, Sally needed to talk. Maxi had to listen intently to understand what she was saying, but understood when she started talking about her life with her husband. When she said how worried she was about her daughter, Maxi's surprised expression told Sally that Maxi hadn't known that she had a daughter.

"You didn't know I had a daughter?"

"No, I didn't. She wasn't in the trailer when I found you. Where is she now?"

"That's just it; I don't know!" Sally sobbed, "I think that Bruce has her with him. I am so afraid for her."

"Have you told the police?"

"Yes, just this morning. I wasn't able to talk enough before that. They told me I had been saying her name when I was delirious from fever and doped up with pain medication. But they couldn't understand me enough to know whose name I was saying."

It was still hard to understand Sally. She couldn't move her wired jaw so words were hard to form.

"What is her name and how old is she?" Maxi could feel how desperate the woman was.

"Hannah. She is four years old. Bruce isn't her father. I was married before and he left me before Hannah was born. Being a father scared him, so he just took off. I filed for divorce and worked two jobs until Hannah was born; then I had to quit one job so I could care for her. A neighbor lady kept her while I worked as a waitress from five to eleven seven days a week. I met Bruce two years ago when he came in the restaurant for dinner. He was very charming and a great tipper and he finally asked me out. I told him I worked every evening and I didn't have time for dates. He kept coming in and took me home one evening.

"He became a regular, and it became routine for him to see me home. He seemed too good to be true. He came during the day on weekends and he was so good with Hannah. She adored him." Sally's hurt and confusion caused her to break down again.

Maxi held her hand, patting it and wishing she could offer more than being a sounding board, but that was all she could do for the moment. She was just glad to be able to understand the garbled talk.

"What happened to change him?"

"He lost his job and couldn't find another. We moved out of a nice apartment into the trailer. He had enough saved to buy it because it was so cheap. I think he started using drugs but I am not sure. I know he was drinking heavily. He said when he got the money for the trailer we would move somewhere else and start over."

"Tell me what happened the day he got the money," Maxi encouraged Sally to get it all out.

"He came home drunk and maybe high on drugs too, I don't know. He was raging when he came in the door. I asked him where we were going now, and he said he was going but I would stay there. When he started taking clothes for Hannah too, I said he couldn't take her and that was when he beat me. After that I could hear him banging at the cupboards and fixtures and shouting obscenities until finally he left, taking Hannah with him. That's all I remember until you came."

"Oh, Sally. How terrible. I thought it was bad enough for you to be hurt so bad but to take your child too. I just can't comprehend the agony you must be going through." Maxi tried to comfort Sally but she felt so useless.

"I'm sure the police will find her soon and return her. I'll pray for you and Hannah."

"Thank you. You are so good to come see me. I would be dead if you hadn't found me that day." Sally's eyes closed in fatigue and she slept.

Maxi stayed by the bed holding her hand until she was sure that Sally was in a deep sleep. Then she got up quietly and left.

It was dark when she left the hospital. She went straight home feeling too burdened to stop anywhere. She craved the solitude of her home and the company of Beau. Thankful that Jeff wasn't waiting for her, she headed for the shower. I guess I am trying to wash away the horribleness of some people.

Still feeling down after hearing Sally's story she opened a can of soup, heated it in the microwave and took it to her bedroom where she sat before the fire to eat. Beau curled up in her lap when she was finished eating, and went to sleep. The fire and Beau's purring lulled her into drowsiness. She soon crawled into bed and slept until her alarm went off at 6:30.

She was dressed and ready to leave for work when Sam and his crew arrived to work on the house. It was their usual starting time. Maxi said good morning and continued out the door but Sam stopped her.

"Hi Maxi. Good morning. I'm glad you are still here."

"Good morning, Sam. Is there something we need to discuss about the work? It seems to be coming along great."

"No, everything is progressing well. No changes that I need to make unless something isn't the way you want it.

"Everything is fine. It looks as if the downstairs will be completed soon."

"Yes, we have concentrated on that area since you are living here. It seemed that was the most important. We won't finish the vestibule yet as we need to go through there for the work upstairs. We will also use the back stairs as much as possible to avoid leaving too much mess in here.

"What I wanted to see you about," Sam continued, "was to ask you to have dinner with me Friday or Saturday evening." Sam smiled in anticipation as he waited for her answer.

"Saturday would be better for me. By Friday I am so tired I can hardly see, much less carry on any kind of conversation." Maxi felt her spirits lift at the thought of going out to dinner Saturday.

"Sure. That would be great. I'll pick you up around 7:30." Sam was just as pleased as Maxi at the thought.

"Okay, see you then. Bye." Maxi was out the door as she said it over her shoulder.

Her day went swiftly. She paid her routine visit to Sally before going home. She didn't seem to have any friends or relatives to visit her. Maxi was becoming fond of her. She seemed to be a very nice person, intelligent and caring. Maxi knew she was worried about Hannah and afraid the police might never find her. Maxi's thoughts went back to when Lorene was four years old. *If she had been taken by anyone, I would have gone crazy.*

She found Sally sitting up in bed; and as Maxi came into the room, her face lit up with an expression that would have been a huge smile, if her jaw weren't still wired. Not waiting to say hello, Sally burst out, "Maxi, they have found Hannah. She is all right and should be back in Forest Hills this evening. I wanted to call you, but I can't get to a telephone. I have been so impatient to tell you the good news."

"That's wonderful! Where did they find her?" Maxi felt nearly as happy as she knew Sally must feel.

"Canton, Ohio. A clerk at a mini mart spotted her when Bruce stopped for gas. He had gotten her a hot dog and then gone to the restroom and the clerk called the police. He had heard about the hunt for the man and child on the morning news. When he saw the Pennsylvania license plate on the car and the little girl fit the description, he was sure enough to notify the police."

"I am so happy for you, Sally. You must be so relieved."

"I'll feel even better when I can see her and hold her," Sally's emotions were raw and it was hard for her to talk.

"Hello. I have a little girl here to see her mama." The voice came from a woman standing in the doorway.

"Mommy! Mommy!" A blond-haired child rushed at the bed trying to climb into it with her mother. It was too high for Hannah, and Maxi helped her up. Both mother and child were sobbing as Sally managed to get her good arm around Hannah.

Maxi slipped quietly into the hallway and motioned for the policewoman to follow her.

Maxi introduced herself and asked, "What will happen with Hannah while her mother has to be hospitalized?"

"It's nice to meet you, Maxi. I'm Sgt. Montgomery. I understand that it was you who found Sally and got help for her." At Maxi's nod of acknowledgement, Sgt. Montgomery continued, "As for Hannah, Children's Services will place her in protective custody. In fact, Mary Hughes should be here any moment. She said she would meet us here. We agreed that Hannah should see her mother before taking her anywhere else. She is a very frightened little girl."

"Hello." A middle-aged woman stopped next to them. "Is this the room where Hannah's mother is?"

"Hello Mary, you got here quickly. I have just brought Hannah in to see her mother. It was quite a reunion." The sergeant nodded to the woman and child on the bed. "It's going to be hard for Hannah to leave her tonight."

As they entered the room, Hannah snuggled closer to her mother and shut her eyes as though to shut everyone else out. Sally had her good arm around her and in spite of her injuries; they looked quite comfortable.

"Can she sleep here tonight?" Sally tightened her arm protectively around her child.

A look of compassionate understanding passed among the three women. Sgt. Montgomery said, "I could ask the Chief if he could post a guard outside the room."

"Well, if the doctor thinks it won't be detrimental to Sally, I suppose we could go along with it," Mary said.

Mary went to talk to the nurses at their station while Sgt. Montgomery pulled her cell phone from her belt and talked to the Chief of Police.

Maxi stayed with Sally and Hannah. Both looked so contented, that Maxi hoped Hannah would be allowed to stay the night with her mother. It would be good for both of them in Maxi's opinion.

"What did Mark say?" Maxi looked up as Sgt. Montgomery came into the room.

"He said he could send a patrolman over if the doctor okays it."

While they all waited to hear from the doctor, they talked in low tones, as Hannah's eyes remained closed. Real sleep had taken over.

"I can't bear to let go of her yet and I am certain that if she has to go to a strange place tonight it will be much harder for her to deal with a foster placement even if it is temporary until I am released."

The nurse came into the room smiling. "Good news. The doctor thinks it will be a good idea for Hannah to stay here tonight. He feels that it will be best for both Sally and Hannah."

"Has Hannah had anything to eat this evening?" The nurse turned to Sgt. Montgomery raising her eyebrows in question.

"Yes, we stopped at McDonald's before coming to the hospital. Hannah was so anxious to see her mother that she didn't eat much but finished a milkshake on the way here."

"If she wakes during the night, I can get her something. Are you settled comfortably, Sally?" At Sally's nod, the nurse opened a warm blanket over the sleeping Hannah, removing her shoes before patting the blanket into place. They all left the room.

Hannah snuggled close. She knew the scent and feel of her mother even with all the hospital smells, just as Sally knew the scent and feel of Hannah's body. They both slept the first deep sleep either had had since the day Hannah was taken away.

Maxi left the hospital in a good mood. Sally and Hannah would be all right. It was Friday and she had the weekend to rest. Her date with Sam came to mind and she smiled in anticipation.

Chapter 21

Saturday morning Maxi woke to sunshine and decided it was time to make a trip to the grocery store. On her way, she took a detour through her old neighborhood. She hadn't been there since her house was destroyed. But she felt drawn there today.

Snow covered the spot where her house had been. Maxi was thankful not to see the blackened ruins. She had been told that all the debris had been removed and the lot graded and seeded. But she was sure that under the snow, grass had not had time to grow much. She had avoided going back before today. It brought to mind all the losses she had suffered in such a short period of time. Engrossed in memories, Maxi didn't notice her former neighbor, Millie Cotter, as she came to stand beside her.

Unaware that Maxi had not noticed her, Mille stood quietly beside her. She wanted to put her arms around Maxi and ease the suffering that showed so plainly on her face, but spoke softly instead.

"I miss you so much, Maxi," Millie said.

Maxi jumped slightly at the interruption of her memories. "Millie! How are you?"

"I'm all right. And you look wonderful in spite of all your misfortune." Millie held out her arms to give Maxi a hug. "I think I need this more than you do."

"I don't know about that," Maxi wrapped Millie in her arms and remembered what good friends she and Millie had been. "Why have I not gotten in touch with you, Millie? I realize that I have missed you very much."

"Thought about calling you so many times, but then I would think that you would be too busy to chat," Millie released Maxi first. She stepped back and looking straight into Maxi's eyes, said, her voice quavering, "I have decided to sell my house. It isn't the same around here without you. All the old neighbors have moved away and the new people aren't very friendly."

"I'm sorry to hear that. Where will you go?"

"Probably to an apartment. I'm not sure."

Maxi eyed the sprawling ranch style house and noted there wasn't yet a for sale sign in the yard. "You haven't made any commitment to sell yet have you?"

"No. I have been procrastinating. It's a hard decision. If I had family it would be easier. Since Joe died, I have been lost. But all the wonderful memories with Joe are here in this house, and I hate to lose those."

Maxi knew Millie had never had children. And she had been an only child so had no brothers or sisters of her own. "Are there any relatives of Joe's around?"

"One sister, but she was never friendly toward me. She thought Joe could have done better than to marry me. She as much as told me so, back years ago, when Joe and I were first married. I was so young and her words really devastated me. I won't approach her now.

"I am thankful that I don't have financial worries. Joe left me well provided for."

An idea skittered across Maxi's thoughts, like a light bulb coming on. "Could you consider taking in a young woman and her four-year-old child for a few weeks?" Maxi related the story of Sally and Hannah.

"I am concerned about where Sally will go when she is discharged from the hospital. With the broken leg she won't be able to handle stairs for several weeks. Also with the trauma of Hannah being taken by her father, it will be hard for both Hannah and Sally to be separated.

At Millie's hesitation, Maxi continued, "Sally is a very nice young woman, who has had a really bad time. And what I have seen of Hannah, she is a well-behaved child."

Maxi inwardly cringed at the stretch of the truth in this. She really didn't know what kind of child Hannah was, but felt sure that she was as her mother Sally had said. She would surely have caught any bad vibes in her visits to Sally.

"It would be only a few weeks until Sally can walk again."

"Let me think about it. Give me your phone number and I'll call you, and maybe go and meet this woman before making a final decision."

Maxi dug in her purse to produce a business card and jotted her home phone number on the back of it. Also, she wrote Sally's full name and the number of her room at the hospital.

Back in her car she watched Millie go toward her house. How old is Millie? I would guess about 58. Maxi thought back to when Millie had coal black hair, the kind that turned white early. So the snow-white hair was not an indication of her age. Maxi's father had had the same kind of hair, and his was white when she was a child.

Wouldn't it be a wonderful solution for all concerned if Sally and Hannah could stay with Millie until Sally is well enough to be on her own again. It would be good for Millie to have someone in the house. And if they don't do well on an everyday basis, it is short term and then they can get on with their individual lives. Maxi's thoughts raced in excited fast forward.

At Wal-Mart she saw several people she knew but no one stopped to chat, just said, "Good Morning." and kept on going. Feeling her loneliness, Maxi continued through the grocery section and headed for the checkout counter.

Back home, her mood lifted as she admired her house bathed in bright February sunshine, and surrounded in snow. She parked her car in the cleared parking area in front. Hefting her shoulder bag with the mail stuffed in one outside pocket onto her shoulder, she gathered two plastic bags by their handles in the other hand and walked up the steps to her front door. She still thrilled at the beauty of the old wood as she used her elbow to keep her shoulder bag from slipping while she searched her pocket for the key to unlock it.

The foyer was still unfinished. She paid little attention to footprints left by the workmen as they carried materials upstairs. She made her way through the dining room lit by bright sunlight spilling through the bay window and continued on through the morning room. She was not at all perturbed by the unfinished state of the house, for her mind's eye saw what it would look like when Sam was finished with the restoration.

But she couldn't help remembering for a moment her ranch home and the luxury of going from her car in the attached garage straight into her kitchen. She breathed a sigh. Nothing was perfect. And she loved this old house already, as she had never loved a house before. Most people had trouble understanding this, and had told her to her face that she was becoming eccentric. *An eccentric old widow in her rocking chair with her cat on her lap.* She smiled contentedly at the thought.

After putting her purchases in the cabinets and refrigerator, she sorted through the mail

- a gas bill and advertisements. She threw the advertisements in the wastebasket and put the bill on the counter. She would write checks next week for the monthly bills.

A cup of coffee would be good, she thought, and had just measured the beans into the grinder when a knock sounded at the kitchen door. Crossing the huge room, she opened the door find Jeff and Major.

"We were out for a walk and saw you come back," Jeff smiled his charming dimpled smile that made him look about 20 years old. Maxi had to smile in spite of feeling a little vexed.

"Perhaps you were waiting for me," Maxi hesitated a few seconds before stepping back so he and the dog could come inside.

"Perhaps," Jeff neither accepted nor rejected the accusation; he just came in and began making himself comfortable. Hanging his coat on a hook just inside the door, he headed toward the coffee maker. "No coffee?"

"I just got home!" Exasperation crept into her voice.

"But, you make coffee before you do anything else. Putting stuff away comes later."

"Not for me, and what business is it of yours how long I've been home?" Maxi was beginning to feel annoyed at all the watching that was going on in her life. This man and his dog were beginning to be too comfortable in her home. She watched him grind the beans, put them into the basket and turn on the coffeemaker. She didn't move to help.

While the coffee was brewing Jeff turned to look at her. His breath caught. Her color was high from being out in the cold this morning, making her complexion glow. *Of course it could be that she is flushed because I am here!* That thought had him stepping toward her.

"I thought maybe we could go to dinner and a movie this evening. What da'ya say?"

"I'm sorry, but I already have dinner arrangements."

"Oh, with Beau?"

"NO! I have friends, you know!" Why did he make her so exasperated?

"Okay. I know you have dinner with Sue and her husband often. Maybe we could make it a foursome?"

"If you must know, I am having dinner with Sam."

A hurt look came over Jeff's face. "I'm sorry; I'm intruding," Jeff headed toward the door, grabbing his coat from the hook and opened the door. "Come, Major."

Chagrined, Maxi headed for the still open door. Leaning into the cold air, she called, "Jeff, I'm sorry, come back. Please."

Jeff trudged on through the ankle-deep snow with Major following in his footsteps. He didn't look back or wave.

"Oh, shit!" Maxi slammed the door, rattling the coffee pot that was just finishing its last gurgle. "And now I have all this coffee and I only wanted one cup." Maxi felt like crying.

It took her all afternoon to get in the mood for her dinner with Sam. *I can't help it if Jeff thinks I only want to do things with him. I don't know where he got the idea that he controls my social life as well as my safety!* Feeling guilty and not liking it one bit, she took a tour through the house. That always cheered her.

Later, humming, she went to her bathroom and drew water in the tub. She would indulge in the luxury of a nice relaxing whirlpool tub bath before dressing to have dinner with Sam.

Chapter 22

Sunday morning dawned clear and bright. Maxi woke feeling so good, it took her a moment to remember the events of the day before. The picture of Sally and Hannah reunited brought a smile. And her dinner with Sam had been very nice. Sam was a nice man. She didn't think of her three dinners with him as dating, but she had gotten the impression last evening that Sam thought of it as exactly that. She was debating how she was going to tell him that she was not interested in more than just a casual dinner now and then. It was too soon after Jim's death. She just didn't want any complications in her private life.

Actually when she thought about it, she didn't think she ever wanted any man as a permanent part of her life. She was content with her work, her home that would soon be finished, and her cat.

She hummed as she made coffee and toast and took it out to the sunroom. The room was completed but lacked furniture except for the folding lounge chair that she had bought the first day she owned the house.

Sitting down, she noted the sunshine reflected off the black water edged with ice and snow. All was peaceful. Life is like a river, she thought. At times it is all sunny, and calm, flowing peacefully. Then there are the rough spots where riffles form and rougher where there is white water as the stream gains momentum over a shallow and rocky streambed. There are the tranquil times like today and there are the raging times when storms or snowmelt swell it to over-flowing in a raging flood, sweeping away anything in its path.

I have lived all my life along this river, Maxi mused. *It has had a major impact on my life and is continuing as I work each day helping families to adjust to a new home away from the threat of flooding.*

As a child, Maxi had loved the river while learning a respect for its power, knowing that the river could take the life of an unwary swimmer. There were dangerously strong currents and places where whirlpools could suck in the weak swimmer. She loved all manner of boating: canoes, rowboats and motorboats. She liked canoes best. Rowboats were a little hard for her to maneuver and she disliked the noise of the motorboats except for water skiing.

The ringing of her cell phone interrupted her thoughts. Digging it out of her robe pocket, she heard Millie's voice come through clear and cheerful. After the usual greetings, Millie continued, "I went to the hospital yesterday afternoon to see Sally. I told her what we had discussed and asked her how she would feel about staying at my house until she could get around enough to be on her own again. That poor girl broke down in tears. She has had a terrible time of it. I felt so sorry for her and I want very much to have them stay with me as soon as she can be released from the hospital.

"I talked to the nurse about when she would be released and she will check with the doctor. They have discussed the situation and were relieved to know there was someplace for Sally and Hannah to go. I also called the social worker that has Hannah in a temporary placement and she is coming here tomorrow afternoon. I do hope that she approves of the plan."

"Millie, that's wonderful news. Please tell Mary to call me when she comes to meet with you. I will be happy to vouch for you."

"I certainly will, Maxi. It seems like our meeting yesterday morning was meant to be. I have been so lonesome since you aren't next door any longer. I feel very good about this. If there are any problems, it is only temporary until Sally can get around. It isn't like it is a permanent situation for either of us."

Maxi felt very good, too, as she flipped the cell phone off. She knew that Sally had been in foster care most of her life and was moved from home to home every few months. She had never had the feeling of 'family'. And Millie had never had a child, so this might just work out for all concerned, at least until Sally was back on her feet and able to work again.

A knock sounded on her kitchen door. She wondered if it would be Jeff. Their Saturday and Sunday morning coffee hour had become a ritual, but after yesterday, she didn't know if he would come again.

"Hi. I wasn't sure if you would stop in this morning after yesterday. I'm sorry. Come in."

"I'm the one who should apologize. I assume things that I shouldn't. You have the right to any friends you want." Jeff hesitated then couldn't help but ask, "Sooo… How was your dinner with Sam?"

"I enjoyed it." Maxi didn't elaborate.

"So, you and Sam, what's going on there?"

"Nothing is 'going on', Jeff. We are just friends. After all, I have been seeing a lot of him, as he works on the house, and I am really pleased at the restorations. That's all."

"Hmm, I wonder if Sam knows that's all?"

"There you go, making assumptions again. You can be so infuriating, Jeff. I am a self-sufficient woman. I don't need a keeper." Maxi was getting angry again.

Briskly, she poured coffee and handed Jeff his mug. "Let's go out to the sunroom. It's a beautiful morning. It almost makes me feel that spring might not be far off."

"Yea, it's melting the snow already this morning. The sun is warm." Jeff accepted the proffered mug of steaming coffee and followed her to the sunroom. "I didn't bring donuts. Haven't been to town yet today."

"That's fine. I have been eating too much junk food anyway."

"Speaking of food, I hear that everyone in town considers you and Sam are becoming an item?"

"What? That's ridiculous!"

"Well you have been seen on at least three occasions having dinner and at least two movies." Sam sipped his coffee and narrowed his eyes at her over the mug.

"You are really hard up for gossip, Jeff. I thought you had a life."

"Well, what can I say, I hear things. I'm observant. So how about going to dinner with me this evening?"

Surprised, Maxi hesitated in answering. *What's going on here? It almost sounds like Jeff is jealous.*

Jeff waited and drank his coffee. They were both still standing never having gotten to the point of sitting down, maybe because there was only one chair.

Tension snapped in the air. Major lifted his head and looked one to the other as if he wondered what was going on.

"Well, is that a bad idea or what? It might stop the gossips about you and Sam, or maybe, start more about you, Sam and me." He wiggled his eyebrows.

Maxi gave a nervous laugh, "Of course it's not a bad idea. I'm just surprised is all, and I really could do without any gossip."

"I'll pick you up at 6. Dress casual." Jeff put his mug down and giving a signal to Major they headed for the door.

Maxi stood rooted to the spot. *What was that all about?* Then, shrugging her shoulders, she walked through her newly restored rooms and a feeling of home settled over her.

The main floor was nearly complete, just needing paint and wallpaper. The foyer and stairway still had only the rough work done, and there was still work to be done on the second floor. Maxi was pleased with the progress Sam and his crew had made. *Maybe I should talk to Sam about finishing the third floor now instead of later, then finishing the foyer and stairway. I'm glad I don't have to cut corners on cost. I also want a garage attached to the side door. The carriage house is too far away in bad weather. I admit I have become accustomed to the convenience of an attached garage. I think it can be done without harm to the integrity of the house. I'll talk to him about it.*

Her thoughts skipped to the carriage house. It was a quaint building and had a lot of potential. Originally housing the horses and carriages of an earlier time, it had never been touched and still contained four box stalls, a tack room and a feed room. The second floor had been used for storage of hay and bedding straw. She could picture it finished as a cottage and a thought popped into her mind. *Wouldn't it be just perfect for Millie?*

Amused by the sudden picture of her friend living nearby again solidified into the thought of *why not?*

Maxi went up the stairs to the second floor. The bedrooms and adjoining baths were nearly completed. Perhaps her dream of having her family home for Easter wasn't a pipe dream after all. Easter was six weeks away.

Back in the sunroom, she picked up the phone and dialed Lorene's number, then hung up before it rang as she realized that Lorene would probably be at church. She would call later. It was too early to call California.

Once again she headed up the stairs for a look at the third floor. There were several rooms there, servants' quarters when the house was built. The rough plumbing had been installed as well as heating ducts when the renovations were first beginning.

There was room for a small kitchen, two bedrooms, a bath and a large room with windows overlooking the river that would be a lovely living room. The chimney that had gone to the now closed off fireplace on the second floor where the two new bathrooms were located could be opened on this floor and a small gas log fireplace built. It could be a complete apartment. Then a picture of Sally and Hannah living there popped into her head.

Laughing at herself as she went back downstairs, she decided she needed something to eat. All this planning had given her an appetite, which reminded her of her dinner plans with Jeff. Too much was happening today.

Chapter 23

Jeff was punctual. "Where are we going?" Maxi asked as she settled into Jeff's car. She noted his black leather jacket over a red knit polo shirt and black chinos. She felt comfortable in her black slacks and turtleneck. They were casual, but she felt she looked good. The evening had become cold, so she had wore her fur-trimmed parka.

"You have probably been there - the Endless Mountain Inn."

For a moment Maxi didn't say anything. She and Jim had gone there many times. They enjoyed the relaxed rustic atmosphere that didn't feel like a stage set. *Can I handle it?*

"Oh yes, Jim and I used to go there a lot. They have good food and an unpretentious atmosphere. I haven't been there since Jim's death."

Jeff gave her a quick look, "Will it be difficult for you?"

"I'll be okay. When you have lived in one place as long as Jim and I did, it is impossible to not go to places where we went together. As a native of Forest Hills, I had taken Jim to my favorite places and they became his favorite places, too."

"We can go somewhere else if you would rather."

"No. I'll be fine. You have seen me through a lot of bad times, and it is good to go there for the first time with you." Maxi smiled at him. She didn't know, but her smile made his heart turn over with love.

"You are a very strong woman, Maxi. I like that about you."

"Thank you. Most of the time I don't feel very strong. I wonder how I'll do when this job is finished."

"How long will that be?"

"By fall I think, maybe before Christmas. I expect the relocations will be finished by then and, of course, my job will be finished. The construction of the dike-levee will take at least another two years."

"Have you thought about what you will do? Look for another job, or retire and enjoy life?"

"I haven't really thought much about it. I've been too busy. I have enjoyed restoring the house so much, but that will be completed, too. I am thinking of having Sam finish the third floor. It could be a complete apartment. Also, the carriage house could be complete living quarters for someone, too."

"What are you going to do with all that space?" Maxi's dreamy look caused Jeff some consternation. What did she have in mind? Maybe she wanted to keep Sam around for a long time.

Seated comfortably in a booth at the inn, Maxi and Jeff both chose steak, baked potato and salad. Jeff ordered a bottle of the house burgundy wine.

"You'd think we were an old married couple the way we order the same thing," Jeff commented, then immediately regretted it.

"You have provided dinner at my house so many times and it seems as though we always enjoy the same foods - except sauerkraut and rhubarb pie," Maxi ended with a laugh.

Picking up her interrupted story, Maxi continued, "Yesterday, I drove by where my old house used to be. I hadn't gone by there since it was destroyed.

"My old neighbor, Millie, saw me and came out to talk. She told me she is thinking of selling her house. When I got home the idea flashed through my mind that the carriage house would be ideal for her. She is in really good health and only a few years older than I, even though she has snow-white hair. I think a retirement community would be too much of a change for her. She has some beautiful antiques. She could keep any of her own furniture that she wanted."

"What about her children. Won't she want to be near them or relatives?"

"She has no one. No children, no relatives, except her husband's sister who always looked down her nose at Millie. While we were talking, I had the idea of asking her to visit Sally in the hospital and consider asking her to come to stay with her while she recuperated enough to look after herself and her daughter.

"She called me this morning to say she had gone to see Sally and they really hit it off. It was agreed that as soon as Sally could be released from the hospital, she and Hannah would stay with her until Sally was well and could decide what she wanted to do. That is, if the social worker gives her okay."

Their food arrived. Maxi breathed a deep breath, enjoying the aroma before picking up her knife and fork.

"This steak is just right. How is yours?" Jeff asked, as he cut a second large bite.

"Wonderful. They have a really fine chef. She is part owner. I have never had a bad meal here. The Italian food is especially good. I almost ordered lasagna, but decided I hadn't had a good steak lately," Maxi's enjoyment of good food was evident. She didn't worry about her weight and order just salads. Jeff liked that about her.

"Then," Maxi continued after a sip of wine, "When I thought of Sally and Hannah, I envisioned them in the third floor apartment." Maxi finished a little breathlessly.

"Wow. You have made a lot of plans. Are you really going to go through with all that?" Jeff's hopes plummeted. It didn't sound as though there would be any place in her life for him.

Maxi laughed and shrugged her shoulders, "I don't really know. The idea excites me, and it feels right. But I will think more about it before making any real plans, or saying anything to either Millie or Sally. I have also thought of opening a bed and breakfast."

As they ate, Jeff sent out some feelers regarding Maxi's feeling for Sam. "Are you getting serious about a relationship with Sam?" He finally asked outright, fearing the worst.

Relief swept through him at her reply. "Sam is good company. I enjoy an occasional dinner with him". After a pause she added, "I'm never going to be in a serious relationship again."

Jeff experienced such a jolt of disappointment that it unsettled him. "You may change you mind when you have more time and are under less pressure from work and the house renovation."

Changing the subject, Maxi said, "I still have that threat hanging over me. If only we could find the bank with the right lockbox we might end it."

"You still have no idea where Jim might have rented a lockbox? Think back, where had he gone just before his death?"

Maxi had done this mind game over and over. "I just don't know."

"Where was Jim raised? Here in Forest City?"

"No. He grew up in Madison. We met at Forest Hills University. He was two years ahead of me and he stayed here until I graduated. By then he was working on the newspaper and was very happy, so we settled permanently."

"Madison. That's just beyond the strip mining area that Jim was investigating, isn't it? Just a village, really. Does Madison have a bank?"

"Yes, in fact there are two. Jim never went back there after his mom died three years ago. She had been a widow for ten years before her death."

Jeff was getting excited, "Think about it. Madison is only a few miles beyond the dump that Jim was investigating. Could he have gone to Madison before starting home that day and rented a lockbox?"

"Yes, it is very likely that he might have done that. But how would we go about finding it? Do we need a court order? And, what name would it be under? Could we ask for a list of all the box holders?" Maxi rattled off the questions.

"I'll talk to Mark tomorrow. Madison is in a different county, so we would need to involve the local officials." Jeff felt real hope that this might be the answer. He desperately wanted Maxi out of danger.

When they arrived back at Maxi's house, Jeff went in with her. Beau came running at the sound of the door opening and leaped at Maxi. She laughed as she caught him in her arms.

"Does he always do that when you come home?" Jeff had never seen this happen before, but then he wasn't usually there when she came home.

"He does sometimes, not always." Maxi gave Beau a hug, set him on the floor to free her hand to punch in the alarm code before it went off and they had the police there.

"I always thought cats were aloof and finicky." Jeff bent to give Beau a rub.

"There are more misconceptions about cats than there are about dogs. Cats are very self-sufficient, but not to the point of not missing someone. Sometimes he ignores me if I have been gone too long to suit him."

After Jeff left, Maxi thought about the possibility of Jim going to Madison. *As Jeff said, it is only a few miles beyond the dump site that Jim was investigating. It could be a real possibility if Jim felt he was in danger and wanted to keep the evidence safe.*

Maxi fell asleep thinking of what Jim's last day had been like. Her dreams were troubled and she woke when the alarm clock went off feeling lonely, tired and anxious. She felt it would be a long and tiring day.

When she drove into the driveway of her house that evening Jeff was waiting. He had papers in his hand.

"We've got a listing of all the names of safety deposit boxes in both banks. Mark and I have looked at them, but can't see anything that would be sufficient to get a court order to open any. And no judge will issue an order to open then all."

Jeff sounded discouraged as he followed Maxi into the house. The day had warmed enough to melt most of the snow, but now that the sun was down it was becoming quite cold again.

Closing the door and turning off the alarm, Maxi reached out for the papers not even removing her coat. She began reading the list, turning over page after page without noting any familiar name. After finishing with the Citizen's Bank list, she started on the list for the Madison Bank and Trust Company. She turned over two pages, then stopped and turned back to the second page. She began to laugh hysterically, which turned into sobbing. Jeff looked on helplessly.

When she finally gained control of her emotions, Maxi dried her eyes and pointed to a name on the list, "Here. This is the box that Jim rented; I'm sure of it – Fred Muggles. Our daughter, Lorene, had a rag doll that she carried everywhere. She named him Mister Muggles. By the time she was six he was quite a ragged sight. When Lorene got the mumps that year and had to miss school, she looked into the mirror to confirm that she was indeed too sick to go to school and said, 'I look as bad as Mister Muggles.' It became a family joke. Two years ago when Jim had his heart attack, he asked me if he looked as bad as Mister Muggles. I was glad that he could joke about his condition and said, of course, you don't."

All the next day, Maxi was on pins and needles. When Mark called her about four o'clock he sounded jubilant.

"We hit the jackpot, Maxi! There were two tapes in the box. We have viewed them with the people from the EPA and the FBI. It is no wonder that the people behind this were so anxious to get rid of any evidence that Jim might have. Arrests will be made within the next 24 hours. In the meantime, I want you to be in protective custody.

Chapter 24

"Protective custody? No way." Maxi wasn't about to give up her privacy in her own home.

"Then the only alternative is to have Jeff and Major stay in the house with you and we will post guards outside." Mark's statement had a finality that left Maxi no alternative.

"Okay. But I have to continue my life. I have a job."

"Wherever you go there will be FBI agents with you: in your office, on appointments, attorney's office, everywhere, Maxi. No alternatives." Mark was determined that she realize the seriousness of her situation.

Maxi had to agree. After all, she wanted Jim's murderers in prison and knew she had to cooperate with the authorities. She knew that it would take time, and that her life was not her own until justice had taken its course.

The 24 hours that Mark had hoped to have jailed the men involved in the case turned into a week, with still no trace of them.

On the weekend following the dinner at the Endless Mountains Inn with Jeff, Maxi, still in her robe, was enjoying a leisurely morning with a cup of coffee that Jeff had made earlier. Jeff was nowhere about. She heard the lock turn in the kitchen door and Jeff came in with Major at his heels.

She was alarmed when she noticed Jeff holding his side. "What's wrong? Are you hurt?"

"No. I brought company." Jeff pulled a small wet bundle from inside his coat where he had been holding it against his body.

"A kitten!" Maxi automatically reached for it. Tucking it against her chest, she could feel the wet seeping into her robe.

"Major and I found her when we went for our morning walk. I think she must have been abandoned. I don't think a kitten this young could travel very far."

"You just now found her?"

"Yes, down by the river road. Major heard her mewing and went to investigate. She wasn't afraid of the dog or me. What do you think?"

"I think we should try to get her warm and dry, and give her something to eat. I don't have any food for one this young, but I have milk and eggs. I'll make her a milk shake. Or, maybe some cream of wheat would be better."

"I wouldn't know. I've never had a cat, much less one this small."

"Hold her while I fix it. I don't know how Beau will react. He may try to hurt her. We'll have to watch her closely. Major seems okay. In fact, he seems kind of protective." Looking at Major, she smiled at the picture Major made as he sat wagging his tail and looking soulfully at the kitten, his ears pointed toward her.

Maxi finished with the cream of wheat and took the kitten into her lap where she fed her with little dabs of the cereal on her fingertip. The kitten was weak but licked her fingertip hungrily.

Beau jumped on the chair next to Maxi and nosed the newcomer.

"I think Beau likes her! He doesn't seem aggressive at all; there is no hissing or spitting or laid-back ears," Maxi noted as she carefully watched to see how Beau would react.

When the kitten turned away from the food, Maxi handed her back to Jeff.

"I am going to find something to make a bed."

Returning with a cardboard box lined with bath towels, she put it on the floor and placed the kitten inside. It mewed weakly, causing Beau to leap into the box. Maxi reached to grab him, but stopped as she watched Beau sniff at the tiny body and begin washing the wet fur. The kitten snuggled up to Beau and they curled up together.

"I think he has adopted the poor little thing." Maxi smiled and watched with a parental affection.

"Do you think she should be checked by a vet?" Jeff still looked concerned. "Is there any chance that she might have a disease that Beau could catch?"

"Beau has had all his shots so he can't get leukemia, rabies or distemper. But we should have her checked. I don't know if we can get an appointment on a Saturday morning or not. I'll go call if you keep watch here. All seems calm but you never know."

Maxi made the call and after hanging up said to Jeff, "If we take her now, he has no appointments scheduled for an hour when the office opens. I'll get dressed and get Beau's carrier."

With the kitten safely inside the carrier, Jeff picked it up and started toward the door.

"You're going with us?"

"Of course I am, after all I rescued her. And I heard you say, 'if WE' take her." Jeff actually felt good when he heard Maxi say 'we' instead of 'I'.

Beau followed them to the door and appeared ready to follow them. "No, Beau, you stay here with Major until we come back."

"Geez, he seems to know what you say to him." Jeff was amazed, as he watched Beau sit down next to Major.

"Of course, he knows. We talk all the time." Maxi smiled at the skeptical look on Jeff's face. Maxi continued, as they put the carrier in the car, "The vet can also tell us if it is a she or he."

"There doesn't seem to be any easy way of telling, like with a dog. Dogs are straightforward in everything. Cats are mysterious even about their being male or female."

"You have a point, Jeff. We'll ask the vet."

An hour later on the way back home, Jeff asked, "So you are going to keep HIM?"

"Of course I'm going to keep him, unless Beau changes his mind about him, since we know that we have a boy instead of a girl. Males don't always get along but since Beau doesn't know that he is a male, maybe it will be all right."

"So what is this one going to be called?"

"I don't know yet. We have to live together for a while and see what develops."

Later, back at the house with the kitten fed and back in the box, Beau again took over the care of the new family member. Maxi beamed like a proud mother, as she looked at the large black cat washing the small buff kitten. Jeff grinned at her.

"What's so funny? You have a goofy look on your face."

"Not half as goofy as you. You look like a smug parent."

"Jeff, I am so glad that you and Major found him. He wouldn't have survived long. There weren't any other kittens or a mother cat around, was there?"

"No, we looked. I am sure Major would have found any others. I don't know what happened. But I think that someone dumped him. How could anyone do that to a little guy like this, but it seems to be the only explanation. I hope the distemper shot and the antibiotic that the vet prescribed keeps him from getting sick. Otherwise, he seems fine now that he has been fed and has a 'mother'." Jeff looked in the box at the two sleeping cats curled together.

"Yes, it will be another two weeks until he can get his other shots. They look so cute together. I have thought that Beau was lonesome when I am gone so much, and I haven't let him outside all winter. The other day I came in and caught him before he could get outside. When I turned and started to walk away, he threw his body at the back of my knees so forcefully that he almost knocked me down. He was really mad at me."

"How did he know that was a good place to hit you?" Jeff looked amazed.

"I don't know. He doesn't think of himself as a cat, he is a 'person'. So maybe he can think like a person, but I think it's instinct," Maxi hurriedly added at Jeff's raised eyebrows

"Well, he knows another of his species, so maybe knows that he is a cat after all," Jeff smiled at her.

By the middle of the week, Maxi had the newcomer named. He was longhaired and a lovely soft, tawny color. He carried his plumy tail high like a banner.

"You are a little prince. How 'bout we call you 'Bonnie Prince Charlie'?"

Later that evening Charlie was playing with a catnip mouse, tossing it in the air and leaping to catch it, Maxi laughed and said, "I think you are 'Good Time Charlie'. So 'Charlie' it is."

Chapter 25

No attempts were made on Maxi's life. Once the tapes were in the hands of the authorities it seemed logical to Maxi that she was no longer a threat; therefore, she wasn't in danger and didn't need guarding. But Jeff and Mark didn't share Maxi's optimism. The guards stayed and so did Jeff.

Two weeks after the tapes were found all the suspects were in jail awaiting trial. Maxi's guards were discontinued, but Jeff continued to occupy a rollaway bed in the library.

"They could hire someone to come after you just for revenge or as a hostage," was Jeff's belief. Mark backed him up, although Mark silently wondered if Jeff was becoming more than just a bodyguard.

Maxi continued her work. She had to keep ahead of the construction. Everything was moving faster than anyone had originally thought. The relocations went well with few complaints. Word had gone around that the money paid for the properties was indeed fair, and that Maxi's ability to help with moving and finding a house could be trusted. To Maxi, their trust alone made her job worthwhile.

But everything cannot go so smoothly. When Maxi went to see Harold Butler for the first time, she had no information that he might be unstable, a fact that she made known to Ken and Jake later.

Maxi introduced herself to Harold when he opened the door at her knock and was invited inside. At her first good look at him she realized his pupils were dilated and that he was probably on some kind of drugs. He had a huge ball of snuff in his lower lip. His black hair was lank and greasy. His faded plaid shirt was open down the front, showing a grayish white undershirt. He was skinny to the point of emaciation. But he was calm, so Maxi continued explaining in her usual way what would take place with his relocation.

He interrupted her, saying, "I'm not goin'a move, you know."

"You're not?"

"No. I thought you should know that upfront so I don't take up your time. I've heard that you are a nice lady and I don't want to hurt you."

"Harold, you don't have a choice. You have to move. The Authority has already bought your house. You had the closing yesterday and they gave you a check for the purchase. You're no longer the owner. This house will be demolished and the dike/levee is going to be built right over this spot. I'll help you find a place that is comparable to this one." Surely he had understood all this when he signed the papers yesterday, Maxi thought.

Instead of replying to her statement, Harold pointed across the room. "See that cabinet over there?"

Maxi looked to where he was pointing while he tipped his head in the same direction and Maxi realized she was staring at a gun cabinet.

"There are assault rifles, pistols, grenades and lots of ammunition. I got a whole arsenal there and I'm not movin'."

This was stated in a calm, flat voice, as detached as if someone else were saying it. He sat down and calmly folded his hands over his stomach as though everything was in his power and nobody would be able to move him.

"Perhaps it would be best if I let you think about it and come back another time." Maxi started edging toward the door. "I'll let myself out."

"Yea. It'd be good if you left, but don't plan on comin' back." Harold stayed seated as she let herself out the door and practically ran to her car.

"Why didn't you tell me about this man?" Maxi stormed into the Jake's office and confronted Ken there, too. She was ready to lay Ken and Jake out in beautiful shades of black, blue and purple.

"I'm sorry, Maxi." Jake really looked concerned and sorry. "I've been so busy keeping up with everything else, that I forgot about this guy."

"Everything went okay yesterday," Ken added, a smug smile on his face. "I thought the stories were exaggerated. He was very calm and reasonable. Didn't say much, but signed the papers and took the check. I didn't give him another thought. You must have upset him."

"I should have told you that he was wounded during the Desert Storm war in the Middle East. He has a plate in his head and is also now a drug addict and very unstable!" Jake said.

"Did you also know that he has a virtual arsenal in his home?" Maxi fumed at them.

"Maxi, I had no idea that you were going there today." Ken sounded contrite but also defensive.

"But you just bought his home. When did you think you would tell me? You know that I always go to the house to begin the relocation plans."

"It slipped my mind, Maxi. I'm sorry."

"Yes, I'm sure it did." Ken seemed oblivious to Maxi's sarcasm. She continued, "Well, I'm just lucky that I didn't get killed." Maxi recounted her visit. "He was calm and just stated he had no intention of moving. Then he showed me his gun cabinet."

"We'll have to turn this over to the police," Jake said. "Maxi, you are not to go there again."

"For your information, I have no intention of getting anywhere near that man," Maxi stated firmly.

Later that week, Maxi was relieved to hear that Harold's father had been contacted and he had helped talk him into coming out of his home. His father had him admitted to a Veteran's Administration Hospital where a psychiatric evaluation would be done and perhaps he could be helped. At least, Maxi hoped so.

"It's not all bad. Maybe now he will get the help he needs." Maxi was talking with Harold's father who had come to her office.

"I'm sorry you were placed in what could have been a very bad situation. I thank God that Harold was in touch with reality enough to not harm you. He was a really good kid before he got messed up in the war."

That evening Maxi was trying to relax from her hectic week at work. But she was too keyed up. Sipping a glass of wine, her thoughts turned to the big party she had hoped to have. First she had thought it would be at Easter - but the work on the house wasn't far enough along to accommodate all the family - so maybe the Fourth of July. Now she changed focus again, moving her plans to Labor Day weekend. Having the third-floor apartment finished for Sally and Hannah and the carriage house for Millie took precedence as they now needed homes. Millie had accepted a good offer on her house. She and Sally were deciding what furnishings Millie would keep for their next home. They were so excited about Maxi's plans for them they could hardly wait.

As it turned out, Millie moved into the carriage house on the Fourth of July along with Sally and Hannah. They would all live there until Sally could manage the stairs to the third-floor apartment. Sally was nearly back to normal, but would require more physical therapy before she could manage so many stairs.

It was an early eight o'clock Saturday morning when Millie came bursting into Maxi's kitchen.

"Maxi, you won't believe this. I just got a call from Howard's sister, the one who always snubbed me. She is demanding all the furniture, claiming they are her family's heirlooms." Millie was so distraught that Maxi had trouble understanding the situation.

"Wait, Millie, slow down. Here, sit at the table and I'll get you a cup of coffee while you calm down. Let me hear what is happening."

"That awful woman wants all my furniture," Millie sobbed. "When Howard's parents died, they left all their furniture to us and their house to Jane. She wasn't interested in the antique furniture or the house, either. She sold it as soon as she could. It was such a beautiful home.

"That furniture belongs in this house, Maxi. It shouldn't be sold to strangers, and that is just what Jane will do. She is only interested in the money. Some of it is worth a great deal."

"Oh, Millie. I'm so sorry. I don't need the furniture, if that's what is causing you so much distress. But you should be able to do with it what you want and keep what you want." Maxi sat with her coffee and put her arms around Millie.

Millie became calmer. "No, that woman won't get a stick of that furniture. I have a copy of the will; I'm sure. It must be in that old file cabinet that I put in storage."

"If you want to go look for it, I can go with you today," Maxi offered.

"Yes, please. I'll go get ready. When do you want to go?"

"Give me an hour." Maxi patted Millie on the back and urged her toward the door. *Poor Millie. She doesn't need this – but neither do I. I have too much on my plate already, but Millie needs me. O Lord, help us get this straightened out.*

Maxi headed toward her bathroom for a hot shower. Hopefully that would get her moving. She was so tired.

It was late afternoon when they finally found the copy of Howard's parents' will and also Howard's will. It bore out Millie's story.

"I'll have my attorney handle this, Millie. Jane needs to hear from an authority figure to set her back so she will leave you alone. I'll see he gets a copy of this Monday morning. He may need to talk to you, too. If he does, I'll have him call you and make an appointment." Maxi was so glad they had found the proof. *It's a wonder that she saved all these old papers. By the looks of things, she never threw anything away. Where will all this stuff end up?*

Sunday morning Maxi slept in. It was noon before she woke up enough to look at the clock. Beau and Charlie were curled up against her legs, sleeping soundly.

"Hey guys, its time we moved a little." She didn't see even a twitch of an ear.

Later, dressed in jeans and red tee shirt, Maxi headed for the kitchen. She smelled bacon frying and discovered Jeff standing at the stove removing the bacon from the frying pan.

"I guess there are some benefits to your staying here. That smells sooo good!"

Beating eggs in a bowl, Jeff smiled. "I knew I might be good for something. Sit down and I'll pour you a cup of coffee."

Coffee cup in hand, Maxi sipped and enjoyed watching Jeff prepare breakfast. He didn't appear to need any help. Even the table was set and orange juice was at each place. Toast popped up just as Jeff was spooning scrambled eggs onto plates.

"Thank you, Jeff. This is wonderful. I can't believe that I slept so long. And how did you know when to start breakfast?"

"I have had everything ready to go since nine o'clock. I peeked into your room at ten and you were still sound asleep. I just waited until I heard you talking to the cats."

"Don't you have to get back to your writing? I feel like I have taken over your life."

"I have been doing my writing when you are at work. I have had plenty of time."

Maxi heaved a sigh, "I am so happy that everything is coming together so well. Everyone is happy. Hannah loves the cats and Charlie had really taken to her. She carries him around with Beau trailing them like an anxious parent," Maxi smiled at Jeff.

"You are really filling up this huge old house. There won't be rooms for bread and breakfast guests like you talked about," Jeff teased.

"Sally goes around as though she can't believe her good luck. She told me yesterday that she felt like Cinderella."

"She should. You have a big heart, Maxi. Not many people would have taken in someone they didn't know - and with a child besides."

"It just seemed like the right thing to do. It was my choice, and it feels like all this has been planned to turn out like this. I'm so glad that I have been able to help Millie, Sally and Hannah. Hannah has become like a grandchild. Have you noticed that she has taken to calling me Grandma Maxi? I just love it."

Maxi had a huge smile on her face, and Jeff wondered if she had any room in her heart for him. He was afraid to ask.

By the middle of August, Sally was able to climb the stairs to the third floor apartment. She loved it at first sight.

After Millie had used what furniture she wanted in her Carriage House, she insisted that Maxi use the rest. Most pieces were antiques that Millie had inherited from Howard's parents, who had inherited them from his grandmother, so it went with the house beautifully. It completed the renovations in a period manner. Maxi now had two bedrooms furnished on the second floor, and the other two would soon be finished.

Sally had asked Maxi to see what could be salvaged from the trailer before it was removed. All that Maxi had been able to salvage were snapshots, a few knickknacks and cooking utensils. Sally's husband hadn't thought to take anything except clothing, Hannah, and, of course, the money for the property. The dishes had been broken when the cupboards were smashed, but again Millie came to the rescue. She had ten complete sets of dishes, all service for twelve. There were sets of delicate china, ironstone, blue willow, Desert Rose Franciscan ware, and pottery as well as several different patterns of Corelle. Sally chose a set of the Corelle. She said she felt more at home using that than the expensive china or pottery.

"You should sell what you don't want to keep and use the money for yourself," Maxi protested to Millie. She loved all the furniture, dishes, and everything but didn't feel Millie should give it all away.

"I would rather see you use it, Maxi. You have given me a wonderful home, rent free, and I feel that now I have something to live for again. You have given me a new life. And if you have these things, then I will see them in use, and it won't feel like I have gotten rid of my old life. You fixed the carriage house so beautiful. I really love it and feel so comfortable and at home there. Since you won't take any rent I feel I owe you something.

"Howard and I certainly didn't need that big house for just the two of us," Millie continued. "When we were young we had hoped for a big family. Howard loved to entertain, so even though the children didn't come along as we had hoped, we were happy there, and I loved keeping all the things handed down in the family." Millie eyes glistened with unshed tears as she gave Maxi a hug, "You are the sister I never had."

Furniture was selected for Sally and Hannah and the apartment was finished. Hannah loved having a room of her own that she helped decorate. Her favorite colors were pink and purple.

Sally said she felt like she was in heaven; everything was so beautiful. She loved the antique brass bed that Millie gave her and the dresser and night stands. She had chosen light cream for the walls, with soft gold, brown and dark green as accent colors. A new chocolate brown leather sofa had been purchased. Light tan carpet completed the apartment.

Millie's antiques consisted mostly of beds, chests, dressers and tables. A few chairs and sofas were reupholstered.

****

Maxi's relocation work was ahead of schedule, the pace being dominated by the construction schedule. Everyone was pleased, the board members as well as the Army Corps of Engineers.

At this rate another 6 months will see the end of my job. Maxi realized with a shock that she was looking at the end of her employment. She had been so involved with the day-to-day work that she really hadn't thought about how much longer she would be working. This was the first time in her life that she had literally worked herself out of a job.

The trial against Jim's murderers had begun the third week of July. Maxi had time off to attend. Because the tapes so well documented everything, Maxi only had to tell what had happened to her home and that Jim was a writer. Also, that she had identified the name that Jim had used for the lockbox. But she couldn't stay away from the trial proceedings. She felt impelled to be there to see justice for Jim's murder.

It was over in two weeks. The ending seemed anticlimactic to Maxi. Dick Sheppard was sentenced to life in prison. Maxi felt that life in prison was perhaps more punishment than the death penalty would have been. That is, until she was told that the prison allowed inmates to live quite well, especially when they had money available for luxuries. It seemed as though Dick Sheppard had plenty of that despite all the fines imposed on his company for the illegal dumping. He had managed to put money in an offshore account in his wife's name. She in turn saw that he had everything he needed that was allowed him in prison. The only thing he lacked was freedom to come and go as he pleased. He even had special meals brought in from a gourmet restaurant.

"It doesn't seem like nearly the punishment he deserves," Maxi fumed to Jeff Saturday morning as they shared their usual coffee and Jeff's inevitable donuts.

Grinding the coffee beans, she dumped them into the filter basket, poured water into the coffee maker then hit the on switch with more force than was necessary.

"No, I agree. It doesn't seem like enough," Jeff said. "As it has worked out, I guess it was a good thing you kicked me out after a month went by with no attempts on your life. If I had continued to live with you, people would have started talking."

"Well, I guess I have given this town enough to talk about," Maxi poured coffee into two mugs and brought them to the table. Declining the donuts, she continued as she pulled out a chair and sat down, "I am very glad that you are my neighbor, Jeff. I don't know if I could have come through all that's happened without you."

"I've been meaning to talk to you about that." Jeff moved closer and put his hands on Maxi's arms. "How would you feel about a permanent arrangement?"

Chapter 26

"Permanent?" Maxi stared at Jeff, uncomprehending.

"Yes. Permanent! As in, 'will you marry me'?" Jeff's hold on her arms tightened and he stared into her eyes.

"I, aaaaaaaaaaammm," Maxi was speechless. She had never considered this possibility. Jeff had just been a very good friend, someone to count on.

"WHAT?" Jeff wasn't getting the response he expected at all. Maybe she was more interested in Sam than he had thought.

"I c-c-can't get married," Maxi finally stuttered. "I'm too old to get married. I'm still married to Jim."

"No you're not! Not too old, for heaven's sake. What on earth do you mean? And you are a widow. That isn't married."

"I've never even thought about such a thing. I am happy with my house, my cats, and my friends. Why can't we just be friends, Jeff?"

"Because it is just too hard to be just friends, that's why." Jeff was getting angry. What was the matter with this woman?

Maxi panicked. She felt as though she was backed against a wall. This shouldn't be happening. Life was just getting sorted out. She needed time, space. "I can't talk to you about this." Maxi turned and went into her bedroom, shutting the door. Jeff heard the click of the lock.

Jeff stared at the closed bedroom door. Then he turned and went out the kitchen door, walking the well-worn path across the meadow toward his house. He walked with his head down; his shoulders slumped. Major kept pace by his side, occasionally whining and looking at his master.

Maxi crawled face down onto her bed. Beau and Charlie had been sleeping in the middle of the bed and Maxi's movement woke them. They both got up to come and rub against her arm, purring and pushing with their noses for petting and attention.

Maxi turned on her side, drawing her knees up and gathering both cats close, smoothing their warm vibrating bodies with her hands.

Misery overwhelmed her. "Why can't he just let things as they are? We were doing just fine!"

The ringing of the phone woke her. A glance at the clock as she picked up the phone told her she had been asleep two hours. A mumbled "Hello", was greeted by Sue's voice.

"Maxi? You sound like you were asleep."

"Mmmm. Yes, I guess I dozed off. Hi, Sue. Wassup?"

"Are you all right, Maxi?"

"I'm fine." Maxi made an effort to pull herself together and sound more normal.

"I thought maybe you were having a rough day. I wanted to ask you to come to dinner tonight."

"Well, I hadn't thought of dinner yet. Yes, I would like that very much, Sue. But what made you think I was having a rough day?" There was no way that Sue could know what had happened with Jeff.

"Just the date, that's all. I know you have been fine, but anniversaries can be rough."

Anniversaries? *Ohmigod. Jim's accident had been a year ago today. And she had forgotten! How rotten could a wife be?* "I'm fine, really Sue. It's a wonder that you remembered. Thanks for the dinner invitation. What time should I be there?"

"Can you be here in an hour? If not, I can hold dinner back."

"No. I'll be there. An hour is fine."

"Okay. See you then. Bye, Maxi."

Maxi rolled off the bed, leaving the cats to move back to their nest between the pillows. Heading for the shower, she was in a daze. *How could I have forgotten? I am a terrible person to not have remembered.*

Later, at Sue's, she had pushed her food around her plate while pretending to eat. She and Sue were sitting on the deck, each holding a glass of wine.

"Maxi, you can stop pretending now. I can see that you are in a bad state. Talk to me!"

Taking a deep shuddering, breath, Maxi let it out, saying, "I forgot, Sue. How could I have done that? How could I have forgotten the date of Jim's death? What kind of person am I?" Maxi was holding back tears, trying desperately for control.

"Maxi, you are a wonderful person, and personally, I think you subconsciously made yourself forget. It's a coping mechanism. You can't bury yourself in grief forever. It's been a year now."

"And on top of that," Maxi continued, not really hearing what Sue had said, "I turned down a marriage proposal today."

Sue's mouth dropped open as she stared at her friend. "A marriage proposal?"

"Yes. Can you believe it?"

"Yes, I can believe it. What I want to know is, was it Sam or Jeff?"

"That's all you can say, Sam or Jeff? And what makes you come up with their names, for chrissake?"

"Because they have both been looking at you with calf eyes and taking you to dinner and all. Well, which one? Come on, tell me! I'm dying here."

"It was Jeff and I couldn't have been more surprised. Why did he have to do that? He was a very good friend and now he has ruined that; and we have to be neighbors, for chrissake," Maxi was near tears again.

"Stop with this 'for chrissake' business. That is not you talking that way." Sue moved over to sit next to Maxi on the glider. Putting her arm around Maxi's shoulders, she said, "Honey, we have been friends all our lives, for as long as we can remember. We were married on the same day in a double ceremony. We celebrated our anniversaries together. No one knows you better than I do. Agreed?"

Maxi nodded, sniffling.

"So tell me why it is that you can't get married again?"

"How can you ask that, Sue? You know!"

"I don't know. Tell me."

"To begin with, I am married. I'll always be married to Jim."

"No Maxi, you were married to Jim. You are a widow now; Jim is not here anymore. He would want you to go on with your life. He wouldn't want you to be alone."

"I still sometimes think he is just away and will be coming in the door any minute. I am 56 years old. I'm too old to get married."

"TOO OLD? And it is 55, not 56."

"Well, almost 56. I can't imagine being intimate with a man. I'm saggy and I'll soon be getting wrinkles and a man would expect to have the whole marriage thing........." Maxi's voice trailed off, and she was crying again.

"Being intimate with a man is just what you need - marriage or not. If you are afraid of marriage, give living together a try to see if it works." Sue added, looking at Maxi with admiration, "and you are not saggy. You are in great shape."

"SUE! I can't believe you said that! 'Try living together.' I couldn't do that. What about the children? What would they think, and what kind of example would that be?"

Sue couldn't help a burst of laughter. "Maxi, your children are adults and married. I think they could stand the shock of you living with someone. I admit it probably would be a terrific shock for them, but they would get over it if you were happy."

"Sue, I can't. I just can't. You realize it would mean sharing a bathroom?"

"Well, you could make arrangements to avoid that if that is the problem." Sue still had trouble containing her laughter.

"Tell me," Sue continued. "Who welcomed you when you first bought your house? Who stayed with you when you were snowed in and sick?"

Maxi looked down at her clenched fists in her lap, "Jeff".

"Who cooked you a Valentine Dinner? Who was concerned when your life was in danger?"

"You would have done the same thing for me if I let you know that I needed you." At Sue's stern look, Maxi relented, "Okay you have made your point. But that still doesn't mean I should get married or worse yet, live with him."

"He lived in your house from the time the tapes were found until after the trial and the men were in prison. Was it difficult?"

"No. It was nice having someone there, but he slept on a rollaway in the library and used the bathroom off the laundry room. That isn't marriage or even 'living together'."

"No it isn't. But it does prove he is an easy man to have around. He is caring and considerate and I think he is in love with you, or he wouldn't have asked you to marry him. And he is a real hunk! I can think of any number of women who would jump at the chance to even have a date with him. Anyway, what did he do when you said no?"

"I didn't actually say no. I panicked and said I couldn't talk about it, and went into my bedroom and locked the door. I guess he went home. I didn't see him when I left to come here."

"Maxi, I want you to do something for me."

"What?"

"Go home and call Jeff and apologize. Tell him you just need time to think about it."

Maxi took a deep breath, "I can't." At another hard look from Sue, Maxi murmured, "I don't know, Sue. I don't want to spoil what we have – or had – but I don't want to mislead him to think I can marry him, either."

"Just do what I ask and give both of you time to think about your relationship. If you really can't consider living with him, then you both have to adjust to that. I don't think he will want to stop being a good neighbor."

A half hour later a subdued Maxi drove her car back home. She sat looking at her magnificent house and a huge sigh escaped her. She put her hand on the door handle to open it and go inside. *What to do? I'm so tired. Why can't life be simple, without big decisions?*

Instead of going in, she sat on the porch steps enjoying the night. The air was soft, warm and fragrant with the scent of honeysuckle. There was no moon and the stars stood out in stark relief against the black sky.

Beau and Charlie came and rubbed against her arms and legs and climbed into her lap, purring all the while.

"You guys really like having a kitty door so you can come and go as you please, don't you?" Their soft fur and warm bodies were comforting.

Chapter 27

Maxi didn't call Jeff as Sue had asked. Instead she went to bed too exhausted to think about any of it. The next morning she still didn't want to think about it.

She distracted herself with plans for her Labor Day party. She wanted an elaborate, gala event.

She called Lorene first and told her what she was planning. Lorene was enthusiastic and said she wanted to come a week early to help get everything ready. Next she called Michael. Eve answered the phone. Maxi told her what she was planning and that she hoped they would be able to come. "It's to be an official open house, too," Maxi explained.

Eve was excited about the plan and said she would tell Mike about it as soon as he came back from golfing. "I am sure he can plan on getting off work for a week or two; I know that I can, since all my work is from home on my computer."

Maxi was pulling out of her lethargy, thrilled that her idea was going over well with Lorene and Eve. Next she called Sue.

"Thanks for listening to me last night, Sue."

"That's what friends are for. Did you call Jeff?"

"Not yet." Maxi wanted to evade that issue so she began to tell Sue about her plans for Labor Day. Sue was enthusiastic, too, and wanted to help in anyway she could. "Let's get together some evening this week, here, and do some brainstorming."

"Any evening is fine with me."

"Okay, I'll call you tomorrow evening after I look at my work schedule for the week. Monday's are always busy and Thursday is the board meeting so Monday and Thursday are out for sure."

Next Maxi went to see Millie, Sally and Hannah. They were having breakfast at the kitchen table in the carriage house. Maxi couldn't help but think they looked like a family: grandmother, daughter and granddaughter. They had were chattering and laughing when Maxi knocked and entered.

"Hello, Maxi. Sit yourself down and I'll give you breakfast." Millie jumped up to give Maxi a hug and went to get the coffee pot and a mug, then busied herself cracking eggs into a bowl and whipping them. "It's French toast this morning."

"Sounds wonderful, Millie." Maxi realized that she hadn't even thought of breakfast, she had been so excited about her plans. Now she was suddenly ravenous.

"I'm planning a party for Labor Day weekend. Who do you want to invite?"

"I can't think of anyone." Millie placed a plate in front of Maxi and continued, "I was never friendly with any of the other neighbors in our old neighborhood. Most of them were there only a short time before they moved on. I would welcome them and before I knew it a new family would move in. I have a few friends from church, though."

"Please invite them, and the pastor and his wife and family - the more the better." Thinking about the old neighborhood, she replied to Millie's statement. "Yes, young executives have to move their families so often; it must be very hard on the children. I remember when Michael and Lorene were growing up; their best friends were made at school, not next door. When I was a kid, Sue and I lived next door to each other and we were in and out of each other's homes all the time. It was like having two homes. It was wonderful - something my kids never had.

"What about you, Sally? Who do you want to invite?"

"I would like to ask my old neighbor, Jean, who used to take care of Hannah for me, and also Florence, who runs the diner where I worked. They were both very good to me." Sally looked anxiously at Maxi, "If that is all right? Maybe they won't fit in with your family and friends."

"It is more than all right and they will fit in just fine. If they have families, please ask them, too."

"I certainly would like to get to know them." Maxi and Millie spoke in unison, looked at each other as they all broke out in laughter.

"We're really gonna have a real party? Will there be hats and whistles?" Hannah was jumping up and down, picking up on the excitement. "I've never had a party. Momma always baked me a cake on my birthday but we never had other people for a party."

"Oh, sweetie," Maxi's heart nearly broke at the thought of a four-year-old never having had a birthday party. "Yes, it is going to be the best party ever. And do you know what? When your next birthday comes we will have a party just for you, with hats and whistles and everything."

"Ooohhh! You promise? Cross your heart and hope to die?" Hannah's look of joyous anticipation had Maxi scooping her up for a hug.

"Cross my heart and hope to die," Maxi made the solemn motions of a cross over chest and then raised her hand palm out to seal the pledge. "Where did you learn that?"

"Oh, Jean said it a lot when she told me we were going to do something. And it worked, because Jean always kept her promises." A look of sadness crossed Hannah's face, "Not like daddy."

The three women exchanged a knowing look and began talking about the plans for Labor Day.

Wednesday evening, Maxi and Sue sat at Maxi's kitchen table making a guest list. "We already have over 100 people on the list and it doesn't have Sam or Jeff. You are planning on inviting them, aren't you?" Sue kept her eyes trained on the paper in front of her, not daring to look at Maxi as she asked.

"Of course they're to be invited. I just didn't get around to it."

"A phone call will do for them. It should come from you since you know them both much better than I and it is your party."

"Sue you are so subtle. And yes, I'll phone them. Tomorrow."

"Tonight! Now!" Sue picked up Maxi's cell phone that was lying on the table and passed it to Maxi, giving her a hard look.

"Okay, okay." Maxi punched Sam's number into her cell phone. A brief conversation assured that Sam would be there. "And feel free to bring a guest, Sam," Maxi added.

"I don't expect to do that, Maxi."

"Okay whatever you want, Sam. I'm glad you will be here. You have done wonders with the house and I want you to have the recognition that you deserve."

Maxi disconnected and put the phone down. Sue wouldn't let her get away with it. "Now Jeff."

"Okay. But I think it would be easier if you called him."

"No way, Maxi. You are not getting out of this. That guy is a prince, and has been so good to you that I am ashamed of you that you haven't talked to him about your feelings. The very least you can do is talk to him, have a discussion about how each of you feel."

"You're right, Sue." Maxi picked up the phone and punched in Jeff's number. He picked up right away.

"Hello Maxi. It's about time you called me."

Maxi's mouth dropped open. "I hate these caller ID phones. I thought I could hang up if you answered instead of your answering machine. I could have left a message on a machine."

"Now you can leave a message with the real thing. Does that scare you too much?"

"No. Of course not. I am calling to invite you to my Labor Day party. You are welcome to bring a guest."

"Oh, a guest, uh. Anyone in mind?"

"No, that is entirely up to you."

"Well, since everyone I know has probably already been invited, I guess I'll come alone."

"You can always team up with Sam." Maxi could have bitten her tongue, but it was already said and she couldn't take it back.

"Sam and I normally get along fine, but somehow I think we will be staying on opposite sides of this party."

"Suit yourself. See you at the party."

"If not before." Jeff had the last word as he hung up.

"He is so infuriating," Maxi fumed. Sue was laughing so hard she had to put her head down on the table.

"Maxi, you have indeed met your match. I can hardly wait for this party."

Chapter 28

Friday of Labor Day Weekend was sunny and warm. The entire weekend was predicted to be wonderful weather.

Michael and Eve had arrived the weekend before, as well as Lorene and Jack. The entire week had been a wonderful reunion. Maxi's family had loved the house, and they were relieved to see their mother looking so happy. They could see that she had put much of herself in restoring this house and making it a real home.

"It's amazing, Mom. How were you able to do all this and do your job at the same time?" Michael could hardly believe his eyes. He missed the home where he had grown up, but under the circumstances he knew he had to overcome that. His mother needed his approval and support.

"Are you sure about having these other people living here?" Lorene was skeptical, especially about Sally and Hannah. They really knew nothing about them, only the story that Sally had told. Millie was a different matter altogether. They had known her when they were teenagers and she was a nice lady -- but would it be a good idea to have her living on her mother's property?

"Yes, I'm very sure, Lorene." Maxi assured her. "Sally is almost like a daughter, and Hanna already is calling me Grandma Maxi. I love her."

Jealousy sizzled in Lorene's consciousness and it startled her to realize it. She was the daughter; she didn't want a stranger for a sister! And someday she would have children and she didn't want her mother to have other grandchildren. Lorene bit her tongue and turned away, not wanting to distress her mother. *After all, she has been through a terrible time. I just hope she hasn't gotten herself into a situation that is going to be a bad scene.*

Everything was in place for Saturday's party. The house, now fully furnished, was sparkling clean. Every piece of furniture was polished, windows sparkled, and hardwood floors gleamed, showing off the beautiful oriental rugs. A florist had placed simple flower arrangements in every room. Garden flowers - roses, daisies, delphinium, hydrangea, baby's breath, phlox, and lilies - were combined with wild flowers from the meadow - Queen Anne's lace, goldenrod and asters.

Outside lights were strung through the trees and shrubs. The Gazebo, which was to be a dance floor, had been strung with hundreds of tiny clear lights combined with Chinese lanterns. Mini lights and Japanese lanterns festooned the patio where a band was to be set up at one end and a bar at the other with tables and chairs in the middle.

"Everything is so beautiful, Maxi, and tonight will be brilliant with all the lights. I can't wait to see it." Sally was in awe. She had never seen such a display. "Even the path to the dock on the river will be lighted, and the patio down there and the dock, too."

"Yes, Sally, I think it will be just as I planned. I'm so glad the landscapers finished with the permanent lighting and all the paths and retaining walls. It will take a couple years before the flower beds and shrubbery will begin to look as I planned, but the annuals have filled in those areas nicely."

"I never thought I would see such a place as this, Maxi," Sally's eyes sparkled. "I can't begin to thank you for taking us in like you did. The third floor apartment is so beautiful. We just love it. Hannah is just as happy as I am. She has never had a pet and she can't be separated from Charlie." Sally was close to tears. "I have never been so happy."

"You have more than earned it, Sally, with all the cleaning and cooking you have been doing. Between you and Millie, I hardly needed caterers. You are more than friends; you are now part of my family. I want you and Millie to enjoy this weekend, too; so-o-o, the caterers stay despite your protests. They will take care of the serving and the cleanup. I don't want either you or Millie even near that part of this party. Do you hear me?" Maxi knew she would have a hard time convincing them of that. Both were hard workers and wanted to do their share.

"The only thing missing is the swimming pool." Recognizing the voice, Maxi turned to face Jeff. It was the first time they had been face to face since Jeff had asked Maxi to marry him. *Come to think of it, did he actually ask me to marry him or just say something about making it 'permanent' - I remember now, he did follow up with 'will you marry me'?*

"Hi. The swimming pool will come next year, and maybe tennis courts." Maxi hoped she wasn't showing her nervousness. This was so awkward!

"Courts? How many do you expect to be playing? All of Forest Hills?"

"I guess we haven't talked recently. I have decided to open a bed and breakfast when my job is finished - probably in a few months."

"Wow. You are a workaholic. When did you decide this?"

"This week. With the kids home, Sue and Rob, Millie and Sally all here working this week, we got to thinking about the possibility. I am really serious about it."

At Jeff's downcast eyes, Maxi was moved to say, "We'll talk later, Jeff. I'm sorry for my behavior when we last talked. I was just caught so off guard. I've never thought of us really dating, let alone anything more than that."

Jeff raised his eyebrows in question, but at Maxi's frown he decided not to press the matter. "Okay. Later it is."

By Saturday afternoon it seemed that most of the population of Forest Hills was there. Food was in plentiful supply on a continuous buffet in the dining room. Maxi had decided to keep food inside near the kitchen in order to make it easier for the catering staff to keep it well supplied with hot food, hot, and cold food, cold. The variety of foods changed from afternoon to evening when a full meal was served.

It was dusk when Lorene caught up with her mother just as all the lights came on. "Oh, it's so beautiful, Mom."

"Yes. It is even better than I expected."

"So, Mom, why didn't you ever mention the men in your life?" Lorene believed the blunt approach would work best with her mother. She was great at sidestepping anything she didn't want to discuss.

"What do you mean, 'the men in my life'?"

"There are at least two who have been keeping you in their sights while avoiding each other."

"Who do you mean?" Maxi's eyes shifted nervously around the various people gathered in groups around them.

"Well, that guy over there, for one." Lorene looked across the lawn to where Sam was talking with several couples.

"Oh, that's Sam, my contractor; we're only friends, that's all. We've gone to dinner and the movies a few times. He's a very nice man and I want him to have all the recognition for his work here. I'm sure he has just been working the crowd and getting lots of compliments, as well as lots of people wanting his services. He is not a 'man in my life'.

"Then why has he been keeping such a close eye on you? Maybe he doesn't know that yet. Then, there is that gorgeous hunk over there, who hasn't taken his eyes off you except now and then to glance at someone who is talking to him."

Maxi blushed. Lorene could detect it even in the dusky evening light, with only the decorative lights giving further illumination.

"O-ho! Bingo! Who is he?"

"Stop it, Lorene. He's just a neighbor."

"Maxi, tell the truth. He is more than just a neighbor." Maxi whirled to face Sue, who was grinning and had a mischievous gleam in her eyes. "Tell her, Maxi, just what a wonderful neighbor he is."

"Really, Sue. Stop it."

"Okay, you had your chance, so now I'll tell Lorene what kind of neighbor he has been and is.

"He met your mom the day she bought this place, with champagne, no less. He kept bringing coffee and donuts every weekend knowing she would be up by nine o'clock. We had a blizzard the first night she stayed here. Jeff braved the storm and four-foot snow to check to see if she was all right. He found that she was very sick with the flu. He stayed and nursed her until she was over it, only then going back to his own home.

"He moved in when the people responsible for your dad's accident were being taken into custody and stayed until after the trial," Sue hadn't paused even to take a breath.

Lorene's eyes got bigger and bigger as the story unfolded. "Mom, you never told us any of this. Your life was in danger?"

"Sue is exaggerating. It wasn't that bad and I didn't want you to worry unnecessarily."

"He stayed with you when you were sick?"

"Well, yes, he did, and we got to be good friends. He slept in the chair, by the way." Maxi was getting indignant over this conversation.

"And what about during the trial?" Lorene was beginning to get a huge kick out of this conversation. She also kept an eye on Jeff, who seemed to be very interested in their group.

"He stayed in the library. And slept on a cot." Maxi turned away and headed toward a nearby group. She was intercepted by Jeff.

"I haven't been introduced to your daughter."

Maxi was caught. She turned and made her way back to Lorene and Sue, with Jeff close by her side. "Jeff, I would like to introduce my daughter, Lorene."

"I'm pleased to meet you, Lorene. I knew who you were, as you and your mom look very much alike. But I wanted an introduction. I have already introduced myself to your husband, your brother and his wife.

Maxi noticed her daughter's reaction and, of course, she knew how Sue felt about Jeff. He is sooo smooth. He has them both wrapped around his little finger.

"Maxi, we need to talk," Jeff took her elbow and guided her toward the path leading down to dock at the river.

"Really, Jeff, this is not the time nor place." Maxi tried to pull her arm from his firm grasp.

"It's beyond the time, Maxi. You do care for me, you are just afraid to admit it. And I am going to convince you." Jeff whirled her around, clasping her close to his chest. He proceeded to kiss her until he felt her relax. When he lifted his head he had to hold on to her to keep her from falling.

Maxi grabbed hold of Jeff and burst into tears.

"What's wrong? I thought it was an incredible kiss. I didn't want to make you cry."

It took awhile before Maxi could say anything. Then it was interrupted with hiccups and sobs. "I didn't want to get romantically involved with anyone. I'm not a young woman. I'm 55 years old, for Chris sake!"

"And I'm 52 but what does that have to do with it?"

"It's diff-ff-erent for a man."

"I don't know why that would be."

"The intimacy. I can't think of sharing a bed, a bathroom or being naked, that's why!" Maxi's voice had risen to a level beyond normal conversation. A couple coming up from the dock and patio below them looked at them and hurried past. Maxi hoped they hadn't recognized her in the dim light.

"I think you embarrassed them," Jeff couldn't help but tease her; he had never seen her flustered before. "And I can't wait to get you naked. As for the bathroom, I can use a separate bathroom. So what other objections do you have?"

"You could have picked a better day to say you wanted to make it permanent."

"Why?"

"Because it was just a year ago that Jim's accident happened." The sobs came again.

Jeff was momentarily stunned, "Oh, no! I should have remembered. I'm so sorry. What can I say?"

"Nothing. I know you didn't deliberately forget, and I didn't expect you to remember. But I was ashamed of myself. I didn't remember until after Sue called to invite me to dinner and asked if I was having a bad day. What kind of person am I to forget something that important?"

"You are human, Maxi. Can we start over?"

"No. We can't start over. Not as far as you thinking we could make it, what was it you said, 'permanent'".

"Why not?"

"And just what does 'permanent' mean anyway? You're just planning to move in and stay?"

"Well, I was thinking a wedding might be nice before I do that."

"Wedding."

"Are you just going to keep parroting me?"

"I can't think. I have to get back to my guests." Maxi pulled away and started up the path.

"Okay. But this conversation is not over, Maxi. You think about a wedding - one that will be soon." Jeff's chuckle followed her up the path.

Chapter 29

People were coming and going all weekend. The biggest crowd had been Saturday as Maxi had planned. Many people had family plans for Labor Day weekend and she knew that Sunday would attract only a few. Sunday was mostly her special friends and family.

Sunday morning the family gathered around the table set up in the sunroom, bringing along plates of scrambled eggs, bacon, sausages, pancakes and blueberry muffins. Maxi had asked Lydia, one of the catering staff, to come back this morning. She thought everyone needed a downtime from Saturday.

"Mom, what would you think of me and Eve moving back here?" Michael asked.

"Oh, my! That would be wonderful, Michael. But what about your jobs?"

"Eve and I discussed it this week. I miss Pennsylvania. California offers many opportunities and beautiful weather, but I find I miss the mountains and the river. Eve loves it here too, even though being a California girl she has never experienced a real winter.

"I've been thinking of having my own computer and consulting business and working out of my home for some time, and I have several contacts that are interested in hiring me as a consultant. It would mean that I would have to travel every few weeks, but I can do that.

"Eve's work is helping people set up web pages for businesses. So she can work from anywhere as long as she has a computer."

"This is so wonderful. I can hardly believe it!" Maxi was nearly speechless and felt like she was hyperventilating.

Not wanting to spoil her brother's time with his news, Lorene waited until the talk had died down before she spoke up.

"We have news, too, Mom," Lorene said from the other side of the table. She and Jack exchanged smiles and Lorene continued, "We are having a baby."

Maxi's mouth dropped open, and then she was on her feet, going around the table to hug Lorene, laughing and crying at the same time. It turned into a group hug as Lorene and Jack were surrounded by Maxi, Michael and Eve.

"May I come in, or is this strictly private?" Jeff's voice came from the French Doors leading to the sunroom.

"Oh, come in, come in," they all chorused as one voice.

"I'm going to be a grandma!" Maxi ran to Jeff, hugging him and wanting to share her happiness, "And Michael and Eve and going to move back here to live. It has been the most amazing morning ever." For the first time it dawned on her that her feelings for Jeff had become very personal - as if he were part of her family.

The others exchanged meaningful looks, nodding approval.

Jeff's arms went around Maxi, hugging her, "Maxi, will you marry me?" His voice was pitched so all could hear him.

All laughter and talking stopped; the sudden silence left Maxi center stage and completely off guard. Her family sat motionless, waiting for her reply. Flustered, she tried to laugh, but it sounded more like a gasp. She looked at Jeff and realized he was tense with nervousness. His raised eyebrows held the question. She looked into his blue eyes and saw the kindness and love.

"Yes," Maxi whispered.

"Yes. Yes." Everyone shouted together, as they all moved to encircle Maxi and Jeff with hugs and kisses and well wishes.

"Are you sure you want to marry a grandma?" Maxi felt like events were moving too fast. She was shaking and moved to sit down before her legs gave way. What had she gotten herself into? She hadn't intended to get married again, and all the reasons she had given Jeff last evening returned full force.

"Maybe we should take more time to think about this. I didn't mean to say that."

But no one was listening to her as they exchanged excited thoughts. "I think a Thanksgiving wedding would be simply wonderful," Lorene was saying. "Mom, what do you think? Doesn't Thanksgiving sound good? We could all be here together again. It would be wonderful."

Maxi's hands were on her face as she looked in shock at the family group. Jeff came to her, and lifting her up by her arms led her into the living room away from all the excited talk. He sat down beside her on the sofa.

"Are you really having second thoughts?"

"I don't know. It's too fast for me to think. I told you last evening that I couldn't even think about marriage, and gave you my reasons and then this morning I said 'yes' without thinking a single thought. What am I doing?"

"Maxi, we got to know each other very well when you were sick with the flu. I like everything about you. We talked about so many things that most couples don't even think to discuss. We have so many things in common. And I do love you very, very much. I didn't think I would ever find anyone that I would feel this way about after my wife died.

"She knew she was dying and told me that I should find someone to share my life with. Her thoughts were more about leaving me alone than facing her own death. She was such a wonderful person. We loved each other passionately, and I couldn't bear the thought of her leaving me. In my grief all I wanted was to continue my writing, and that was all I needed.

"Since I met you that has changed. I want to spend my life with you, Maxi. I don't feel like a complete person without you."

By the time he was finished speaking, Maxi was sobbing softly. "I didn't want to think about my feelings for you. I felt guilty, that I was forgetting Jim and being disloyal. And I didn't think the children would approve, so I pushed all my personal feelings aside. I was going to be strong and go on with my life alone.

"This morning I was carried away with all the good feelings about my family and I guess it just released my real feelings about you. If you can take a 55-year-old grandma as a wife, I can accept you as my husband. I love you too, Jeff."

Jeff and Maxi stood and embraced. Applause erupted from the doorway.

"You are all just awful. Not giving a person any privacy at all," Maxi scolded with a huge smile. "And I think a Thanksgiving wedding sounds wonderful. We will get married right here in the parlor with a fire blazing in the fireplace and we will give thanks for all our many blessings."

At that moment, Lydia appeared in the doorway from the dining room carrying a bottle of champagne with a silver tray loaded with champagne glasses balanced on one arm.

"I brought champagne hoping we would be celebrating," Jeff said as he took the bottle and proceeded to open it with only a little pop of the cork. "I didn't want to waste any champagne by giving it the famous loud pop, spraying champagne all over everything. It's more dramatic, but we need all this to celebrate properly."

He indicated a table where Lydia was to put the tray of glasses. "Stay, Lydia, and celebrate with us."

"Michael, would you please call Sally and Hannah and then call the carriage house and ask Millie to come over." It was a directive, not a question. Maxi wanted everyone she felt was family to be there.

Hannah came running down the stairs, eyes wide with excitement. "Are we having another party? I think you have the most wonderful parties, Grandma Maxi."

Before anyone could answer, Millie came hurrying through the dining room and was joined by Sally at the same time. "What is all the excitement?" They asked in unison as though they were choreographed.

Jeff took charge. "We have announcements and toasts to be made. First, Maxi has agreed to marry me." Raised voices, with Hannah's high pitch rising above everyone, echoed their joy. Jeff continued, "To my lovely wife-to-be."

"To the bride and groom-to-be." Everyone raised their glasses in salute, even Hannah whose champagne glass had been filled with punch.

"I'm next," Maxi raised her glass, "To Lorene and Jack, our new parents-to-be."

"What does that mean?" At Hannah's question the group paused with glasses at their lips. A ripple of laughter preceded Maxi's explanation. "Hannah, Lorene and Jack are going to have a baby. And that will make me a grandma."

Hannah smiled and raised her glass with the others, "I love babies."

"Hear, hear!"

"And there is one more. Last, but not least - a rather trite phrase, but all I can think of now - to Michael and Eve who are coming home." Maxi raised her glass and everyone echoed, to "Michael and Eve."

Later, when everyone had calmed down, Maxi noticed Hannah sitting off by herself, looking sad.

Going over to her, Maxi asked, "Is something wrong, Hannah?"

Sniffles and shudders shook Hannah's body as she shook her head.

"Come on; tell me what has you so upset. It has been such a happy morning," Maxi coaxed, lifting Hannah and settling her on her lap.

"You said you are going to be a Grandma."

"Yes, my daughter Lorene and her husband Jack are going to have a baby. We are all very happy about it. You like Lorene and Jack, don't you?"

With downcast face and another sniffle, Hannah said softly, "I thought you wanted to be my grandma, since we live here now; but you will be too busy being a grandma to the new baby."

"Oh, honey. I will never be too busy for you, and I love being your grandma." Maxi was nearly overcome with emotion. She didn't think she could take much more today.

"Really, truly, cross your heart and hope to die?"

"Really, truly, cross my heart and hope to die. I love you, Hannah. Love is multiplied, never subtracted. Do you know anything about adding, subtracting and multiplying?"

"A little, I think. Multiply means to make more. In Sunday school the teacher said the people were told to 'go fourth and multiply'. The teacher said that meant they were to have big families and to ask other people to believe in God so there would be more Christians. That is what missionaries do."

"Exactly. Love always has room for more. It never gives out."

"Can I call you Nana? That is what Emily calls her grandma."

"Yes, I would love to have you call me Nana."

Hannah raced over to where the others were talking and hugged her mother, "Mama, Maxi is going to multiply."

"What on earth do you mean, Hannah? What is Maxi going to multiply?" Sally was laughing, wondering what her precocious daughter was talking about.

"She is going to multiply grandma. That means she will be my grandma, too, not just the new baby's grandma. She said I could call her Nana.

"That's wonderful, Hannah. Now you have two grandmas. Millie is Gran, and Maxi is Nana." Sally hugged Hannah and looked over her head at the two new grandmas. Her smile thanked both of them.

Chapter 30

Maxi's nervousness increased proportionately to the number of days until Thanksgiving. Her work pace was frantic as those displaced wanted to be moved before the holidays and before cold weather. It seemed her job would be over sooner than she had expected. She was looking forward to retirement, at least from the Flood Protection Authority. Some changes in administration, as the project neared completion, had made her work less enjoyable and more of something to just get through and be finished with it all.

Maxi wanted to change the wedding plans. She thought Easter would be better. Her job would be finished by then and she wouldn't have the distractions of work while planning a wedding, even though she wanted it to be simple with only immediate family and close friends. She definitely wanted to have it in her newly renovated home.

"We will still have a family Thanksgiving," Maxi explained to Jeff as they sat in front of the fire in the library, enjoying an after-dinner glass of wine. "It just won't include a wedding. I just can't handle that right now. I want to be able to relax and enjoy it."

"Is that the real reason, or are you having second thoughts?" Jeff had been lounging in a club chair, but as Maxi continued with her 'plans' he stood, turning his back to her and staring into the fire.

"Of course it is. Maybe you just don't want to understand! You don't have the pressure of a job that I have. You just do your writing when you feel like it." Maxi's temper flared.

"What does your family think about it? I suppose you have discussed this with them before saying anything to me." Jeff sounded bitter as he continued, "It seems your family comes first with you when you have decisions to make."

"That's not fair! I just happened to be talking to Lorene today and said to her what I just told you. Mothers and daughters do discuss things, you know."

"And who else? Sue, too, I suppose."

"Well, yes, I did say something to her yesterday. She is my best friend. Has been almost all my life. And while you are counting, I was talking to Michael yesterday, too. You are sounding jealous, Jeff."

"No, I am pissed off, that's what! I am only your husband-to-be, but I am the last one you talk to about our marriage plans. It seems to me that I should be the first, not the last. Maybe I just don't mean that much to you and maybe the wedding should just be cancelled, period."

Maxi's mouth dropped open in total surprise. She was not able to respond to this outburst. Jeff put his wine glass gently on the table, turned and walked out. Maxi heard the front door close softly. Suddenly the house seemed too empty and Jeff's exit seemed so final that she couldn't comprehend what had just happened. She was exhausted. *I can't deal with this! What just happened? All I was saying was that I wanted to wait a few months until I am finished with my job!*

The little voice in her head asked, *is that really what you were saying? Be honest now, maybe Jeff is right and I am having second thoughts about the whole thing.*

She put her wine glass on the table next to Jeff's and curled up on the sofa, pulling the afghan over her to stop the sudden chill. She was too tired to move any further. She was asleep in minutes.

Sun shining on her face woke her. She felt disoriented as she slowly sat up. Why was she in the library? Seeing the two half full wine glasses on the coffee table brought back the memory of what had happened last evening. Tears stung her eyes, but she refused to give in to them.

She glanced at her watch. She was already late for work and she still had to shower and get dressed. A half hour later she was in her car, still dazed and barely functioning. She pulled into the Dunkin Donut drive thru and ordered a black coffee. *I hope this gets me back into focus. I can't work this way.*

At the office things got worse. Jake had left last week to take a position that too good to pass up, as his job as executive director was nearing completion. He had explained to the staff and the board of directors that there was only clerical work to be completed, and there were any number of people who would be qualified to complete it. His last day had been Friday. Maxi felt abandoned. Ken was appointed as the new director, and Maxi found him to be an officious and condescending. Some people can't handle titles.

After all the responsibility Maxi had shouldered and the really great job she had done, she was now being questioned on everything that had already been approved. She had been responsible for over $3 million paid for the relocation of over 200 families and 17 businesses. The final payments and moves were all that was left to do.

She had not yet hung up her coat when Ken called her into his office and for more than an hour went on and on, questioning the last three checks she had requested to be drawn.

"They have been approved by the Corps of Engineers, and Jake approved everything as documented and in order. I don't understand your questions and obvious reluctance to have these checks drawn." Maxi was close to losing her patience.

"Perhaps you don't understand that I am the director now and expect to be included in decisions."

"But this was all decided before you were the director. To make changes now would not be fair to the people involved. They are ready to move into their new homes, and I have to stand up for their rights."

"I still have the final okay, and I feel you are trying to go around me. I won't have that. You should have brought the vouchers to me before taking them to the accountant." Ken's face had turned hard.

"I'm sorry. These are the last relocation checks. Let me finish with these families and I'll give you my resignation today, to be effective in two weeks. That will give me enough time to finish up all the remaining paper work."

He agreed that he would accept that, and Maxi watched as he donned his hardhat to go on his daily parade around the walkway on top of the levee as if he was personally responsible for the entire project. What he didn't know or refused to acknowledge was that none of the other staff or board members wanted the job. There was nothing of real importance left to do. A secretary could work with the Corps to finalize any remaining paper work. Jake had asked her if she would finish out the project as director prior to telling the board he was leaving, but she had turned the offer down. That was before the board decided Ken would fill the vacancy. But there was nothing she could do about that now. She probably wouldn't have wanted the job in any event; she was eager to get on with her new life.

The relief that Maxi felt was immediate as she went back to her office. It was like a black cloud had lifted and she felt free and energetic again. There was no way she would have walked away from the last three families before they received their moving expenses which were scheduled for this afternoon. With that settled, the secretary could complete any remaining work.

Sarah, the secretary, was competent and really needed the job as a single mother with two children. When this position ran out, she would be able to draw unemployment for six months or until she found another position. Maxi had already given her a reference and suggested a couple of places where she might apply.

Maxi settled at her desk and began a list of things to complete within the next two weeks. It was mostly being sure her files were in order, boxed and labeled for storage, and any reports that the Board of Directors needed were prepared. Nothing remained for her to get approval on from the Army Corps of Engineers. She would wipe her computer hard drive clean as the last remaining task. She had no idea what would be done with the computer. There was nothing on it that was not contained in the files, but she felt it was best to wipe it clean.

Picking up her phone, she punched in Jeff's number. His answering machine picked up her call and she left a short message that she needed to talk to him, "Please call me, Jeff."

She waited for his call all day. He did not call and she felt despondent as she drove home. Thank goodness Millie was nearby in the carriage house and Sally and Hannah were in their apartment, otherwise she felt she would have been going home to an empty house except for Beau and Charlie.

She let herself into the kitchen by the side door. Almost immediately Beau materialized with Charlie right behind him. "Hi, guys." She scooped one up in each arm and headed for her bedroom to change into more comfortable clothing.

Returning to the kitchen ten minutes later, dressed in a yellow sweat suit and booty-type slippers, she immediately checked the answering machine. No messages. Disappointed but determined to talk to Jeff, she dialed his number again. His machine picked up on the fourth ring. "Jeff, if you are there, please pick up. I really need to talk to you – we need to talk. Last night was a mistake. I'm sorry."

After waiting a few seconds with no reply, she said to the machine, "Oh shit, be that way and sulk all you want. Maybe I'll decide not to talk to you after all. Maybe this is all a big, big mistake!" She slammed down her phone and let out a scream that sent both cats diving for cover.

Catching her breath, she turned to find Jeff behind her in the kitchen. She spoke in a quavering voice, "I didn't hear you come in. You scared me to death! Haven't you heard of knocking or calling out as you come in?"

"I'm sorry I scared you, and I did knock before opening the door. You were so busy screaming into the phone you didn't hear me." Jeff leaned against the kitchen counter as he waited for her to regain her composure.

But it didn't happen. What composure she had evaporated. Maxi started to shake and tears rolled down her cheeks. She couldn't move her feet, her knees felt weak. She gradually slid down the cabinet until she was sitting on the floor. Her head bowed and her shoulders shook with sobs, hard tearing sobs that made her throat feel swollen and raw but she couldn't stop.

Through her tears she saw Jeff cross the kitchen to her. He seemed to be moving slowly as if she were a wild animal that had to be approached cautiously. She felt a cold, wet knob touch her cheek, and then a warm smooth tongue swiped the side of her face, catching some of the tears. Maxi looked up directly into Major's big face with his dark brown eyes looking worried. He whined and licked her face again. Maxi locked her arms around Major's big neck, buried her face in his coarse fur and cried harder.

"I wish you would do that to me."

"Do what?" Maxi sobbed.

"Wrap your arms around my neck and let me hold you. I have arms and Major doesn't."

"I trust Major."

"And you don't trust me?"

Maxi hiccupped, wrapped her arms tighter around the dog and shook her head vigorously.

"Okay. What can I do to gain your trust again? You used to trust me. I'm sorry if I abused that trust. I want it back again."

"Well, that won't happen. I am tired of being hurt and abandoned. I'll take care of myself. I don't need you. I'll be fine without you, Jeff Knowles."

"Well, I'm not fine without you."

"You were the one who walked out on me. And you didn't call me and I am tired, so tired."

Her arms slid from Major's neck and she began to collapse sideways. Jeff quickly ran to catch her before her head hit the floor. He sat beside her with her head and upper body leaning into his lap and his arms around her. She stopped crying and raised herself to nestle her head on his chest. Soon her deep, even breathing told him she was asleep.

Jeff sat motionless, not wanting to wake her. After a while his back against the hard cabinet began to hurt, the leg Maxi leaned against began to cramp, and his arms felt numb. Her hair covered his mouth and nose. He considered his options. *I could lay her down on the floor until I can stand and get my circulation going again? No, that would wake her. She might start bawling again and I couldn't stand that. Prop her against the cabinet and hold her with one hand so she won't fall sideways while I get up? No, that would probably wake her, too.*

"Major, come here." The big dog crept on his belly closer to Jeff, whining softly until he was pressed again Jeff's leg. "That's it. Good boy. I'm going to shift Maxi so she is lying across you until I can get up and have my arms and legs back again." Jeff talked softly and moved slowly until he had Maxi sitting on the floor and leaning against the dog, her head pillowed by the fur on Major's back.

Jeff hoped the continued feel of warmth would keep her from waking up.

Jeff slowly stood up, grasping the counter as he steadied his numb legs. The stinging sensation told him the blood was flowing again. After a couple of minutes of stretching stiff muscles, he turned and opened the cabinet where he knew she kept her supply of liquor. Selecting a bottle of Jack Daniels, he set a double shot glass on the counter and filled it. He drank it in one gulp, then leaned over the counter while it burned its way down his throat and settled warmly in his stomach. He hadn't eaten all day and it caused an immediate buzz. Fortified, he looked at Maxi curled into the warmth of Major who lay as still as a statue, looking at Jeff as if to say "Now what?"

"Now we lift her and get her to bed, boy." Jeff knelt, slipping his arms under Maxi. Lifting her from the floor, he wobbled a bit as he stood. "You're heavier than you look, or else I'm not as strong as I used to be," he mumbled to himself. Mumbling as he went, he focused on getting her to her bedroom where he laid her down gently. He took an afghan from the chair next to the fireplace and covered her, pushing a pillow under her head. He lit the gas log and settled down in the club chair with his feet propped on the ottoman. Relaxed by the liquor, he soon fell asleep.

Charlie and Beau crept cautiously into the bedroom, keeping an eye on Major who was lying on the floor beside Jeff. He watched as they jumped up and made their way across the bed until they were beside Maxi. Beau curled up in the bend of her knees and Charlie curled into the curve of her stomach. Major joined the others in sleep.

Chapter 31

They all awakened with the ringing of the phone. Maxi stared at her bedside clock - nine o'clock - morning or evening? She didn't know. Maxi felt almost drugged, definitely confused.

Jeff rose from the chair just as Maxi reached for the phone. She froze, looking at Jeff. He nodded toward the phone. Maxi jerked herself upright and picked it up.

"Why are you still at home? You are not finished here for two weeks." Ken's belligerent voice roared through the phone, causing Maxi to hold it away from her ear.

"Ken, I'm not coming in today. I am taking a sick day. I have weeks of sick time coming."

"Sick, my eye. You get in here. There are people here to see you. Be here in a half hour." Ken slammed down the phone.

She tried calling the office back and got a busy signal. Banging down her phone, Maxi scowled at Jeff, "I don't know who could be at the office to see me."

"Are you going to go in?" Jeff didn't need to ask what it was all about; Ken had been shouting so loud that he could hear him all the way across the room.

"Yea," Maxi sighed as she got off the bed and realized she was dressed in last night's attire. "I look like a Chiquita banana. What happened last night, and why are you here so early in the morning?"

"Last evening I came into the kitchen and startled you, while you were busy screaming into my answering machine. Then you just kind of collapsed. I brought you in here and just covered you up. I didn't want to wake you. You looked completely exhausted."

Maxi closed her eyes as it all started coming back. Jeff walking out the night before last, her telling Ken she was quitting, trying to call Jeff and not getting an answer, then coming home to an empty house feeling so very, very tired. She only vaguely remembered what happened after that.

"I have to get dressed for work." Maxi headed for the walk-in closet, saying over her shoulder, "I wanted to talk to you yesterday to tell you that I gave my two week notice at work."

Jeff stood spellbound and watched as she came out of the closet with clothes over her arm and walked into the bathroom, closing the door firmly.

He waited through the sound of the shower and the following silence, which he supposed meant she was getting dressed. Twenty minutes later she came out wearing a bright red suit, perfect makeup - as much as Maxi ever wore - and with her hair still a little damp picked up her purse and was out the door, pulling on her coat as she went.

"Hey, wait a minute. We have to talk. What do you mean you quit your job? I thought you still had three months to go." He trailed after her, but she kept going at a fast pace and was off down the drive in her car before he had a chance to do anything.

"Hell!" He looked at Major. "What now? Have we screwed up big-time? Are we ever going to understand that woman?" Major whined and leaned against Jeff's leg. "Guess we better lock up and go home."

As Maxi walked into the reception area, she heard loud voices and shouting coming from her office.

"What is going on here?" Maxi shouted, too, but couldn't be heard. She was ignored. She slammed the door, hard. That got the attention of everyone.

Ken stood with hands on his hips, his elbows out in an 'I won't budge' attitude, the scowl on his face reinforcing his stance as he glared at the man and woman standing across the room from him.

Oh, no! Maxi took in the situation and roared into action.

Marching between them to stand behind her desk, she pointed to Ken, "You go over there. This is my office and I'll take charge here."

Ken looking stubborn, at first stood his ground then under Maxi glaring look, moved to the side of the room. The office was small with only two chairs across from the desk. Maxi indicated that the couple should sit.

"Now, tell me what is going on here, Beth. You look like the only one calm enough to get it straight."

Beth took a deep breath in an effort to calm herself. "I don't feel all that calm, but I'll try;

he makes me so mad I want to hit him." Beth shot a deadly glance at Ken before continuing. "Last night, about 5:10 he came into our deli. It was crowded as it usually is at that time of day, with people stopping in after work. A lot of people buy our take-out for their dinner, or get milk and bread, that sort of thing and we also had a long line waiting to buy lottery tickets. You know what our business is like, Maxi."

At Maxi's nod, Beth point at Ken, "He came stomping in and saying in a loud voice how the flood protection project had put people in a lot better situation than they had before and they still moaned and groaned about being uprooted and they didn't get enough money."

Beth looked at her husband who had an expression of pure hatred on his face as he stared at Ken. "I had to call the police to get Ken out of there, before Mike physically hurt him. Mike tried to reason with him and asked him to leave, but he just got louder."

"I was only stating the truth. I am tired of hearing you people bad mouth us when we have really done you a favor and you are in better circumstances now than before." Ken defended himself.

Mike was getting up, his fists clenched and a scowl on his face. Maxi motioned for him to sit back down and turned to Ken, "I think you owe them an apology, Ken."

"Apology, my foot. They'll get nothing from me."

"Yes they will, Ken. You were way out of line. In fact, a 'Letter to the Editor' will do fine. I think that is appropriate. Do you two agree? Will that settle this incident in a reasonable manner for you? Anyone who was in your store or has heard about it will read the apology in the newspaper, and you can cut it out and post it in your store for anyone who misses it."

Beth and Mike looked at each other, and then nodded at Maxi.

"Great. I am glad you are both being so reasonable. We all know that you only got what you were legally entitled to, nothing more. And I have not known you to complain about your new business location; in fact, you have been very cooperative and have thanked me numerous times. I hope your business continues to thrive." Maxi stood up and steered Ken to the door. She almost had to push him out as she hissed in his ear, 'Go, you have done enough for one day. I'll come talk to you when they have left."

Maxi walked Beth and Mike to the reception area.

"Thanks, Maxi. We appreciate all you have done for us. But we felt we had to come in this morning and talk to you about it. We didn't expect to run into Ken."

"I'm sorry I was late getting here today. I am usually here by eight o'clock. I'm glad we got it straightened out. You were right to come in." Maxi shook hands with them and ushered them out the door.

Marching back the corridor, she went straight to Ken's office. "I'll write the apology letter for the newspaper and, you will sign it." It wasn't a question.

Ken had paper spread across his desk, looking extremely busy. "Well, get to it then, you have already wasted half a day being late. That was your business I had to deal with this morning and it wouldn't have happened if you had been here in the first place."

Maxi's mouth dropped open. Clamping her jaw closed, she turned and left. Any attempt to make him admit the truth would only prolong the unpleasantness with this man.

Half an hour later Maxi presented Ken with the apology letter for his signature. "I won't sign this. This is absolutely ridiculous."

"Okay if you don't want to sign it then I will add a couple of paragraphs explaining just what happened and sign it myself." Maxi scooped the letter off his desk and turned toward the door.

"Now wait a minute! I won't permit you to do that. I'm in charge here and I will not allow it!" Ken stood behind his desk and pulled himself to his full 5'4" height.

"Ken, what you don't realize is that I gave you my resignation yesterday with two weeks notice."

"Exactly, two more weeks and you're gone!"

"No, Ken, I'm gone today. I have three weeks vacation time and 21 days of sick time. I will get this news release to the newspaper, wipe my computer drive clean and then I am out of here." Maxi stood facing Ken, looking him squarely in the eye with a grim, determined set to her mouth.

"Leave you computer as it is. I'll have Sarah take care of the computer. I don't want anything erased." Maxi heard him mutter under his breath something about 'who knows what she's afraid I'll find'.

"And give me that dammed letter to sign. Then I'll be rid of you!"

Maxi handed the letter to him and waited until he had signed it; then took it off his desk. She wasn't going to let him keep it; she knew where it would end up. She would deliver it to the newspaper office herself.

Back in her office, she took her personal items from the desk drawers, her desk accessories and her coffee mug, found a box for everything and carried it to her car. Remembering the two pictures on the wall, she made a second trip back for them. Taking a last look at her computer, she decided not to bother with it. If she erased it now, Ken would manufacture a story about what had on it. *He would probably file a lawsuit against me for things that never happened and it would be a nightmare to disprove. I'll leave it.* Maxi was muttering to herself as she headed down the corridor.

Stopping briefly to let Sarah know that she was not coming back to work, but had in fact resigned, Maxi carried the pictures to her car. As she drove from the parking lot she realized that a heavy weight had been lifted from her shoulders. She felt lighter and freer than she had in months. Breathing a huge sigh, she thought, *Thank goodness that's over. Now I can get on with my life.*

Chapter 32

Two weeks before the wedding, Maxi declared a girl's only shopping trip to New York City, and at her expense. She asked Lorene to be their guide as she was the only one who had knowledge of the city.

"First, we must consider that we are taking Hannah with us, so we don't want to go to a really fancy restaurant where we can't get something a child would enjoy. What is your budget, Mom?"

"I want first class, Lorene. This is my treat for all the help everyone has given me this past year." Maxi replied. "Also, this is the first trip to New York City for everyone except you, Lorene."

"Okay, then. We will stay at The Four Seasons. We'll check out their restaurant for breakfast so we don't waste a lot of time going from place to place first thing in the morning."

Lorene was making notes on a large, yellow legal pad. "I want to take you all to Saks Fifth Avenue, Jeffrey New York, Macy's, Bergdorf-Goodman, Bloomingdale's, and Century 21. We'll find time to take Hannah to the zoo, Victorian Gardens in Central Park, FAO Swartz, the Empire State Building and the Staten Island Ferry." Can you think of anywhere you want to go, Mom?"

"I would like to see a Broadway Play and Radio City Music Hall," Maxi replied.

"Okay. Are we going to take Hannah, or do we do a strictly adult play?"

"Can we see The Lion King? I think we would all like that one. I would like to see Phantom of the Opera, but that would never do for Hannah." Maxi replied.

"The hotel will be able to provide someone reliable to stay with Hannah. Maybe that would be good while we do some of the department stores, too," Lorene was jotting down notes as fast as she could write.

"I don't want Hannah to feel left out. She has not had any childhood to speak of, and I know Sally won't want to leave her with a stranger."

"Oh, and I want to invite Sue, too. She was my maid of honor when Jim and I were married. I want her here for this wedding, too. So include her in our trip, Lorene. She has been there, but I think she would like to go with us. And we'll include Mark's wife, Anna, and also Eleanor, the wife of Jeff's FBI friend. Jeff will want them to be at the wedding. So the wives should be included in the New York trip."

As they were gathering to leave for New York, Jeff pulled Maxi aside, "Thank you for including Brian's wife in this trip, Maxi. It means a lot to me."

"Brian was so wonderful in dealing with everything connected to getting Jim's killers in prison. I can never thank him enough. I have gotten to know his wife, Eleanor, too, and I like her very much. I hope we can see more of them in the future."

The time in New York was wonderful. Hannah was delighted and proved to be no trouble at all, even during the two hours they were trying on dresses. She 'oood' and 'aaad' with each dress tried on.

Finally, each chose a dress. Appointments were made at the hotel salon for hair styling, manicures and make-up sessions, Hannah included, except she didn't need make-up; but she did have her nails done in a pale pink polish, hands and feet. Hannah giggled as she admired her pedicure and tried to look very grown up, causing smiles among the staff as well as her companions.

A week later, Maxi and Jeff stood before the parlor fireplace, waiting as all the guests gathered before being seated around the living room where sofas and chairs had been re-arranged for the wedding. Swags of Champagne roses hung from the fireplace mantel with greens and miniature lights. Maxi had had a difficult time deciding on the decorations. Since it was Thanksgiving, she had thought pumpkins, colored leaves and berries were appropriate but what she really wanted were roses on the mantel as well as in her bouquet.

When Jeff first saw Maxi a few moments ago, he was stunned by her appearance. He had never seen her in a formal dress. He was momentarily speechless as he took in her floor-length, gold lame' sheath and its elegant simplicity; gold and diamond earrings were her only jewelry.

Maxi was holding a boutonnière of a single rose, the same as those in her bouquet. Laying her flowers on a side table, she reached up and pinned it to his lapel.

"You are so handsome in your tux," Maxi whispered as she patted the flower into place on his lapel.

"I'm no match for you! You're absolutely gorgeous; you take my breath away. I want to hug you but I'm afraid to touch you. You're so lovely, Maxi".

"I'm huggable in this dress, Jeff." Maxi smiled and reached up to put her arms around his shoulders. "You don't get away that easily."

Maxi and Jeff turned to look around the room, enjoying the thrill of having everyone there with them. There were no attendants, just guests. But they were all dressed in formal attire, Maxi's gift to each of them, dresses for the ladies and tuxedoes for the men.

Maxi was noting each lady's appearance.

Lorene was lovely in a dusty apricot sequined gown, trimmed in pale turquoise with turquoise sequins; her hair, a natural light blonde, skimmed her bare shoulders. Gold and diamond jewelry gleamed at her throat and ears as well as around her wrist and on her fingers.

Eve had chosen royal blue as her color; the strapless gown, trimmed with sequins and black beads, complimented her dark complexion and black hair that she pulled back into a chignon. She had earrings of blue sapphires and diamonds. Maxi thought she looked beautiful.

Millie was elegant in a lovely silver-gray satin gown, with ropes of pearls around her throat and a long strand that went to her waist. Her crown of pure white hair had grown longer and was now up in a French twist showing off her pearl earrings and, Maxi noted, her elegant neck.

Anna, a beautiful, petite brunette, had chosen a mauve brocade sheath with an off-the-shoulder boat neckline. Her pearl choker necklace looked wonderful, Maxi noted.

Eleanor, looking regal and sophisticated with her sleek, short cap of black hair, wore a black, figure-hugging, crepe gown that flared just below the knees. The neckline was high in front and plunged to her waist in back. She had objected to the dress saying, "I can't wear black to a wedding."

"Of course you can. The dress is perfect for you. The only criteria are whether or not you like it," Maxi had replied.

Eleanor's only jewelry was diamond and black pearl earrings that she had told Maxi were ones that had been her great, great grandmother's. She had refused the offer of jewelry from Maxi, saying she didn't wear jewelry much and had told her of the earrings she had inherited, adding "They will look perfect with this dress. They are so elegant that I have never had anything appropriate to wear them with."

Eleanor's other concern was her new hairstyle. "I don't know if Brian will like it. Like many men, he always liked my hair long. But I am so pleased with it. I feel like a new woman, sort of dark, mysterious and elegant," Eleanor had confided, with a giggle. As it turned out, her husband had been delighted when he saw her, being heard to comment, "You look fabulous!"

Sally and Hannah came in last. Sally looked radiant, shy and joyful, all at the same time. Her shoulder-length, dark brown hair with natural, red highlights gave her a lovely, girl-next-door look. Her Chinese red satin sheath flared at the knees to a full flounce. Maxi noted that she looked stunning.

While in New York, Sally had confided to Maxi, "I never even had a high school prom dress. This one is so beautiful, I feel like a queen with my princess by my side," Sally put her arm around Hanna and gave her a squeeze.

Now, Hannah was thoroughly delighted with herself. She wore a floor length dress of deep red velvet trimmed with white fur. It featured a circle skirt that had weighted tape sewn in the hem to cause the fabric to swirl out as Hannah twirled around and around giggling and laughing causing everyone to laugh with her. She carried a white fur muff. Her long, light blonde curls bounced as she danced to her seat next to her mother. She looked like a Christmas doll.

Maxi left her place beside Jeff to go and hug each one in turn, Hannah last. "You look like a princess, Hannah."

"I know. I'm bootiful. Momma said so," Hanna replied modestly.

A photographer mingled among the guests taking candid shots. Later, he would take formal photos of everyone.

The men all in tuxedos joined the ladies, while Jeff waited for Maxi to join him in front of the pastor. The ceremony began.

Later, on the sun porch, Maxi and Jeff were spellbound as they gazed at the glorious golden sky. It was sunset, but the sun was not visible through the low hanging clouds. There had been a light mist all day but that had stopped. Now the setting sun had turned the entire sky into a luminous golden dome. The bare tree branches stood starkly black against the gold.

"Its beautiful, more beautiful than a rainbow. I feel like it is an omen, a wondrous omen for our new life together." Maxi allowed a little romantic fantasy to color her dreaming and leaned into Jeff's encircling arms, letting her head rest on his shoulder.

"I've never seen anything like it before," Jeff murmured, his chin resting on top of her head.

"We've only just been married; and I feel it is like a blessing on us".

"Okay, you two, Thanksgiving Dinner is served." Lorene stood in the French doorway, smiling.

As the entire family gathered around the table, Maxi at the one end and Jeff at the other, Maxi held out her hands to clasp those on either side of her and a circle was formed as they gave thanks. "Let each of us say what we are most thankful for. I will start," Maxi bowed her head.

"Dear Lord, on this wonderful Thanksgiving Day I have so much to be thankful for: Jeff, my wonderful new husband, all my family and a new member on the way, our new extended family - Millie, Sally and Hannah – our friends Brian and Eleanor, Mark and Anna. Thank you for our good health and I pray for your love to surround those who are sick or without family."

The murmured thanks continued around the table. Hannah was last and was not to be passed over. She squeezed her mother's hand on her right and Maxi's on her left. "I am thankful for my mommy and all my new family; grandma Maxi and Grandpa Jeff, Grandma Millie and all my new aunts and uncles. Please don't let anything bad happen to them or take them away. I have never been so happy."

"Amen" was a chorus around the table.

Happy chatter continued throughout the delicious meal that had been prepared by Millie and Sally, with help from Lorene and Eve.

After dinner, Jeff and Maxi left the table and headed for the parlor where a fire blazed in the fireplace.

"I think I want to celebrate our anniversary on Thanksgiving Day in the future rather than on the actual date." Maxi declared.

"That sounds good to me." Jeff settled on the sofa and pulled Maxi down beside him. They were alone as all the others were chattering away while clearing the table of the leftover food and dirty dishes.

"I never expected my life to take a turn like this. When Jim died, I thought I would sell my home, buy a small cottage with a wide front porch that had room for a swing for summer days and evenings; plant a flower garden. It would have a fireplace for winter with a rocking chair, two or three cats and maybe a dog or two. I thought eventually I would have grandchildren who would visit me and stay in the summer and maybe the family would come for holidays or I would visit them."

"Instead you got me," Jeff smiled. "And a huge house and now your family is moving back"

"I'm afraid I will wake up and it will all be a dream. Just imagine, Michael and Eve moving in here until their new house is built. And Lorene and Jack told me this morning that they are looking into buying the farm next door. I hope it works out; it will be wonderful to have them and a new grandbaby next door."

"Jeff, do you really want a honeymoon away from here?" Maxi asked, glancing sideways to watch his reaction.

"I think we could wait until February, if you would like that."

"Yes! That would be much better. I am so happy getting settled here, and there are so many plans to make. February can be rather a cold and boring, and it would be nice to go somewhere sunny and warm. When we get back it will be nearly spring. Jeff, I am so happy! Everything is perfect! And that scares me a little! Nothing is ever perfect - at least, not for long."

"But you can't let the unknown spoil what you have today", Jeff replied. "Today we have it all; and we'll handle all our 'tomorrows' together."

About The Author:

In 1972, the author and her family experienced the devastating flood that affected the Susquehanna River Valley. Years later, the resulting dike/levee flood protection project was built by the Army Corps of Engineers. The author was the relocation specialist for that project. She and her late husband restored a 100-year-old Victorian house, and as a widow she renovated a 50-year-old house. She is a lifelong resident of Pennsylvania.

Printed in the United States
103871LV00005B/91-267/P